THE TRAGEDY QUEEN

THE TRAGEDY QUEEN

LINDA LEITH

NUAGE
EDITIONS

© 1995, Linda Leith

All rights reserved. No part of this book may be reproduced, for any reason, by any means, without the permission of the publisher.

Cover art by Gina Georgousis.
Cover typography by Kate McDonnell.
Photo of Linda Leith by Louis Desjardins.

Acknowledgements
My thanks are due to Anne McLean, Ron Rower, Beverley Story and Janet Coutts, as well as to my editor, Karen Haughian.

Published with the assistance of The Canada Council.

Printed and bound in Canada
by Les Ateliers Graphiques Marc Veilleux Inc.

Dépôt légal, Bibliothèque nationale du Québec and the National Library of Canada.

Canadian Cataloguing in Publication Data

    Leith, Linda
    The tragedy queen

    ISBN 0-921833-37-7

    I. Title

PS8573.E49T73 1995   C813'.54   C95-900301-0
PR9199.3.L44T73 1995

NuAge Editions, P.O. Box 8, Station E
Montréal, Québec H2T 3A5

This book is dedicated to my sons—
Adam Leith, Michael András, and Julian Desmond Barnabás Göllner

The Tragedy Queen is a work of fiction. While some of the events of the novel were inspired by actual events, they have assumed another, fictional life of their own in the pages of this novel. The black garden in the novel is based on a real garden in Pointe Claire, the creation of my friend and colleague, Rod Smith. The character of the gardener, the other characters, and all their names, circumstances, histories, habits, and foibles, are of my own invention, and any similarity to any individual, living or dead, is purely coincidental.

The hostess, already of imposing size, her face heavily powdered, her looped hair parted in the middle, saw herself as an allegorical figure—sometimes with a crown of laurels on her head as Corinna, on other occasions, dressed all in white, with mistletoe twined in her glossy hair, as Norma. One ungrateful guest likened her to "a tragedy queen at a suburban theatre."

> A description of Speranza, Lady Wilde,
> at 1 Merrion Square, Dublin
> from *Oscar Wilde*, by Philippe Jullian

The rooms, sagely and soberly furnished, held an engraving of a young woman standing on her hands, her heels in the air. The young person was Salome, Princess of Judaea, as she appears in Flaubert's *Hérodias*.... Wilde had not previously met that young woman. When on this night he did meet her he bowed and exclaimed, *"La bella donna della mia mente!"*—a phrase of Petrarch which, being translated, means: The fair lady of my dreams.

> Edgar Saltus, introduction,
> *The Plays of Oscar Wilde*, 1900

PART I

1

Vince Carlson prides himself on knowing a lot about middle-aged women. Young women are easy enough, but they bore him. They have no character, no money, and no proper sense of gratitude. What interests Vince is the affluent middle-aged woman who's already half in love with danger.

Put five women in front of him, all of a certain age. Two are terminally innocent. One has become a shrew. Another one is sure to be a nympho. Which can be useful, but the nympho is about as uninteresting as the young woman she wishes she still were. At least one of them—one woman out of the five—is just out of reach. And ripe for the plucking.

There are tidy lawns to the right of him, barrels of petunias to the left of him, ancient, sweeping maples and apple trees in front of him. This place could fool you. Norman Rockwell country: all picket fences and family values, flower beds and gingham. If you don't watch yourself, Vinskie my lad, you could end up here overdosing on Harvest Crunch.

But look closer, and it's a hair's breadth from Gomorrah. Take that short, ample woman over there, carrying her blue recycling bin from the side of the road back up her driveway. White pleated shorts, long-sleeved madras blouse hiding securely restrained breasts. She walks briskly, as though she's busy, with an almost imperceptible limp. Straight, mouse-coloured hair trails over her shoulders.

She's probably worn her hair like that since she was thirteen. In the sixties, when Vince was in high school about a mile from this very spot, lots of the girls used to wear their hair long and straight like that. Yet, judging by the dimples on those thighs, this is a woman whose own kids must be in high school by now.

Who does she dream about? When she's lying awake in bed, folding laundry, standing in line at the bank—who does she think about?

The man next door? Her best friend's husband? Unlikely. Her own husband has commuted to Montreal for the past twenty years, and has caught the 5:16 home every weekday evening. Her dreams are of a riskier man. The star of a movie she saw when she was seventeen. The voice behind a song she can't get out of her head. His name hardly matters. Even his looks hardly matter. What matters is unpredictability. And a streak of ruthlessness.

The briskness is for the neighbours' benefit. When she's in her immaculate white kitchen, she sits down at the table where *The Gazette* is spread out in front of her, and she puts her head in her hands. She wants a job. Or meaning. Or a lover.

He can't see her face. Everything depends on the face. Vince revs the engine to catch her attention, but he is too late. By the time she turns around, she is already closing the front door behind her. So she'll watch him through the window, she'll stare at him in disbelief—his Harley, his Ray-Bans, his leathers—as she would stare at a bluebottle in her kitchen.

Vince grins. He has paused at the Stop sign on the corner of Lakeview and St. John's. It doesn't say STOP at all; it says ARRET. And the ARRET is blackened out. Which is about the only sign that Vince is still in Quebec. And about the only thing that has changed since Vince was a teenager here.

But not quite the only thing. That recycling bin, for a start. And that woman. How old would she be? How old would she have been in 1965? That was the year Vince was supposed to graduate from Beaconsfield High School and never did.

Vince pulls the Harley away from the Stop sign. He is in no hurry. It's barely nine o'clock, already hot, more humid with every passing minute. The lights at the corner of the Lakeshore Road are red.

Pointe Claire village. Vince stares. He had forgotten this scene. When Carrie, the real estate agent, drove him over here to show him the house, they came from the other direction, out from the village.

The silver-spired church, the greystone convent and the windmill on the point look no different from this distance than they looked thirty years before.

The *pointe* itself—the cape—juts out into the St. Lawrence and affords a clear view up and down river—west to Ste. Anne de Bellevue on the tip of the island of Montreal, and east to the Lachine Rapids and, beyond them, to the centre of Montreal. Far away in the distance a black tanker is churning its way slowly down the Seaway past the long line of trees on the far shore.

The Indians were the first to admire the view up and down river. The Indians who never were Indian. Lachine which is not China—nor India either, for that matter. And—Vince realizes for the first time—the lake which is not a lake. It's steaming, now, sullen in the accumulating heat of the summer morning. Vince must have always known that this was the St. Lawrence, at least to the extent that he would probably have been able to give the right answer if someone had insisted he explain exactly what Lake St. Louis was. A bay in the St. Lawrence.

As the lights change, and he rounds the bend, the sun catches the chrome and dazzles Vince. He pulls over to the side of the road, and the traffic trundles past him towards the village.

Boulevard St-Jean. That's what the street sign says, though Carrie herself called it St. John's. And Lakeshore—the Lakeshore Road—is really Chemin du Bord du Lac. Everything here has two names, sometimes three or more. French names, English names, abbreviated names, hyphenated names, jumbled-up or largely forgotten names. You name it. Why not? Everybody else seems to. Everyone, all the time, is translating. But the one is never quite the same as the other, and nothing, ever, is quite what it seems to be. A pretty shifty spot.

Coming back feels right. There's a kind of inevitability about it that appeals to Vince. He realizes he's been working up to this.

Moving in with a woman has lots of advantages, as no one knows better than Vince. But often it means putting up with the kids—teenagers, most likely, or worse, adult kids with an eye on the family fortune.

Moving into an empty house is even better. The house he rented in Dollard from the Xavier woman was a kind of dry run. In Dollard he not only had the house; he had his freedom, too. He made the most of it, using the house as a warehouse for the goods he'd scored, hiding the TR6 in the garage until he'd found the right buyer, making his deals in private, and basking in the luxury of having no one around to ask irritating questions.

The Xavier witch didn't take it lying down, of course. Vince enjoyed watching her struggle, especially when she practically bankrupted herself with legal fees trying to nail him. And she couldn't get him out, not even when she swore she had to move back into the house herself. Vince owed her five months' rent when he got the letter from his mother's lawyer two weeks ago. It was that very afternoon he picked up *The Chronicle* and noticed the ad for this house on the Lakeshore. It felt as though all the pieces of a puzzle were falling into place. That's when he poured the sugar into the witch's steam iron. She'll be surprised when she finds herself smearing caramel over some pricey silk dress. As his parting shot, Vince punched holes in the bottom of a dozen cans of sardines and left one inside every closet in the house.

He didn't mention a word of any of this to pretty little Carrie. It was enough for her to know he'd lived in the area as a kid. On Golf Avenue, actually. Oh yes, lovely street. She'd found that reassuring, added it to the short mental list that would convince her she could rent the house to him, pocket the first month's rent as her fee, and get on with the more lucrative business of selling. She'd agreed to rent the house only because the owner was her next-door neighbour; rentals were a waste of her time, especially in this recession-wracked economy, in a buyers' market, in a middle-class suburb littered with Montreal Trust signs, Royal Lepage signs, Century 21 signs and several of the kind of *A vendre* signs you can buy at the hardware store when you don't want to see another real estate agent for as long as you live.

Pretty Carrie wasn't going to ask any more questions than necessary. And the ins and outs of Vince's career, so to speak, are none of her business. If he doesn't tell her he used to be a lawyer, she'll never find out he was disbarred, let alone that he was jailed. It's not her business, none of it. Vince has the lease inside his black leather jacket. The house is his now. They'll never get him to pay another penny. And they'll never get him out.

A bank of cloud moves over the sun, softening the outlines of the day. There's a gust of wind, and the muggy air is filled with puffs of tree pollen swirling around like snow in a blizzard. Vince starts up again, cruising slowly between half a dozen well-spaced houses and the plots of weedless grass that divide the road from the lake, and then nosing into the driveway he'll be sharing with the house in front.

The massive stone and brick houses crowded together here on the corner of Cedar are an affront to the standoffish manners of most of these Lakeshore homes. Sal's house, the one Vince is renting, is an enormous bunker so well hidden behind the house in front as to be invisible from the road. That's one of the features that appealed to Vince about it from the start.

Vince pulls up at the door to the wide garage and eases off his black helmet. He sucks in his gut and worms his fingers into his pants pocket for the housekey. At the top of the stone steps, he pauses to survey the scene. It's taken him a long time to make his way back to these shores. This will be his view every morning now. Through these tall maples, past these towering pines, all the way across the St. Lawrence. Vince is home. Home free.

2

There are two letters on the floor just inside the front door. Vince picks them up and studies them. Both are addressed to Sal.

The one on top—now isn't this a bonus!—is from MasterCard. Kicking the door closed behind him, Vince tears off the end of the envelope and pulls out a statement. Ha! He examines it closely. Not only a statement, but Sal's very first statement. She must have gotten the card just before leaving for Europe. $1,500 credit limit. And all she's put on it so far is $56, at Archambault Musique. He'll need her expiry date. Yes. But knowing when she got her card will give him good odds on that one. Vince snorts. Things are going his way.

The other envelope is pale green, addressed in clearly legible handwriting, a woman's writing. A Canadian stamp postmarked Mississauga, Ontario, July something 1993. Sal must have had her mail redirected—there was none last week when Vince looked around the house with Carrie—but postal employees are fallible.

The letter is signed: loveLillianxxx. An account of Lillian's home decorating idea, questions about Sal's cello, about Slovakia. Vince already knows about Sal spending the year in Bratislava. There's nothing interesting in the letter at all. Nothing useful. Just greetings and chirpiness. Lillian Gush, Vince says out loud, tearing the letter and the envelope in half. He's just about to toss them onto the floor when, on second thought—there may be spying eyes in this house before long—he stuffs the pieces into his pocket.

The telephone rings. He walks over to the phone in the hall. That'll be Yolanda. Sweet, pathetic Yolanda. Where most of them try to put their most brazen foot forward in their Personals ad, Yolanda came across as a little lost lamb, as bewildered on the eve of her forty-sixth birthday as she might have been on her sixth. So he wrote to her. And she went for it. They all do, every time.

"Mr. Windle?"

"Yolanda!" he exclaims, flipping through the Yellow Pages next to the phone.

She burbles.

"A *rendez-vous*," he says. "The Ritz Garden? One o'clock tomorrow? Perfect. Did I mention? I may have to be out of town later in the week… Oh, it's too soon to say. Exciting, though, an exciting opportunity," he concludes.

No sooner has Yolanda bid him *adieu* than he dials the number of a florist on Ile des Soeurs. That's where Yolanda's condo clings to the side of a pyramid.

"Le Tulipier." A woman's voice answers.

"Forty-six long-stemmed red roses."

"And a message?"

"Happy Birthday, Yolanda."

"And that's from…," the voice is unctuous, practised.

"From You Know Who.'"

"You will be paying for this with…"

"MasterCard."

"Your name?"

"Schleiermacher."

"First name?"

"Sal." Sol would be more plausible as a man's name, but the slightest change can cause a computer to hiccup. Vince wants this to go smoothly.

"Sal? S-a-l?"

"That's it." Salman? Maybe. But Salman Schleiermacher might be pushing the limits of credibility. "Sal short for Salvador." Vince smiles into the receiver. He can still surprise himself. Salvador Schleiermacher! Where did he dredge up a name like that?

"Card number, Mr. Schleiermacher?"

"5258," Vince begins, reading off Sal's statement. And then hesitates. A beat. "My eyes! Yes. 5258 9493 9282 7458."

"Expiry date?"

"05/96." No hesitation this time. That's his best guess. Three years from the date when this card was most likely issued.

"Very good, sir. I'll need your telephone number, and the address and telephone number of the lady."

He'll know soon enough if he's wrong. Salvador. Ha! Isn't that a Spanish name?

And why not? Vince thinks. His own father was Spanish. Carlos. A refugee from the Basque. A socialist and a painter. Vince remembers little about him, but what memories he has are vivid. A big, loud man, smearing black and red paint over tortured canvases. Vince remembers late nights in the apartments and studios of new-found friends, visits to galleries, concerts, plays—even, once, the opera. That was something. Vince remembers the heavily made-up faces and unnatural voices of the women. Alarming, exciting, unforgettable. Carlos worked as a diver for the Port of Montreal. He drowned in the harbour when Vince was six years old. The only real regret of Vince's life is that he has nothing of his father's. His mother chose to forget that whole period when she remarried.

His mother.

She'd been Teresa, once, when she stepped off a boat from Poland at the end of the war. She was Teresa when she taught Russian on Park Avenue, Teresa when she married Carlos, Teresa when Vince was born. But after Carlos died, she turned herself into a stranger. By the time she'd latched on to Ted Cunningham, she'd taught herself English and was calling herself Thea. In less than a year she was Mrs. Ted Cunningham— and she'd tacked Cunningham onto the end of Vince's name too, so that they would all be Cunninghams, for all the world a real family.

Vince was to call him Dad. He is your father now.

Vince was fifteen when he ran away. Already tall, not yet big, with a zit the size of a pea at the side of his mouth, and a football uniform and a sketchbook hidden away in the schoolbag on his back.

Vince hasn't given that kid a second thought in nearly thirty years. He has never been a man to dwell on the past. What for? Vince has lived an unconventional life, living off his wits and his women. There is nothing in his past he has needed, nothing useful, so he's kept the door to it closed all these years, just nursing the one or two old resentments that have served him nicely.

His mother is dead now, too. Dead and buried. Has been for the better part of a year, but Vince has only just found out. It took her lawyer all this time to track Vince down.

And now he's back. Money, for a change, is no object. Between them, fate and his mother's lawyer have fixed it so Vince is going to be able to live a life of leisure out here in Pointe Claire. Leisure. And pleasure. This place is one big garden of earthly delights, just crawling with lonely, underappreciated women. And Vince has some plans of his very own. He has time to spare, energy to burn, and a whole village full of women to toy with.

And Sal, in her own distant and unsuspecting way, is one of those women. While he's waiting for Le Tulipier to phone back—better to expect a refusal and be prepared to bounce back convincingly—Vince tunes the radio to Oldies 990 and begins his first unimpeded survey of the house.

He noticed one or two saleable items when Carrie was showing him around last week, but he wasn't about to let her see him inspecting the weave of the Persian carpet. "So the house is fully furnished?" he had asked casually. "Yes," Carrie had smiled prettily; "Sal didn't want to put everything she owned into storage for the year." Furnished the house admittedly is. But not fully. The cabinet in the dining room is empty, the kitchen is barely equipped, and the beds are unmade. So where are the rest of Sal's belongings? There must be a stash somewhere.

In the bedroom Vince stops. On the wall above the queen-size bed, there's an engraving of a turbaned woman in harem pants doing a handstand. Vince lifts it off the hook and examines it. Donald Rimmer might give him a couple of thousand for this. If Vince decides to sell it. Maybe that's one thing he'll hold on to, keep for himself. That and the Tiffany lamp in the hall.

Vince's expenses will be low, thanks to his gracious hostess. Pin money's about all he's going to need, especially if Yolanda comes across— as she probably will. Just a bit of effort should cover his day-to-day expenses. He's expecting his mother's legacy by August, anyway, all $186,000 and 23 cents of it. A tidy sum. He won't fritter that away. That's going to set him up for the rest of his life.

So what's he going to sell? Those murky oil paintings in the dining room, certainly. He won't share his living quarters with those. Most of the furniture can go. There'll be more, once he's had a chance to explore more thoroughly. And if he stores it downstairs in the family room for a while, he'll be able to move it all into a truck inside the garage without anyone seeing.

Sal had lived here in lollipop land far too long. If it weren't for the fact that she had an alarm system installed, he'd figure she must be insanely trusting. Maybe she is anyway, like those people with guard dogs the size of ponies who leave their jewellery lying around when they invite people over for dinner. She didn't even bother hiding most things before she left, just trusted in standard filing-cabinet keys, Scotch tape, and human goodness to protect her most intimate belongings from prying eyes. Vince could almost begin to fear for her.

He moves the Tiffany lamp and the Persian carpet into the bedroom, removes the paintings from the walls and stacks them in the family room, and has carried down two or three more loads when the telephone rings again. Vince is in the kitchen, where Sal has considerately provided him with a telephone that displays the number along with the name of the caller. And lists previous callers. Le Tulipier.

"Mr. Schleiermacher?" What an annoying voice the woman has.
"Speaking."
"There's a problem, sir. The expiry date you gave me on your MasterCard is not correct…"
"Not correct? Let me see. 06/96?"
"06/96, sir? You told me 05/96."
"Did I? It's my eyes. I don't see as well as I used to." This much is true. His eyes are not what they used to be. After a lifetime of perfect vision, Vince is increasingly presbyopic. Nothing unusual, of course, for a man in his forties.
"That's quite all right, sir. I'll try again."

It'll work this time, Vince feels sure. He opens the back door and steps out onto a fenced-in deck hung with a profusion of flowering vines that someone—it must be Sal herself—has gone to the trouble of training along lengths of twine and attaching with plastic-coated ties.

Vince can't risk a third try at the expiry date, not for a week at least. That might alert the bank to an illicit use of the card, and that's the last thing Vince wants, especially when he's divulged his phone number and made it easy to track him down. Not that anyone is likely to bother. But it would be a pity to ruin this cosy little set-up by being greedy.

So, it had better work this time. Otherwise he just might feel irritated. Irritated with Le Tulipier, with the bank, with Yolanda herself—and even with Sal, whose name just happens to be attached to this little adventure and whose belongings are at hand. Casually Vince trails his hand through the vine leaves.

Really a most secluded deck, considering the proximity of the neighbours. Sal's is one of four diPietro houses built as a family compound in the fifties. Even as a kid Vince knew a bit about the diPietros. The father was a stonemason, the owner of a construction company, and Frank was the original owner of the Edgewater Hotel. His house, the one right in front of Sal's, is now owned by a family called Remillard. These houses are practically on top of one another. Solidly built, too, as befits the family of a stonemason. What was it Carrie said when she showed him the thickness of the interior walls? You could huff and you could puff, and you'd never blow this house down. Baby talk and threats. A bad combination, Vince had thought, smiling at her indulgently.

Provisions. Vince isn't going to hang around any longer waiting for Le Tulipier to phone back. He picks up his helmet and keys, and rolls the Harley down to the end of the driveway, where he stops beside the blue minivan parked at the side door of the Remillard house. There's another whole driveway for those people, a semi-circular one. What are they doing, blocking half of the driveway they share with Sal? Bet they wouldn't do that if she still had a man about the house.

The lake looks pure. You'd never guess there's a sink of PCBs out there somewhere near Dorval Island. Or that the river is swimming with them all the way out to the sea. The wind is coming up. Out on the lake a windsurfer in a rubber wetsuit is skimming over the sandbar. He looks as though he's in control, but he's just riding the wind, at the mercy of the elements. As Vince watches, he topples backwards with the sail on top of him. The world is full of fools, Vince thinks. And a good thing too.

Vince mounts the Harley and turns out onto the Lakeshore Road. Past Cedar, Killarney Gardens, Bowling Green. Bowling Green is a long oblong crescent edging a wide strip of well-tended grass that must once really have been a bowling green stretching up from the Lakeshore. The houses here are all on the outer rim of the crescent, old wooden houses with creaking porches facing the bowling green. A bit like Golf Avenue, it occurs to Vince briefly, before he banishes the thought, crossing over to the parking lot of the ruined Edgewater Hotel. He's not ready for Golf Avenue.

No wonder he didn't recognize the Edgewater. The original building must have been destroyed. Yet it, too, was solidly built. So what happened? Was there a fire? Had they stopped paying protection? Judging by the style of the three godawful turrets over the hotel's main entrance, unmistakable products of the sixties—and the bits of broken furniture he can see through the big, dirty windows of the old bar-room at the side—the "Edge," that's what they used to call it, must have been rebuilt not long after Vince fled Pointe Claire.

And now it's derelict. The rebuilt hotel must have gone bankrupt, or maybe it was closed down. No more afternoon drunks, no more sleazy doormen, no more bouncers, no more white limos. On summer afternoons when he had nothing to do except ride his bicycle around and avoid going home, Vince used to sit on the grass sometimes, watching the action in the parking lot and staring through the railings at the patio decorated with yellow umbrellas, angular women, and tall, unlikely coloured drinks. Even the pool is unrecognizable now, though, and the patio is littered with garbage.

Vince doesn't like to see sixties products falling into disrepair. He caught *2001: A Space Odyssey* on TV a while back. That was a film that had swept him away when first he saw it. But, this second time, he found that everything from the costumes and the furniture to the computers and the spaceships looked like junk. A glistening future transformed into a pathetic past.

The Harley growls away from the Edgewater, past the post office and the Esso station on the corner of Cartier Avenue. There's a snack bar, a Caisse Populaire, and then a row of cutesy little shops—Dutch tiles in the window of one, handmade lampshades in another, raffia and stencils in the crafts shop—near the bus stop on rue de Lourdes. A dozen seniors are congregating outside the new Lawn Bowling Club at the top of de Lourdes, exercising failing skills, clinging to a semblance of control. Vince eyes them coldly. He would rather die.

Back to the Lakeshore and right through the village. The Marché Seaubois may be his best bet for groceries. The closest, anyway. No fewer than three Italian restaurants, a couple of minuscule beauty salons, a tea room, a string of ice-cream parlors and precious little gift shops with windows stuffed with pewter reproductions of art nouveau picture frames. A village oversupplied with useless items; good for groceries but not much else.

In Vince's day it was a real village, with a pharmacy, a jeweller, a hardware store, and a movie theatre, even, that had been taken over by Rossy's, a dry goods store presided over by a round, impassive woman. And, Vince realizes—seeing the old stone house that's a restaurant now, on the corner of rue Ste-Anne, and reminded of Mme. Portelance—a dressmaker.

But the shoemakers, the Boisvert Frères, are still there, with the very same kind of display in the window, and—Vince pulls over and peers at the shoes lined up side by side in neat little rows—for all anyone knows, with some of the very same shoes. Only their *CHAUSSURES* sign seems larger now than it was thirty years ago. Aren't things supposed to look smaller than you remembered?

These all are anodyne thoughts, manageable kinds of memories. Vince is doing just fine—and why shouldn't he? But enough is enough. It's time to turn around. He wheels around in front of the IGA supermarket, which has had an ugly facelift since he last saw it, but still has R. Déry's name on it, and cruises down to the *pointe*. The church of St. Joachim looks unchanged, and Vince has no memory of the squat manse or of Ecole Marguerite-Bourgeoys, though surely they already existed when he was a teenager.

The greystone convent is quiet, and the sails of the old windmill are fixed and still. Vince remembers the convent as a substantial community. You'd never walk through the village without seeing two or three or more well-scrubbed nuns. After a while they vanished into thin air. Vince stares at the convent. *Congrégation de Notre-Dame.* Does anyone at all live there anymore? Is it haunted by the spirits of all those nuns?

There's a rope now across the grass in front of the windmill, and a *Propriété Privée* sign. You can't get out to the *pointe* and, with the trees in the way, you can't even see the clear view up river anymore. So much for *claire*. And the frail little clapboard houses themselves with the *fleur-de-lys* fluttering outside look more than ever as though a strong wind would blow them all away.

Turning to face the other way, Vince watches half a dozen children clutching flyaway towels around the village pool, on the far side of the church. Parc Bourget is the limit of the French-Canadian Pointe Claire. This is the French swimming pool, this the French school, the French church, the French park. The French-speaking population of the village used gather here with their skittery little flags and light a bonfire on the evening of June 24, Quebec's *Fête nationale*. It was called St-Jean Baptiste Day then. Not a soul speaking English down here, either then or on any other day of the year.

Not a soul other than Vince. He had high school French in those days, not at all fluent. But he was curious. And he was sympathetic. He has his stepfather, Ted Cunningham, to thank for that. Ted Cunningham had only contempt for French Canadians, their speech, their church, their sins, their fun, their anxieties over their language. Vince, who had only contempt for Ted Cunningham, has chosen to live closer to francophones than to English Canadians for most of his life.

There's a Canadian flag outside the teashop, a leftover from Canada Day, Vince notices as he cruises back up to the Lakeshore Road. Probably a flag is never innocuous, but here, a stone's throw from those little wooden houses down on the *pointe*, the red maple leaf on the white background is like a red rag: a provocation. This village may have a whole lot to say about Quebec, about what's happened to it in the past thirty years. But, at the same time, Pointe Claire is a kind of little Canada. That's what that article in *l'Actualité* magazine decided last winter.

Vince was in La Malbaie at the time—he'd followed Lucette back there. That's where he'd seen the magazine announcing that Pointe Claire was the most desirable place to live in Quebec. It was the first time in years that he'd heard of Pointe Claire. The article was packed with charts and tables. The marriage of French and English who live here side by side. The relative affluence, shopping facilities, entertainment, libraries, sports facilities and cleanliness and recycling and God knows what all else. The journalist snidely concluded that Pointe Claire was the most Canadian of Quebec communities.

So what is Pointe Claire, anyway? Typical of Quebec? Or of Canada?

Eh?

Vince pulls up in front of La Bouffe. The real answer, he figures, is that it's typical of both. And how Canadian that is. How Québécois. You see? There isn't even a name that covers both. At least none that does so satisfactorily. Canada seems to deny Quebec. And Quebec certainly doesn't cover Canada. So how about "Canada and Quebec"? If Trinidad and Tobago can do it, why not Canada and Quebec? Or would that be Quebec and Canada? Ha. Someone would be sure to feel humiliated at taking second place. What a quandary. This place is like one of those irritating little puzzles that can never be solved.

Vince orders himself a cheeseburger all dressed, a *poutine*, and a large Coke, and sits down beside the Harley.

A half dozen village matrons are grouped under candy-striped umbrellas outside the café on the other corner of rue de Lourdes, sipping bowls of capuccino, sharing confidences, and glancing in Vince's direction. Feeling more than ever a cat among the pigeons, Vince stares at them more closely, wondering if perhaps he knew any of them, if any of them were in school with him. They're speaking in low voices, but in the moments of laughter and loudness he can hear they're speaking English. No matter how well they can speak French, English is the language they speak among themselves, all these women. Sal too, of course. A woman whose friends call her Sal is no francophone. What kind of name is Sal anyway? The name on the lease was Katarina something von something Schleiermacher. No mention of anything even remotely like Sal. Sarah? Sally? Probably. There were Sallys at school with Vince, and some of them were Sally short for Sarah. There was a big crop of Sallys and Cathies and Debbies at Beaconsfield High School in Vince's day. No shortage of diminutives. Bonnies, too. Vince hasn't thought of the name Bonnie in nearly thirty years. The one in his class was Bonnie short for Bonita, but no one ever called her Bonita.

What other possibilities are there?

Salome? Ha! A severed head, madam? On a salver, madam? Vince doesn't think so. He raises a sceptical eyebrow at the mild suburban matrons under their gaily striped umbrellas. Not a *femme fatale* among them.

The closest thing to a *femme fatale* around here would be some businesswoman type desperate to prove her mettle in a man's world. The type Vince can't stand. He prefers women who aren't too sure of themselves. Diffident, lonely women. No, that's not quite it. There's more to it than that. He likes the great opera singer Jessye Norman too—he loves Jessye Norman, he would die for Jessye Norman—and you could hardly call her diffident. But she isn't what you'd call a business type either. And there's no way she's trying to be like a man. Jessye Norman is all woman, and what a woman—a real *femme fatale*. But that's neither here nor there. Vince doesn't expect to meet up with the likes of Jessye Norman any day soon. More's the pity.

Vince leaves his bike beside La Bouffe and is conscious of eyes following him as he crosses the road and heads into the Marché Seaubois.

The signs emblazoned all over the front windows, of course, are in French only. That's what the law requires. If there's any English, anywhere, it's inside the store, far enough inside as to be well out of sight of passersby. Surprisingly, there's none. Not one English sign anywhere. And quite right too. Is there a single soul who can't figure out that the sign over the eggplant means eggplant even if it says *aubergine*? Vince picks up an iceberg lettuce, some minced beef, bacon, ketchup, yellow mustard, sweet pickles, coffee, beer, frozen fries, milk. Among the plastic cheeses in the fridge a roll of *chèvre* catches his eye. He could pocket it, easy as pie.

No.

Oh, no. Not *chèvre*. That's a whole other story. A whole other Vince.

There are only three other men in the store, the two managers and their teenaged helper. The older manager, behind the meat counter, is exchanging pleasantries in French with a dumpy little housewife waiting for her sliced bologna. She can't be a regular customer, and she can't have much of an ear for French accents, or she'd have figured out the manager is an Italian who is no happier in French than he is in English. But then, perhaps she likes to practise her French with the village shopkeepers.

Vince listens to her hesitant phrases as he picks up a baguette, some hamburger buns... he wants some kind of pastry too, and picks up a box of those raisin squares his grandmother used to call fly's cemetery—he hasn't had those in years. Anything else? He heads over to the cans of sardines and, with the suggestion of a smile on his big face, picks up a whole case. And then a bag of sugar. Vince detests sardines, and he doesn't take sugar in his coffee. It's never too soon to be ready for the *dénouement*, though, even when you're hoping there won't be one.

The younger of the managers is at the cash where a petite, dark-haired matron is calling him Mike. She has her back to Vince, reaching into her purse for her wallet, but when she straightens he can see it's pretty little Carrie.

Vince watches her leave the store. She's dolled up in a small pink sundress and matching pink sandals, lipstick, and dangly earrings. She isn't Vince's type at all. And it's easy enough to sneer at her. She'd look all wrong downtown. She'd look all wrong in the countryside, like an ice cream cone in the middle of winter.

Through the shop window Vince watches Mike's assistant fill the back of her beige minivan—why they call a vehicle that size a minivan is beyond Vince—with seven or eight bags of groceries. How big a family does she have, anyway? And why's she so edgy? Even from this distance Vince can sense her nervousness. Vince can imagine several reasons for it. Her little French, her children, her mother, her house, her garden, her budget, her waistline, her husband's cholesterol level. But none of these reasons is sufficient to explain the way she's put herself together—what's she trying so hard for, anyway?—or the way she glances around her to see who's watching. The women with stories worth hearing aren't the ones sharing confidences over bowls of capuccino. The women with stories worth hearing are the ones like Carrie.

Outside, with one bag of groceries in each arm, Vince walks over to Carrie's minivan, which she is just beginning to move out of her parking space. She looks like a little girl perched up high in the big vehicle. "Hi there, Carrie," he says.

"Oh, hi!" Carrie straightens in surprise and tucks her dyed black hair behind her ear. Her fingers are bony, her fingernails bleached white. Her foot slips off the brake—she can hardly reach the pedals, he sees, leaning in through the window—and the van lurches back an inch or two before she steadies it. She says nothing more, though. Has she forgotten his name?

"Vince," he says, reaching a big hand out towards her.

"Yeah, I know. Hi, Vince," she answers. Her hand is cool and dry, her voice casual, almost careless. But she meets his eye boldly. And holds his gaze.

Vince knows an opportunity when he sees one.

"Are you on your way to the house? I have to stop off at the gas station, but then I'm going home. Can I give you a ride?" She pulls her eyes away and looks doubtfully around the parking lot full of minivans. All these women drive minivans. The very idea that Vince might not own a car is giving Carrie pause. Only teenagers and cleaning women use the buses in Pointe Claire. Everyone else drives.

"No car," Vince drawls, enjoying this. "My bike's over there." He jerks his head in the direction of the Bouffe.

"Your bike?" Carrie asks, dismay vying with disbelief. But Vince is already on his way.

As she backs the van up, Vince loads the bags, mounts and starts up the Harley. He revs it just to show off while a couple of cars pass slowly, and then roars down the deserted Lakeshore Road, knowing full well the expression on Carrie's face without having to see it. In his rearview mirror he watches her beige minivan slide out of the parking lot like an overgrown slug. That is one desperate dame.

3

Taking the scenic route home through the backstreets, Vince has just turned down Wilton towards the lake when a rabbit races across his path. He brakes even before it dawns on him this must be a pet; there are no wild rabbits in Pointe Claire. And, sure enough, there at the back of the garden on his left is a hutch. The rabbit has crawled in underneath the hedge on the other side of the road—a huge, brazenly unkempt cedar hedge, ten feet or more high, obscuring whatever house lies behind. Something odd about it, though. It isn't only its raggedness that stands out here among the manicured lawns. And it isn't only the water that's gushing out of a hose on the driveway. Vince looks more closely, and then finds himself staring.

On this side of the hedge, for a start, is an intricate pattern of stones. One loop of large flat grey stones outside a loop of smaller, pinkish stones. Another loop of round pebbles, another... The driveway, too, what *is* it made of? It's some kind of fabric, almost like some sodden, weather-blackened carpeting. Something else catches his eye, something about the gate. Vince inches his bike back to get a better look at the rough wooden gate, over which a length of driftwood curves in such a way as to create the effect of a Japanese temple. There's some other structure behind that, but it's obscured by the hedge and gate.

Vince turns his head, feeling someone's eyes on him. It's a fierce, fit, short-haired blonde standing outside the front door of a house across the road, and she's glaring at him.

"Wanna buy a house?" she shouts over at him. A middle-aged woman in short shorts with a crazy glint in her eye.

Vince looks behind him. No one. The termagant really is addressing him. Now that's a good word that Vince doesn't often get to use. Vince loves to find a use for a good word.

"I said," she repeats more slowly, more loudly, even more deliberately, "DO YOU WANT TO BUY A HOUSE?"

This is what they're like when they've gone completely berserk. Vince hasn't often had much to do with this type. He's made good and sure that he's long gone by the time they become like this.

"Of course you don't. No one wants to live across from this—" and the woman casts her left arm out, incorporating the whole of the property with the Japanese entrance. "Just think what it would be like, living here, and pity us."

Vince is at a loss for words. But he's loath just to roll on his way. The termagant is just warming up, and Vince—well, he's not to blame for this little drama. He finds he has to remind himself of this. The role of innocent bystander is not one he's found himself playing too often.

"I'll sell to you. If you love it so much, why don't you put your money where your mouth is? Come and live in our house. We can have the papers drawn up in a trice. Come on in and sign on the dotted line."

Vince decides to play along. "Why do you want to sell?"

He's hardly opened his mouth when he notices the hose moving. He can't see anyone, but someone must be standing further up the sodden driveway, out of sight, pulling the hose. Playing a little game, in fact.

"Why?" the woman repeats. "WHY?—"

But she gets no further. She's caught sight of whoever is in the driveway. She doesn't lose interest in Vince, though. She seems to assume he's implicated in whatever it is that's going on here.

"Look at this!" she screams at Vince. "He's soaking everything. My lawn, the road. He's been running that water all day. He's doing it to annoy me. On purpose. That's why I want to sell. I want out of here. I want him out of my life!"

The response is silence. But the hose is poking out again now, and gushing stronger than ever.

"You see? He's doing it deliberately." Her voice is cracking with anger and frustration.

Vince can't resist. He moves the Harley forward to see up the driveway.

And there, in the shadow of the huge cedars, stands a short, slight man of about fifty with a bemused smile on his face, playing the woman with the hose as though teasing a kitten with a length of yarn. His face, peppered with freckles, has the roundness and the charm of childhood—and the pallor of the grave. He straightens when he sees Vince.

"So you're the lucky guy," he smiles, gesturing for Vince to pull into the driveway. "I'm Scott MacLuhan."

Scott MacLuhan. What a quintessentially English-Canadian name, Vince thinks, for such a lunatic. Scott MacLunatic. MacLoon.

There's a car at the back of the driveway, an old Pontiac, and tucked away behind that, under a tarpaulin, is a motorbike. Not a Harley, for sure not a Harley. Some Japanese job. Vince cuts his motor, pulls off his helmet and puts out his hand, but MacLoon is shouting back at the termagant and doesn't notice.

"We used to be friends, believe it or not," he tells Vince, gesturing towards the woman. His stained pants are held up by a curled leather belt, his T-shirt is faded and shrunken. The raggedly cut dark hair at the nape of his neck sticks out sideways like the boughs of a tree in a child's drawing of Christmas.

"And now she's hounding me out of here. You wouldn't believe what she says about me these days. All kinds of accusations. She's even accused me of Satanism."

He seems genuinely bewildered, and Vince, who has known Satanists, can understand why.

"And that," he seems to assume that Vince must know his story, "is just what City Hall wants to hear. Any enemy of that woman's, though, is welcome in my garden."

Vince dismounts. The driveway *is* covered in a kind of carpeting, or matting. The brown-shingled shack to the right of the driveway is on its last legs. It wouldn't take much to blow this house down. And there's debris everywhere—bits of broken window frames, old cardboard boxes, piles of bricks, stones, bottles. But MacLoon is leading the way past the shack and along the path, and Vince, bowing his head to pass under the gate, begins to see that he is in the company of a master.

The garden is on many levels, stretching around the little shack all the way to the back yard, with more substances and more variety than any other garden Vince can remember seeing. There are little patches of vivid green moss, strips of blue-green grass, lines of bricks, rubber tires, pools of water, little plastic dinosaurs on ledges of bleached driftwood, curved wooden bridges, deliberately uneven pathways, all manner of recycled, precisely arranged junk.

This man is a real artist. No wonder he has enemies. Vince looks at him in awe. Before he can speak, though, a car pulls up in the driveway, and three men in suits clamber out. Vince nods to them in passing and climbs back on the Harley. The termagant watches in silence from her doorstep as he turns back onto the road.

"I would *love* to buy your house!" he calls over to her, the engine idling. "How much are you asking?" Probably not that much, in fact. Property prices have been depressed for years by the threat of Quebec separating. It's so easy to paint Quebec the devil. As though English Canada hadn't effectively separated from Quebec years ago. And as if Quebec separation would really, in the end, make the slightest difference to man or beast. With the money Vince's mother has left him, he could afford the house, too.

But the woman looks away, pretends she hasn't heard.

"You mean you weren't serious?" he taunts. "Well, I am. I'd love to live next door to that place. It would be a privilege."

At the corner he pauses for long enough to read the name of the street. Wilton. Someone should put a plaque on the gate to that garden, the way they do in the States on heritage houses. Here in Pointe Claire, though, they're more likely to raze it.

One of the Remillard kids is hunkered down right in the middle of the driveway studying a caterpillar when Vince rolls up to the house. Vince accelerates and misses the little darling by several inches—he just wanted to give her a scare—but gets the caterpillar. The kid goes screaming to her *maman*, and if her *maman* knows her business, she'll now make *very* sure to keep her little cabbage out of Vince's way.

When he dismounts, he sticks his wad of well-chewed gum on the windshield of the blue van just where it should melt nicely in the sunshine. Then he takes his groceries indoors and checks out the phone in the kitchen to see if anyone called while he was out. No. A good sign, that. If everything works out the way he hopes, Vince is going to have time on his hands. Time, energy—when has he ever lacked for energy?—and inspiration. And talent, too. He cracks open a beer. This is his chance. This is what he's wanted. A window, a breather, the time and the opportunity to see what he can do. For Vince fancies himself an artist too. MacLoon will be his inspiration. MacLoon is a kindred spirit in the suburban wasteland.

Vince has just taken his beer out to the porch to study the Harley when he sees Carrie pulling into her driveway.

He cups his hands behind his head and stretches briefly. Then it's into his Los Angeles cop stance—actually it's his Tim-Robbins-in-*Short-Cuts*-stance—hands on hips, legs apart, as he waits for her to make a move.

"Some bike," she calls to Vince over the hedge that surrounds her back yard. She almost succeeds in getting the tone right.

"Yeah." He doesn't move. It would be neighbourly of her to invite him over to her place. If she has the guts.

"I'm just going to put these groceries away—" she says nervously as he sidles over towards her, his hands still on his hips.

The effect of this is lost on her, he realizes, as he walks alongside the high hedge towards Carrie's driveway. Better that, though, than having to strike the pose all over again. It has to look casual, comfortable, natural.

"—and then I'm going over to the pool for a swim."

"What pool's that?" Somehow Vince can't picture Carrie at the village pool in the company of all those windblown children.

"Oh, it's the Lakeshore Swim Club, an outdoor pool we belong to...." Then, she adds, "There's a Ladies' Swim between noon and one."

"For ladies only?" He leans on the word "ladies." And it hardly seems necessary to add, "How sexist," but he does so anyway. The joys of the moral high road are as limited, Vince has always found, as those of an endless stretch of unbending highway, but he experiences them seldom enough that he can relish the moment.

Carrie lifts two grocery bags out of the van and turns her back on Vince as he closes in on her. "There are only women around at that time of day," she explains matter-of-factly, as though she would never, for the life of her, use the word "ladies." She's unbelievably small-boned, this particular little lady, with wrists about the width of Vince's big toe. Everything is good and big out here in Pointe Claire—except for some of the minikins who live here. Minikins. That's another good word.

"Hey, whaddya say I give you a hand with all those bags, and then you show me this swim club of yours. Can I join too?"

"Most of the members are families with kids..."

But Vince is not a man to take a hint. He looks at her quizzically, wanting an answer to his question.

"But I guess there's no reason you couldn't join," she says doubtfully. "There are some single members, I think. I could give you the phone number of the woman who's in charge of membership this year."

"Sounds like it's got all kinds of prejudices, this pool of yours. Kind of like those apartment buildings that you can't keep pets in, or children."

"The house is in a big mess," she says, ignoring this. She's fumbling with her front door key as if she had never used it in her life before. "Teenagers," she adds, as though that were explanation enough. Which it just might be. The idea of having kids has always appalled Vince, especially during those times when he's been living with a woman who is saddled with some.

Inside, Vince is surprised to smell tobacco. The house is enormous, solid, mostly emptly, and seemingly indestructible. Wall-to-wall green carpeting, imitation wood panelling, and late IKEA furnishings. And every light in the place is hanging from the middle of a ceiling. But a mess? The only sign he can see that the house is even lived in is the mug of tea in the sink. There are women who die of starvation thinking they're too fat. Maybe Carrie is one of them, too.

Carrie is munching on carrot sticks and stashing boxes of lasagna in the freezer when he carries in the last three grocery bags.

"You must really like Pizza Pockets," he marvels, catching a glimpse of the inside of the freezer.

"Not me. These are for my husband. And for the kids. The price was right, so I thought I'd stock up. I'd like to do more of that. Bulk buying, I mean. It's the only way to beat the system. And I'm not short of space. I could store a lot more in this house. If there's one thing I'd really like, it's to be a really well-organized bulk buyer."

She's dead serious.

"Here, could you put these in the big freezer? Downstairs, on your left." She hands him a case of frozen grape juice, and he goes down to the basement, where the smell of tobacco smoke is even stronger. The basement is as big as a supermarket—and nearly as well-stocked, with walk-in storage closets, a freezer that could hold several corpses, and neatly stacked shelves groaning under the weight of gallon tubs of peanut butter, canned vegetables, bottled water, diet soft drinks, pickles, paper towels, soap, serviettes, giftwrap, and enough rolls of three-ply toilet paper to supply a small army for the better part of a year.

Following the smell of tobacco from one cavernous room to another, Vince finds himself face to face with a small, round, gaudily red-headed woman dressed in dove-grey chiffon and holding a thin black and gold filtered cigarette in an ebony holder.

"A new man!" She smiles as he stops in the doorway. The room is hung with a hundred or more expensively framed colour photographs of glamorous women in extraordinary hats. "Oh, I *do* like to meet a new man!"

"Vince is the name."

"Janet," she says, reaching out her hand. Nothing standoffish about this one. "A pleasure, I'm sure. Oh, yes, definitely a pleasure." She smiles. "Well, well, well. What a surprise. A nice surprise, I should add, and a nice change from the men Carmen usually brings home. And from that feeble little White Rabbit husband of hers too, I should say. *If* I might be so bold."

What a card.

"Will you?" Janet asks, offering Vince a Balkan Sobranie.

"Gladly."

"Good. I thought you just might like one. I can't abide these pious people and their fanaticism over what they think of as their Health with a Capital H. I'm seventy-six years old. And I've been enjoying my Sobranies for more than half a century."

Janet's hair may be thinning, but it is piled high on her head and held together with pins topped with what just might be real pearls. Vince is impressed. She's worked hard putting herself together. The blue of her eyes is faded, but her mascara is the colour of midnight, and the red on her lips is a true red, smudged only slightly near the corner of her mouth. Not bad, for seventy-six. Her ears are studded with the same pearls that her neck is swathed in, her wrists drip with golden bangles and charm bracelets, her fingers are busy with rings of gold and amethyst, opals, turquoises, and sapphires, and her fingernails, though cracked and split, gleam bright red.

"Let me guess. You're the man who's moved in next door."

"I am."

"And what brings you here?" She's watching him like a hawk. And he's estimating the value of her jewellery—but he's doing so unobtrusively. Something tells him to tread warily with this one. Vince decides to risk the truth. He looks her straight in the eye.

"Art," he says, dropping his voice.

"Art? Is that what you said? Are you an artist?"

Vince has never described himself as an artist before. Yet it's true. He's a real artist, a consummate artist, really. And what he creates is himself, over and over again, persona after persona, fiction after fiction. His work requires talent and skill and inspiration and flexibility and nerve, all of which he has in abundance.

It'll be months before any of these women realizes what kind of artist Vince is, exactly, before someone actually uses the words "con artist," and figures out that they apply to Vince. In the meantime they'll just assume that he's the kind of artist who paints pictures. And that's OK, that isn't a lie. That's exactly what he wants, now. It's high time he got used to the idea.

"Yes," he says, "an artist." It's satisfying to tell the truth once in a while. Satisfying to be able to tell the truth with impunity. There is something risky about this, though. It's all just a bit close to the bone. He's going to need all his wits about him to keep control of this character. Living a lie is one thing. Living a pun is another.

"Well, good for you. What kind of artist?"

"Drawing, painting," he says hesitantly. Too hesitantly. This is an unfamiliar vocabulary. "Oils. I work mostly in oils," he continues more confidently. It's a lie. Vince hasn't sat at an easel since he was fifteen. But he wants to be that kind of artist, too. He's promised himself to get started again, to become a real artist, just like his real father. That's been his plan, coming back here to Pointe Claire: live off the fat of the land and become an artist.

Janet has noticed his hesitation. "This is a new departure for you?"

"It'll be the first time I devote myself full time to my art."

"Aha! A change of direction. It happens to the best of us. My first career was as a fan dancer. Do they still use that term? Probably today they'd call me an exotic dancer."

Vince stares at her.

"Oh yes, that's how I started out," she continues blithely, pleased at Vince's reaction. "Now that's an art, I can tell you. A fan dancer. A performance artist. I never liked the word stripper. *La stripteaseuse* is better. *La stripteaseuse* has a nice sultry feel to it. English is so crude, isn't it? I was never a hooker, oh no, a fan dancer's a different kind of calling altogether. Although in a sense you could say we're all hookers, aren't we? Men and women both. We all have our price, as it were, in whatever currency we value the most."

Vince is having difficulty imagining Janet young, on stage, scantily clad.

"But there was no false intimacy. I never led the customers on. Sex is practically all in the mind anyway, you know. Jeannette was my professional name. Janet just wouldn't do, you see."

Vince nods. He can see that. Yes. Jeannette, draped in a long feather boa, vulnerable to the slightest breath of wind.

"I specialized in stimulating the imagination. Men are much more imaginative than women usually give them credit for. I worked with suggestion, metaphor. This was in the forties. Montreal was a very different city then. Oh, it was a grand place then. Very drab now, so I gather, very dull. It doesn't sound like my kind of town at all anymore… This was before Carmen, of course." Janet looks up sharply. "Don't let on I told you this. She hates it when I talk about my life. She thinks of it as my 'past,' can you imagine! Amazing, really, that I should have had such a conventional child. She's always been like that. Colleen, now, is more my kind of girl."

Vince looks uncomprehending.

"Carmen's daughter," she explains. "Colleen's the youngest of my grandchildren. I have nothing in common with the boys. Nothing at all. Hockey, beer, and coarse jokes. That about sums them up, both of them. But Colleen's a great girl. Funny, isn't it, how these things can skip a generation and then pop up again unexpectedly?"

From upstairs comes the noise of voices raised.

"Oh, yes," Janet is continuing, ignoring the sound. "I'm the madwoman in the basement. Attics are getting rare, so there's nothing else for it: they have to stash us in the basement. And even fan dancers get old, sad to say. Not too many people wonder about what happens to us after we step out of the limelight. It might be easier all round if we just vanished into thin air. But we don't. Too much vitality. But where was I? A new departure, yes. Just the ticket. How are you going to feed yourself?"

Vince shrugs. "I have some savings."

"Savings don't last. Sooner or later, you'll need an income. And you won't make an income from painting."

She's right, of course. Vince will have to keep his expenses low. Or be distracted forever with bread-and-butter deals.

"Art for art's sake is quite a luxury," Janet is continuing. "More than I could ever afford. I favour"—she gestures around the room with her ringed hands—"the kind of art that pays the rent. I designed every one of these. Sold them all too. Very expensive they were, but no one complained. They were worth every penny."

"The hats?" he asks.

"That's right. That was my business after I stopped dancing. Brim's at first. Brim is my surname, hard to believe, but there it is. Then, later on, after the language law came in, it was Brims, without the apostrophe. It suited me just fine when we were told to stop using apostrophes. What matters is doing a good job. And I did. I had a secret."

There's a high-pitched voice shouting somewhere. Carrie's? It doesn't sound like Carrie. Janet raises one eyebrow but makes no comment. Perhaps it happens often.

"You see," Janet explains, "I saw the millinery in the same light as the stripping. Both create an illusion, but there's more to it than that. What makes a great hat is flamboyance—and peekaboo."

From upstairs comes the sound of a door slamming. Janet falls silent, waits. This is one lady who knows the score. She looks up wryly as Carrie bursts into the room.

"I have to be on my way," Carrie says to Vince.

Janet blows smoke as Vince stubs out his Sobranie. "Come back and chat some other day," she says.

"I'll do that."

"But not in the afternoon," she calls after him. "Mornings are better. Or evenings. I'm often busy in the afternoon."

Carrie is silent on the way back upstairs.

"What keeps your mother busy in the afternoon?"

"She has," Carrie purses her lips, "a gentleman friend."

Vince wonders if that is irony he's hearing in her enunciation of the word "gentleman."

"Oh yeah?" he asks, hoping for more.

"He's a history teacher. They just talk about movies," she adds quickly, closing a door on that subject.

There's another silence.

"My daughter was just here," she says finally.

"Here?"

Carrie leads him along the hall upstairs where she pushes open the door to a girl's bedroom littered with clothing and bedclothes and cassette tapes and cans of Coke and ashtrays and pizza crusts and magazines and boxes of tampons and used tissues and worn panties shaped like a figure-eight and earrings and tubes and bottles and lotions and lipsticks. On the radiator under the window are two crisp squiggles of dirty tube socks.

"Want to see more?" Carrie asks, closing the door with some difficulty. "There's more. The house may look neat, but that's because I just close the door on all the messes."

"And they never spill out into the hall and the kitchen?"

"Of course they do. And that's where I draw the line. I want those parts of the house tidy. That's not such an unreasonable thing to ask, is it? Most of the time I just bung anything that doesn't belong into the closet, but surely I can ask my own daughter to pick up some of her own garbage once in a while..."

"Oh, I think you can." And obviously do, he thinks.

She smiles plaintively. She's been wanting an ally for so long, and she chooses to find one in Vince. "But really it's easier for me to do it myself than to get the kids to do it," she sighs.

"And your husband?"

"Oh, Reed—" Reed! He would be called Reed! "—most of the time he doesn't even notice it. And when he does, all he does is politely ask whoever's around to tidy up—and then he forgets all about it. So of course nothing gets done."

"Of course," he echoes. Deaf to irony, she seems to like it when he repeats what she says. There's a name—what is it?—for the tendency to repeat what someone else has said to you. "How many children do you have, anyway?"

"Five, counting their father and my mother." This trips off her tongue in a way that suggests she's said it more than once before. But not even repetition can dull the bitterness behind her words.

"Five," he echoes again. Then, to draw her out, he adds, "Lots of company."

"Company! Oh! Sometimes it's so lonely I could scream. It's bad enough when they're small. Small children are no better company than dogs—"

A lot worse company, Vince would have said. He nods understandingly.

"—but what they don't tell you is that, the older they get, the more children start behaving like husbands—sticking around only long enough to put together a snack, and then skulking downstairs to the TV and the company of their favourite assassins."

What a tough, uptight, angry little cookie. What would Reed have to say for himself? Who knows? Who cares? But it always takes two. When you listen to a certain kind of woman for long enough, you can get a pretty bad impression of men. Vince has no illusions at all about men. But long-suffering women are vipers.

"Wanna ride over to the pool on the Harley?"

Carrie recoils as though he were proposing a dirty weekend. And this is the very lady who would love a dirty weekend. What *is* he going to do with her? Turn into Little Sir Echo?

"No!" she blurts out. "No... thanks, er, I don't have time now. I'm going to be late, I have to get back to the office by two o'clock. I'm on my lunch break."

"Tomorrow, then?" It won't be a bad idea for Vince to cultivate Carrie. She's his contact with Sal. And Vince is going to want to keep Sal at bay for as long as possible.

"Oh. Well. Maybe. I don't know."

Has she always been like this? Vince wonders as he walks back to Sal's. Surely not. She'd have exploded by now. You can't live in such a state of nervous tension indefinitely.

Chances are, then, that she'll explode soon.

"Back to the Garden" is blaring from the radio, and Vince is flipping through an old copy of *Saturday Night* that he found in a pile of magazines downstairs, when the telephone rings. A full-page photograph has just caught his eye. David. Yes, the marble original. Michaelangelo's David on display in some domed Italian alcove—in Rome, isn't the original in Rome?—the pedestal partly obscured by a dozen or more museum-goers, the young man himself fully visible, from the top of his beautiful curls all the way down to his toes. The perfection of manly form. Almost naked, but not quite. For in this picture—it's an advertisement for Canadian Airlines—David's nakedness is covered. And not by a fig leaf, but by a large, gilded maple leaf. "We Bring Canada to the Rest of the World," reads the caption. And yes, it must be Rome. "Canadian provides direct service to Rome and Milan." David certainly isn't in Milan.

Vince reaches over for the phone without bothering to read the display.

"The roses are magnificent!"

"Yolanda!" he whoops. It's a win! "They arrived. I'm delighted."

"How extravagant of you. How kind!"

"I wanted to give you—" his voice is deep again, controlled "—a small token."

"And we haven't even met."

"But we will. A small token of the hopes I attach to our meeting."

"Until tomorrow, then."

"*À demain.*"

Vince sets the magazine to one side and picks up the Yellow Pages. He wants to send flowers to Carrie, too, and Le Tulipier isn't about to deliver out here. There's a florist in the village... No. He'd better be careful patronizing the local merchants. Some of them may know the name Schleiermacher, know that Sal is no Salvador. There must be a florist in the Fairview Pointe Claire mall. That should be big enough, impersonal enough.

Fairview. Vince glances at the magazine again. The original of the statue may be in Rome. But once, many years ago, for a period of no more than a few weeks, David was in Fairview. That was when Fairview first opened, 1965 or so—70 stores, 70 degrees, that was the slogan they used to lure customers in. Someone had the bright idea that a shopping centre—and especially so huge and well-appointed a shopping centre as Fairview Pointe Claire—should not only be a commercial space but, as in European squares, a centre for culture as well. So they built enormous fountains at each end of the mall and, in a bold and unprecedented move, unprecedented in Canada, anyway, set plaster copies of two of Michaelangelo's masterpieces—one of Moses and one of David—on pedestals for the shoppers' edification and delight.

Which was fine except for one thing. Moses posed no problem, for Moses was clothed. The problem was David. David's unadorned, alert little penis. Not even that little, really, for the statues were both full-sized, and therefore larger than life. The suburban matrons were appalled. They didn't know where to look, what to tell their children. Vince overheard his mother agreeing with a neighbour about it on the phone one afternoon, and then talking it over with Ted Cunningham in hushed tones that evening after dinner. She was outraged, Vince remembers her saying. How could she be outraged? Vince wonders now, staring at the magazine in front of him. Did she remember nothing of Carlos? Nothing at all? And what about Ted Cunningham? Vince doesn't remember how he reacted. Probably he said nothing. The suburban dads were less vocal, less brave, than their wives. God only knows what would have happened if it had been Moses's phallus unveiled instead of the boy's.

Letters poured into *The Chronicle*, or whatever it was called in those days. The talk show lines hummed with the scandal. On CJAD and—what was that other station? the one based in Pointe Claire that played popular music?—CFOX.

Art? Who gave a damn about art? These people were talking about decency. The statue was stark, staring naked, and the upstanding English-speaking citizens of the West Island—by far the majority in those days—wanted it out of their spanking new mall. Pronto. And they got what they wanted. In fact, they got more than they wanted, for no one could see any point in keeping Moses in the mall without David. So, in no time at all, both Moses and David were removed from the Fairview mall. Vince doesn't know what happened to Moses, but David had a bad time. First he was painted green in some student prank, and then he spent a few years in the library at Loyola College. That's where Vince lost track of him.

And now, all these decades later, Canadian Airlines has come up with the solution that no one thought about. Keep the statues, but hide David's penis behind a maple leaf! How very Canadian. Canada Customs officials stop sexy books at the border. Canadians put artists on trial for displaying erotic paintings. "We bring Canada to the rest of the world." Then as now. The enemies of art thrive then as now. How smug. How Philistine.

Do they not know what they do? Oh, let the world beware.

"McKenna," says the voice on the other end of the line.

"I want to send a potted plant as a gift." Nothing too extravagant for Carrie, or he'll just create suspicion.

"Yes, sir. We have a nice orchid in a clay pot for $60."

"Perfect."

What else can he buy over the phone? There's a time line with the MasterCard, and the sooner he spends, the better. There won't be another statement for weeks, and it'll be nearly a month before it reaches Sal. But who knows what Sal herself might spend, over there in Europe wherever she is. And the minute she's told she's over her credit limit, the card will be worse than useless to Vince.

So he orders a carton of frozen steaks, one of frozen shrimp, and one of lamb chops to be delivered tomorrow morning. $313. That'll keep the wolf from the door for a month or two. Ha. What was it Carrie said about bulk buying? And just look at him!

And what about his supplies? Back to the Yellow Pages. Vince wouldn't mind looking around an art supply store. But he wants to put this on MasterCard too, and that means using the phone. Some things are pretty standard, anyway. He picks up the receiver. The best easel they've got is $89. He takes the man's advice on brushes. Sketchbooks in three sizes, finest quality. Charcoal, pens, ink, canvas, oils... a total of $463 including taxes. To be delivered.

That'll do for now. He doesn't have to spend the whole amount this afternoon.

There is one more little housekeeping task. He takes out his own notebook, finds Donald Rimmer's number, and dials again. Vince is cooking on all burners, laying plans. He loves laying plans. Not that you can plan for every eventuality. That, in fact, is the pleasure of it. There is a risk. He has to stay on his toes. He isn't right in his calculations all the time. But he's right most of the time.

"You there tomorrow at eleven?" he asks.

"What ff...for?" A good fence, one of the best, but such an irritating stutter. There must be some way of coping with a stutter. Vince knows he'd find a way.

"I want a price on a couple of paintings."

"Th..that's all?" Donald asks. He uses words sparingly, and hesitates over them, too, avoiding words he's afraid of. Like a man for whom English is an alien tongue.

"And some ID."

"N...name?" Singing might help. That's supposed to work like a charm. Even people—men, really, they're nearly always men—with the most debilitating stutters can manage a song. Why is that, anyway? Is it the rhythm? Whatever it is, it works. And if singing works, surely some kind of chanting would get him over those consonants, rid him of that stupid echo.

"Wincenty Tadeusz Cunningham." Fake ID. He needs it for when his big cheque arrives. Vince has had lots of fake IDs over the years, but this is the first time he's ever arranged for a fake ID in his real name. He loves it.

A quick deal tomorrow morning will whet his appetite for lunch with Yolanda. The paintings are small. He can manage them on the Harley. But he will be needing a car again. Perhaps Yolanda will come in handy there too. Why not? Vince is on a roll.

The doorbell rings, and he opens it to a plump woman in white pleated shorts and a long-sleeved madras blouse.

4

"Hi." She smiles tentatively. "You must be the tenant." In one hand she is carrying a white plastic bag and, in the other, the leash of a yellow Labrador. The dog bristles. Vince bristles too. Dogs have tended, in the main, to be his enemies' best friends.

Vince inclines his head slightly and says nothing, not quite sure what is coming next. When in doubt, wait it out. And never, ever let a stranger know your name.

"Madeleine," she says. "Madeleine McNichol. I promised Sal I would help out if there was any need while she's away." She pronounces her name like a francophone but speaks English without a trace of an accent.

"Vince," he says, gesturing for her to come inside. In the background, the radio is now playing the Beach Boys. Sunny music, that's how Vince thinks of all these old songs. Music for when you're feeling purposeful and energetic.

Madeleine's face is a surprise. Round and gentle and beautiful, with the diffident smile of a woman who would clip recipes for pineapple upside-down cake and rinse out her empty milk cartons. Light makeup—foundation, eyebrow pencil, no lipstick. Almost as nature intended.

The dog is starting to bark. That dog has more sense than its owner.

"Mitsou!" she remonstrates, as the dog strains at the leash.

"Such a sweet dog." He grimaces apologetically, with just a hint of sadness. "And I'm sure I'll get used to her. But I'm sorry to say I'm nervous about dogs." He hesitates. "I was bitten once," he adds confidentially, pulling up his shirt to show the stitches on his side.

Madeleine gasps satisfactorily. She'd gasp a lot more if she knew why he really needed those stitches. But some of Vince's adventures will not go over well in this kind of neighbourhood, and the knifing is one of them.

"Would you like me to leave the dog outside?" she asks.

Vince thinks quickly. What's going to do him the most good? That's the bottom line. He doesn't care one way or the other about the bitch. But he's a great believer in keeping his options open. Madeleine's evidently a friend of Sal's; that's one consideration. There might, Vince muses, eyeing Madeleine's high-necked blouse, be others. It might just suit him for Madeleine to stop by on her daily walks with Mitsou.

"Even the sweetest dogs know when we're afraid of them," he begins. The "we" is a nice touch, he thinks. He's going to have fun making himself part of this upstanding little community.

"Oh, dear." Madeleine is pulling the dog away from the front door. She's such an innocent. The kind of woman a sensible man should hire to cook his meals, manage his household, and raise his kids. With her long straight girlish hair and her shoulders rounded to discourage lewd imaginings, she is the very image of a good woman. Vince knows the type well, and this is the genuine article. Sympathetic to just about everyone. A giver. Just dying to help out, lend an ear, lead her life vicariously.

Only her eyes hint at the possibility of a different kind of story. Friendly enough, certainly. Warm, dark, and not entirely uninteresting. There's sorrow there, and wistfulness, a hope so forlorn and so well hidden that she is holding his eyes in hers before properly realizing that she's supposed to be looking away. And the realization, when it comes, takes her breath away. Vince grins. Madeleine may be an innocent, but with a little nudge in the right direction she might not be an innocent for ever.

"There's no need to leave her outside, I'm sure," he sighs uncertainly. Don't overdo it. This new persona can be vulnerable, but he's not to be a wimp. He bends down to stroke the dog's head calmly, adding, more decisively, "No. There's no need for that. I'd like to win her over." And you too, sugar, he thinks, catching Madeleine's eye again, I'd like to win you over too. This time she looks away instantly. The dog is quiet, expectant. "Bring her inside."

She waves her little white plastic bag—it's weighted down with what looks like a pound of sausages—in the direction of the garage. "OK. I'll just put this in your garbage first."

"Fine," Vince says, it finally dawning on him that the little bag is full of Mitsou's shit. That this woman has been picking her dog's turds off the ground and bagging them. So, people really do that.

He watches as she disposes of the bag and lets Mitsou off the leash. The dog considers first Madeleine and then Vince before deciding to follow them into the house where, ignoring Vince, she sniffs around the kitchen.

The song has ended, and the radio announcer is going on about some guy in San Francisco who's an expert on flirting. "According to this guy," she says in a bored whine that she probably thinks is alluring, but which reminds Vince of nothing so much as a trapped housefly, "top-notch flirters realize that the first step is to stare at people. You can't be ambiguous about it. You stare for exactly two seconds. Anything less doesn't work. Anything more, they may call the cops on you."

Vince acts as though he hasn't heard. Madeleine is getting edgy. That's quite enough of Oldies 990 for one day, he decides, sidling over to the counter. Arousing her interest is one thing; terrorizing her is another.

But this is one announcer who knows how to make herself heard. "Two seconds," she has repeated—"A hint for cautious Canadians, count 'one Saskatchewan, two Saskatchewan'"—before Vince finally succeeds in swatting her.

"I would offer you some coffee if I thought I knew how to work this machine…" Vince says helplessly. He figures the best way to make Madeleine comfortable is to let her know he needs the help she is programmed to provide.

"Oh, thank you," Madeleine says, as Mitsou slumps down heavily on the dining room floor and rests her head on her front paws, "but no. I've had enough coffee for today. And besides," she checks her watch, "I have a *rendez-vous* this aft." Vince hasn't heard anyone say "this aft" since he was fifteen. "I promised a friend I would stop in to see her. But I can show you how to work the machine, if you like."

"Sure." Vince accepts all donations. He's a taker from way back. And then, as she opens the bag of coffee he's handed her, he adds, "Say, would you give me a hand here? The living room is so bright, I want to use it as my studio, and I wouldn't want to damage any of Sal's things. Do you think we could manage to move the furniture downstairs into the family room?"

"You want to use the living room as a studio?" Madeleine asks as they're carrying the end table downstairs.

"I'm an artist," he explains. This time it trips off his tongue.

Madeleine looks quite impressed. "Oh, yeah? What kind of artist?" she asks.

What, Vince wonders, can the word artist mean to her? What can art mean to her? A watercolour of a perennial garden in full bloom, perhaps. Wide-eyed children. Woebegone women. Something blowzy, Vince would bet on it. Something just like Madeleine herself. What's that saying? The thought is father to the deed. Something like that. No. Vince doesn't want to say that. He doesn't mean that at all. That's one of Ted Cunningham's sayings, just another shorthand substitute for thought and feeling.

How did it happen that Vince got into the habit of doing the very same thing? How did he get into the habit of finding a saying for every occasion? Powerful habit, too. He's never managed to shake it off. That, he's sure, is behind his resentment of English—and has a lot to do with his sympathy for francophone Québécois. For Vince, English isn't even second-hand. It's third-hand, a borrowed language, and an alien one— the language he learned because of Ted Cunningham. But somehow indispensable, such is the power of English. And he learned how to use it, oh didn't he just! The best defence against English is knowing how to use it. Some francophones know that. Jacques Parizeau, for example, the leader of the Parti Québécois. Lucien Bouchard of the Bloc Québécois. No stauncher *indépendantistes* than these, no truer defenders of the French language in Quebec. And they speak better English than most English Canadians.

English does have its uses, and Vince uses it like a rapier. Precisely so. Like a well-honed weapon. With the right haircut and the right clothes, Vince can pass for Anglo-Saxon and Protestant. That's another skill he learned from Ted Cunningham. In fact, when you come right down to it, Vince owes a lot to Ted Cunningham. And he resents it all.

What would his real father have said? How did his real father speak? Vince doesn't know. He has so few memories of his father.

Vince looks over at Madeleine, but she hasn't noticed his preoccupation.

Where were they, anyway? Artist. He's an artist.

"A painter. I work in oils... But I find it very difficult to talk about my work," he says. "Talent is fickle. I have a superstitious fear that if I say too much it will fly away and be lost forever."

"Oh," says Madeleine. "But why here? What brings you out here to Pointe Claire?"

"I lived out here on the West Island as a kid," Vince says breezily.

"Really? Me too!" she says. And just as he figures she's about to ask him a question he won't want to answer, she adds, "I wasn't born here, but we—my family—moved here when I was a teenager. And I never left. I've been here practically all my life. Isn't that terrible?"

He touches her shoulder. This is dangerous territory for Vince. The last thing he wants is anyone connecting Vince Carlson with that fifteen-year-old Wincenty Cunningham who ran away in 1965. That would do his reputation around here no good at all. Heading Madeleine off in a less risky direction, he continues, "I came back here to work. And to get in touch with my roots."

She nods as though she understands.

"I've reached a time in my life when I wanted to pause, take stock, decide how I want to proceed from here on in." Vince is enjoying this risky new game. He likes it when the things he says mean more to him than they do to his audience. He likes skirting honesty, being the only one who knows where the truth ends and imagination begins. In short, he realises, he likes telling the truth, if not exactly the whole truth. He is taking stock. That much is true. He's a middle-aged man, and it isn't only his eyesight that's starting to fail him. He is thinking about how he's going to proceed from here on in. That's true too. "I have had many sadnesses in my life," he tells Madeleine, "some heartbreaks, some bad luck. Haven't we all?" How much longer can he keep this up? He touches Madeleine's hand lightly with his fingertips. She wavers.

Vince presses his advantage. "Perhaps I have had more than my share, but who can really say? We have all had more than enough pain, haven't we? I needed a change. Not too drastic a change, but an important change all the same. I feel it's time for some calm, some reflection, some…" he looks searchingly at Madeleine, reaches for the right kind of word, "some consolation." It isn't the right word, but it may do.

"There are times in one's life when one needs that," Madeleine agrees gently, meeting his eyes.

The plants stay, and the track lights, and between them he and Madeleine move two chairs from the kitchen and a small dresser from the back bedroom. The oil paintings go downstairs too, because Vince needs plain white walls to be able to do his own work.

"Sal loves these…*toiles*," Madeleine says as she lifts one off its hook in the dining room. "They were hers, they had belonged to someone in her family. I guess she thought the paintings would be safer on the wall than stacked up against boxes in the storage area."

"Storage area," Vince repeats in a neutral tone of voice, betraying none of the excitement he feels.

"Yeah. Up in the attic. She put a lot of stuff up there. And out in the locked area in the garage."

"Right." *Yes!*

"There are probably two dozen fans out in the garage," she giggles.

"Fans?"

"Yeah. Wolf kept bringing fans home. All kinds of fans."

"Wolf?"

"Sal's ex-husband."

"The big bad Wolf?"

"Yes! How did you know? She did start calling him that—we all did, really—after he ran off with that girl…"

That old story, thinks Vince. "And the fans are his?"

She nods. "His company had started manufacturing fans. He was always bringing home the latest model. Of course, that was *avant*." She pauses. "But he left them here. Sal kept meaning to get rid of them, but she ran out of time, and they just ended up in the garage."

"Your first language...?" Vince asks. He can usually tell, but there's something unusual about her accent in French. Is that European? And what about her husband? McNichol could mean anything. Up in Charlevoix, where Vince spent four months with Lucette, McNichol has been a French name for two hundred years. All thanks to some soldier who stormed the Citadel with General Wolfe and then stormed a *Canadienne* and fathered countless little French-speaking McNichols. So Madeleine's husband might well be a francophone.

Lucette. Madeleine reminds him a bit of Lucette. Though Madeleine doesn't have Lucette's sheen, the sheen of the well-to-do widow. Vince worked hard on Lucette. She welcomed him into her house and her bed. And if it hadn't been for that spendthrift son of hers, Jean-Yves, she would have put the considerable assets of La Poulette Grise into that ski resort development scheme the way Vince wanted. Vince was annoyed when she turned him down. So he forged Lucette's name on an application for a supplementary American Express card especially for Jean-Yves. Then, on a business trip with her to Montreal, Vince ran up nearly $30,000 on plastic before tucking it into a greeting card, which he signed *"ta petite maman,"* and mailed to Jean-Yves for his twenty-first birthday.

Madeleine may look a bit like Lucette, but financially she isn't in Lucette's league at all. It won't be money, not with Madeleine.

"My father is francophone, my mother English," she says. "English from England. We lived there for a while, in London. Then we came back here. And Pierre, my husband, *il est Acadien*, an Acadian, from Moncton. So I speak French more than English now, I guess, but I'm happy to speak English too."

No linguistic hardball for this little innocent. Why is Vince not surprised?

"Can I see some of your work?" she asks as they come back upstairs to the kitchen. Mitsou hoists herself to her feet at their approach and gazes at them expectantly.

"You'll see it," he says cryptically, pouring himself a mug of coffee. Is there no limit to the amount of bullshit this babe will put up with? And then he has the day's very best idea. Why didn't he think of this before? An artist needs a model. Vince needs... well, what? A victim? Yes. But he has Yolanda all lined up already. There has never been any shortage of willing victims like Yolanda, just dying for Vince. And he couldn't care less about them. What Vince needs is a challenge. A woman who takes a bit of persuading.

And what better way than by getting her to model for him? It's so obvious—and so full of potential—that it takes his breath away. Why didn't he think of it before? He must have been inspired by that MacLoon guy.

Madeleine will take some persuading. He eyes her speculatively. Just maybe.

"Actually," he says eagerly, "I wonder if I could ask you to sit for me."

"Sit for you? You mean you want to paint me?"

"Well, I want to begin by drawing you, really. I'll be working with oils too, but later. Charcoal to begin with. Or pencil. Maybe even"—the thought surfacing from long ago—"pen and wash. There's nothing subtler than pen and wash."

Madeleine says nothing.

"Would your husband mind?" Vince ventures.

"Oh, no," she says, "it's not that." She doesn't sound very sure.

"Are you worried about what people would say?" he asks considerately.

"There is that," she concedes. "You wouldn't believe how quick people are to talk. Especially you being a single man…and with a Harley, and all."

And all. He likes that. He shrugs as if it matters not at all to him. "It's up to you."

She's tempted. Some part of her is tempted. But she's so very timid, so very conventional.

"If you're not comfortable with the idea, just forget it." He can afford to be gracious, and to show a little disappointment. He has time. And even if she never comes around, someone else will.

Madeleine has had the very same thought. "I bet Carrie would sit for you," she says suddenly, in a new voice.

Vince looks at her sharply. So. Madeleine doesn't like Carrie. All is not quite as cosy in this neighbourhood as it seems.

Vince is thinking fast. With his bread and butter so nicely taken care of, all Vince really needs from a woman is diversion. And Carrie, certainly, would not be his first choice for that. But Carrie could be useful. Far too easy, of course, and not much fun. But, as Sal's real estate agent, she will be useful in keeping Sal at bay.

So it will be worth Vince's while to work on her. To work on her and to play her. Getting her to model for him will be easy. He'll pay her more attention than she's had in decades, flatter her senseless. He figures he has about one week before she's begging for him. One week max. She'll be putty in his hands. And—this is the beauty of the plan—he'll be a real artist too, just as he's always wanted. An artist like his father. Two birds. One stone. It's perfect.

Madeleine is a different story. She'll take longer. But there isn't a woman alive who isn't susceptible to Vince's undivided attention. Madeleine will model for him, too. She may be balking at it now, but she's going to give it some thought. A lot of thought. Vince likes a challenge. And he has a hunch that there may be more to Madeleine than meets the eye. She might be worth the wait.

As if it were the most natural thing in the world, Vince takes Madeleine's hands in his.

She's pulling away. He holds on tighter. "Yes," he says. "Beautiful skin," he says thoughtfully.

"Skin?"

"Yes." He looks up at her, as though surprised that she heard what he said. "Skin is so important, and you have beautiful skin—hands, face, surely the rest of your body, too." He is watching her carefully. The merest mention of her body is enough to set some women aflutter. Especially women who keep their bodies this well hidden. And, sure enough, she's looking terrified.

He lets her go. "You must use some wonderful lotions," he says, "to keep your skin so soft in this climate, with such dry air to contend with, holes in the ozone layer, overheated winter rooms…"

"Oh," she says. She doesn't know what to say.

"I'm sorry." He smiles at her as naturally as can be. "I guess I'm not supposed to know about lotions and moisturizers and sun-blocks…" But, as Vince knows well, women love it when a man knows about such things. And they find it so disappointing to realize, time after time, that the men who take an interest in cosmetics are men with no interest in women. Vince wasn't out of his teens before he recognized that here was a niche he could fill.

"No. That's all right," she lies. Her voice is back almost to normal. "I'm just surprised." They always are.

"And I'm probably being impertinent. I know. But—I can't help it—I'm always interested in the things we find ourselves up against. And the ways we protect ourselves. Of course, we have all been hurt."

Madeleine flinches, stares at him.

"We get hurt, and then scar tissue closes over the hurt, so that no one knows, or almost no one. We all do it. We have to protect ourselves, to keep things hidden. All the important stuff gets hidden. That's what makes us so much more interesting now than we were as kids. It may be the only consolation of getting older. I'm afraid," he goes on, his voice deep, sincere and sensitive, "that I am not used to having casual acquaintances. I like intimacy in my relationships, especially with women, and I like intensity. I have enemies, and I have very close friends." "Have had" would at least contain a grain of truth. The whole truth is that there have been people, women mostly, who have made the disastrous mistake of thinking he was a close friend. Details like that do not trouble Vince. "And I feel sure you will not be my enemy."

"Oh, no." Madeleine is appalled at the very idea. She is innocent of evil. She lives in a world without enemies. Or so she thinks. Vince smiles his most open smile. In reality, I am your enemy, sweetheart, your natural enemy. I may be your lover, but I will still be your enemy, more than ever your enemy. And there is no protection against me.

"Are you happily married?" he asks.

"Mm, yes," she mumbles in her confusion, wondering why he's asking, not ready yet to realize that it's because he's considering the possibility of unbuttoning that high-necked blouse of hers.

"And faithful?"

"Yes," she squeaks.

"What a shame," he says.

Opening the fridge, Vince pulls out the package of hot dogs and snips the end off with the kitchen scissors. Mitsou is instantly on the alert. Vince waves a hot dog around a bit. The last traces of wariness disappear from the dog's eyes, and she eats out of his hand.

"Any problems with the alarm system?" Madeleine asks, peering at the panel behind the front door as she goes on her way.

"Uh, no." The alarm system is one thing Vince isn't going to worry about. And it isn't going to do Sal one bit of good either. It isn't designed for a Trojan horse.

"Well, I have the same kind in my house. Let me know if you need any help with it."

"Thanks." Vince makes a mental note that Madeleine knows how the alarm system works. "So, where does that friend of yours live?" he asks.

"On Golf Avenue. It's a ten-minute walk for me. My house is just up the road from here," she adds chattily. "On the corner of Lakeview and St. John's." And suddenly she blushes, thinking she's being forward.

Golf Avenue. Vince hesitates, but then can't resist taking advantage of Madeleine's confusion. "Want a ride over?"

"Ride?"

"Sure. I'll take you." And why not? Vince can handle it. He's on top of the world, N. Vince Ybl.

"No. How silly of me. I have to take Mitsou home..."

"That's fine. Whatever you like. You walk her home…" He pauses, and then leaves it at that. She tries to read his eyes, fails, and then limps on her way with Mitsou beside her.

The middle of the garage floor consists of wooden planks covering a pit that must be a car mechanic's dream—but that Sal has used for storing firewood. At least, one end is stacked with a couple of cords of wood. The other is empty except for a greasy-looking puddle of water. There must be a leak in the roof. To make some more room in the garage—he'll need it for a load of hot electronic equipment that's being delivered next week—Vince moves aside the wooden planks and tosses the three mountain bikes that are neatly lined up in the back of the garage down into the puddle at the far end of the pit. He eyes the storage area Sal has barricaded with a length of wood nailed across the door, but decides that's a job for another day.

What's urgent is to get everything he can sell from the house itself into one spot. So he goes back indoors and moves all the goods he won't himself use into the family room. Then he closes the door, locks it, and adds the key to his own key ring. He doesn't want anyone wandering in here unexpectedly.

Then he glances at his watch. That's about right. Madeleine should have had time to get home by now.

He dons his helmet, starts the Harley, and heads straight for Madeleine's. Mitsou bounds over to greet him when Madeleine opens the door. Vince says nothing, just hands Madeleine the spare helmet. She's as thrilled as a teenager. That's the great advantage of middle-aged women. They're appreciative. She climbs onto the bitch pad behind him.

5

And they're off, back to the Lakeshore, right through the village—Madeleine holding onto Vince so tightly he can hardly breathe—and as far as Golf Avenue. There he leans into the bend between the old corner store with a hand-scrawled sign that used to advertise "*Vers à vendre*" all year round—it's now an art gallery—and the house opposite that's been tarted up as the Piazza Romana restaurant—

—and there he gasps, loses control of the Harley, and, with Madeleine's scream reverberating in his ear, barely succeeds in pulling over to the side of the road without keeling over completely.

Vince really can't breathe now. He's gasping for air. It's Madeleine's fault. Stupid fucking bitch. He rips Madeleine's arms off his chest—and she half falls, half jumps off the bike. In the same move, he yanks loose the strap around his neck and pulls his helmet off.

But it doesn't help.

What's going on? What's happened to him?

He closes his eyes, breathing with difficulty. When he looks up, leaning unsteadily on the handlebars, Madeleine has picked herself up and is gesticulating at him. Is she speaking? What is she saying? Her face is distorted, but he can't hear her at all. Now she's pulled off her helmet and is turning away, running away.

Vince frowns. What has happened to him? What is this? Vince has never felt like this before, never.

No. That's untrue, he suddenly realizes. There's something familiar about all this.

And all at once he knows. It's something he once knew, an echo of something powerful he once knew.

The accident.

It's what people call an accident. But in some way it was inevitable, not an accident at all. If that hadn't happened, something else would have.

Something had to give, eventually. It was inevitable that something happen, something dramatic and final. That's why he doesn't think it was really an accident.

Pull yourself together, Vince. Pull yourself together. Go after Madeleine. You've got to go after Madeleine. Go after Madeleine…

He can't do it. He just can't. He sits down beside the Harley on the side of the road, holds his head in his hands, and concentrates on breathing.

What if the fifteen-year-old Vince had taken a different route home that afternoon? What if he had been nowhere near the corner of Golf and Lakeshore when that girl came tearing out onto the road? What if he hadn't run straight into her?

But he did. He knocked her over, hard. And then a passing car smashed into his bicycle and into the girl, careening on down the road before the driver, it was a woman, finally pulled up near the corner of Lanthier, flung open the door of the car, and started running back to where Vince and the girl were lying.

Vince can see the scene in his mind's eye as clearly as if it happened yesterday. The car, the woman, the girl, the smashed bicycle.

The boy? There's something shadowy, almost ghostly about the boy. Vince can't see him clearly, face to face. No. That isn't it. Vince doesn't want to see the boy clearly. Doesn't dare. This is bad enough as it is.

Vince was hurt—his shoulder hurt, and his elbow, and the side of his head. But the girl—it would be that girl, the only girl who had ever interested him, what *was* her name, anyway?—was hurt worse, how badly he couldn't tell, but she wasn't moving at all. She'd been barrelling out of her driveway straight onto the road, full tilt, completely oblivious.

What the hell had she been doing? She wasn't two years old. She was Vince's own age, a girl of fifteen. Had she gone berserk?

The only thing Vince has ever been able to come up with to understand what she did is that maybe it had something to do with her mother. Had they just had a fight? Her mother was there, for sure. He remembers her running down the driveway towards them, shrieking like a madwoman. And the driver of the car had nearly made it back, too, to where she'd run into them.

Vince looked around him wildly as the mother and the driver closed in on him.

He had had to get out of there. He didn't feel crazy at all, just desperate and hopeless and absolutely sure that he had to get out of there. He had no business being so close to home this early in the afternoon. He had been planning to go to the golf course to finish the drawing he was working on—and to kick his unused football uniform around in the sand trap a few times. And now his mother would find him out.

He couldn't deal with the fallout from this. No. He would not face the consequences. He had lost his real father, his first language, his real name, his mother's attention, his sense of his own importance, even his grandmother. He had so little of his very own. Nothing, really, other than his art class once a week. If his mother found him out, she'd put a stop to that. Vince was sure of it. And he would not let anyone take anything away from him, ever again. It was a blanket refusal, a turning point.

Go after Madeleine. Go.
Where is she, anyway?
Slowly Vince picks himself up, gets on the Harley, and kick-starts it. He's aware of faces staring at him through the windows of the restaurant.
Fuck it.
He tries to marshall his energies.
But he isn't ready to head off yet. Another minute. He needs another minute. Behind him cars are stretched all the way up to the stone gates to the golf course, vehicle after vehicle insisting *"Je me souviens."* He's seen this for so many years—how long it is, anyway, since Quebec changed its licence plate motto from *"La belle province"* to *"Je me souviens"*?—without ever really noticing it before. He notices it now. "I remember." Vince just sits there on Golf Avenue, staring into the rearview mirror.

The girl. He'd never spoken to her, but he'd liked her. He'd been fascinated by her, really. And now here she was lying in a heap on the road. She was perfectly still. Numbly, he stared at her, and slowly the numbness turned cold, then he felt impatient, finally angry. Why did she have to get in his way? Still staring, he found he didn't care whether she was alive or dead. She didn't matter. He, Vince, was the one who mattered.

And then, on an impulse—is there a more impulsive age than fifteen?—Vince picked up his mangled bicycle and then, seeing it was damaged beyond repair, let it drop before taking off at a run up Golf, along Lanthier to Cartier, up towards the highway where he hitched a ride downtown.

It was the beginning of his real education, the end of the timid Vince, the birth of a new, tough, single-mindedly selfish young man.

He had some luck. The man who stopped for him spoke no English. Vince, who had rarely spoken French outside of school, stumbled over his words at first, so that it looked like a language problem rather than confusion and aimlessness when he couldn't immediately say where he was headed. Gare Centrale, he finally said, the train station being one of the few places he could name in Montreal. So the man never realized that Vince was a runaway. They rode in silence most of the way, Vince staring out at the world as though seeing it for the first time.

The man dropped Vince off on the corner of Atwater, and Vince drifted through the bustling after-work crowd, first this way and then that, up this street and along that, until the crowds had dispersed, night had fallen, and he finally arrived at Central Station.

He sat on a bench and watched the ticket collectors guard the gates to the platforms. He was hungry.

Food. He was going to need food. A place to stay. Clothes, eventually. A new identity, too. Some kind of ID card. It all meant money. He eyed the travellers near him. A fool and his money are soon parted, he told himself. None of the men paid Vince the slightest attention, but one or two motherly women glanced at him, seemed to wonder about him, and one smiled at him kindly. A fool and *her* money? But how? How? Vince knew he had better be careful. It wouldn't take long till his mother would be looking for him, alerting the police, giving them photographs of him, a description of what he was wearing. But they wouldn't know where to start, where he would be, unless he gave himself away. Vince himself didn't know where he would be.

Ottawa. Quebec. Toronto. Or all the way out west.

A train pulled into its spot near where Vince was sitting. He watched the last passengers trail through the gate and disperse, listened to the railwaymen slamming doors. As the last of them shuffled on their way, the guard leant against the railing and lit himself a cigarette.

That was when Vince made his move. The man's back was to Vince, and as he pulled on his cigarette, Vince slipped past him, down the platform, and flattened himself against the door to the first carriage. No one had seen him. He quietly opened the door, as quietly closed it behind him, and looked around for a place to hide.

Was the train leaving again that night? For what destination? Or was it here for the night? Vince had no way of knowing. He lay down under one of the seats and eventually fell asleep. Awakened when the cleaning staff turned on the lights, he succeeded in dodging them, and was still in Montreal when the doors opened to let the passengers in next morning.

That's how it was decided. He would stay in Montreal.

He stole food off a restaurant table that morning, made a run for it, and got away easily. But he knew that was no way to get on. He'd have to be more devious than that.

He wandered east along Craig, down to the Port of Montreal where his father had drowned. Carlos. Vince Carlson. That would be his new name, he decided there and then. He wandered further, far into the east end until there was no more English. At the entrance to one of the oil refineries a leaflet was pushed into his hand as the day shift moved through the fresher ranks of the evening shift. He glanced at the leaflet, listened to a young American woman proselytize in a French clumsier than his own, and finally dared to speak to her. Socialists, of a kind, explained her Québécois partner, who came over to join them. Communists, of a kind. Vince's interest was piqued—his father had been a socialist—and he stayed to talk.

He spent six months with the Maoists, learning doctrine, a woman's love, and—when the man, too, became his lover—cunning. Amazing how easy it is to forge your way through life when you have a place to stay, food to eat, and the answer to every question you can think of. He made his escape from the Maoists when he had what he needed: two ideas, each as clear as crystal. The first one was in the book. "To each according to his needs." Vince's own needs were boundless. "Charity begins at home" was the other. To these he would later add a third. "There's one law for the lion, and one for the lamb." *Voilà!* The perfect recipe for a man on the make. And freedom to boot.

But nowhere to spend the night. So he went up to a woman outside Morgan's. He'd been robbed, he said, his voice sincere, pleading. He had no way to get home to Toronto where his mother had just died, he needed help, money to phone his sister, find a place to stay overnight, buy his ticket home. It worked. He was on his way.

Women, he soon learned, were easier, a softer touch than men. And he was so young, so very needy, so good at getting what he wanted—well, they just fell over themselves trying to help him. Vince can remember only a few names, a few moments. And then he met Constance. Someone—Vince doesn't remember who it was, how it happened—must have introduced him to Constance. Vince searches his memory. He must have been seventeen when he met Constance.

She had never married. There had been a young man, once, and a long engagement, but something had gone wrong, and she had never married. Financially she had never needed to. She'd never needed to work, either, but she gave piano lessons for something to do. That must have been it, Vince realizes. It must have been the mother of one of her pupils who sent him to Constance.

She was worried about living alone in her big Outremont house. She wanted a young man to occupy the basement apartment. Rent-free. This suited Vince fine. Especially when she introduced him to her friends, her world. Vincent—he was now Vincent—allowed her to take him under her wing, show him off to her circle of friends. Allowed her to take him to plays, concerts, the opera. To artists' studios, *vernissages* and dinner parties. On vacation to Provincetown and the Florida Keys. Vince was a keen student. And then she ruined it.

Most of her friends were discreet, but one wealthy gentleman—the owner of a gallery on St. Denis—went too far, talking to Vince for too long and in too low a voice in Constance's living room. The rows started that night. Constance started watching Vince more closely. She became dependent, obsessed, jealous. Vince left, in the end, only when she lent him $5,000 to complete his education. He opened his first bank account under the name Vince Carlson. He was nineteen.

What if Vince had stayed in Pointe Claire? Or gone home again a week after the accident? A year later? How would his life have been different?

Vince has always refused to entertain questions like this. But right now, in the glare of the sunlight, within view of the golf course for the first time in nearly thirty years, he asks himself what would have become of him if he'd stayed on.

Would he be heading home tired and spent at 5:16? Surely not.

If it hadn't been the accident, it would have been something else. One way or another he'd have got out. He had to. He didn't know it at the time, not consciously, anyway, but he had to get out. Why did nobody see that? The signs were all there, if only they'd known what to look for. Did they think he was just another sullen, awkward kid who happened to have a funny laugh? Yeah, that laugh. How could he forget that laugh? It mattered so much at the time.

He had two laughs in those days, his regular laugh and a laugh he hardly recognized as his own. At school no one mentioned it. They figured he must have been born that way and just felt sorry for him.

But he hadn't been born that way. Vince can't remember when, but it must have been after they'd moved out to Pointe Claire. The laugh would start for no reason at all. First he'd feel his face splitting into a big wide grin, and then he'd start laughing this big, cavernous laugh that rolled and roared and even hissed.

His mother couldn't stand it. She figured that if it could start, it could stop too. She wanted it to stop. Vince would tremble every time she went to the school, every time she set up some new appointment for him. At home neither she nor Ted Cunningham bothered to hide their contempt for him; in front of strangers they disguised it as concern for his welfare.

His mother—this occurs to Vince now for the first time—must have died thinking he still had that laugh.

It isn't like Vince to think like this.

So what's going on here? Why is he thinking this way now? It's temporary, that's what it is. Like having a tooth filled. It'll only hurt a bit. Not much. A twinge here and there, just to make sure it doesn't get worse. And then he'll be able to forget all about it again.

Vince is beginning to feel better, more himself.

If he doesn't get a move on, Madeleine will have made it back to her house before he catches up with her.

He shakes his head. That was a bad mistake, bringing Madeleine along on his first visit back to Golf Avenue.

But how was he to know that it would hit him like this?

Only now he's got to pick up the pieces with Madeleine. Explain himself, somehow. Oh, that's not much of a problem. He'll think of a way to do that. He's explained his way out of a lot trickier situations than this. He's good at taking care of himself, taking care of number one.

That's where his mother went wrong. She forgot that Vince was number one.

It could have been OK, back then. If only his mother had been looking out for Vince. It could have been her and Vince against the world. But no. She threw her lot in with Ted Cunningham instead.

Vince could understand why she married again. That wasn't it. He had more trouble understanding why she married Ted Cunningham. But she did. And though Vince never had any use for Ted Cunningham, he could see there were some good reasons for his mother's marrying onto easy street.

She was some kind of chameleon, his mother—thin, anxious, and adaptable. That was her protection. She was pretty enough, too, but unremarkably. She went unnoticed. Which was smart, up to a point. Only she got carried away, and Vince was plunged into darkness. She stopped speaking Spanish the day Carlos died. Vince had never heard her actually speak anything else, for she never brought her Polish or her Russian—the languages she taught for a living at that language school on Park Avenue—home to where Carlos used to wrestle with gaudily painted demons. By the time the Cunninghams had moved into the middle-class area of Montreal known to its mostly English-speaking population as NDG, to its few francophones as Notre-Dame de Grâce, Thea had turned herself into an English Canadian, and Vince, who had never heard his real mother tongue, never afterwards heard her speak anything but English.

Had she struggled with her accent in English? Had Ted Cunningham helped her with that? And what, after all, had possessed this costive, round-faced English Canadian to marry a displaced Polish widow with a son named Wincenty? These are mysteries that Vince has never been inclined to explore. He just might have to conclude that there was, once, something spontaneous and real and even appealing about Ted Cunningham.

Vince is happier believing his own fiction. That his mother was resourceful, clever, probably manipulative. And that Ted Cunningham was a dullard. One thing is sure. Whatever need—whatever weakness— it was that persuaded Ted Cunningham to marry Teresa Jimenez, *née* Malinowska, he was careful never to show it again. Who was this man, really, in the core of his being? Vince doesn't know. He was a book Vince never bothered to open. There was nothing original about Ted Cunningham, nothing fresh, nothing interesting. Even his thoughts were someone else's. Don't look a gift horse in the mouth. He who pays the piper calls the tune. Hoist with your own petard. Ted Cunningham had a saying to match every occasion. Vince's childhood was punctuated with such sayings.

As Vince lurched into adolescence, he learned to fear his stepfather, in some ways to hate him. Vince wished he had never been born, and he knew Ted Cunningham wished that too. With his mother and Ted Cunningham more and more a team, Vince himself more and more an outsider, Vince felt sure that his mother would have left him behind on the Plateau Mont Royal along with Carlos' ashes, his canvases, and his old records if she could have got away with it. He remembered so little of Teresa, so little of Carlos. These two strangers, Thea and Ted Cunningham, were the only parents he now knew, and some part of him was convinced they must be right to despise him. He was sure his life would end in disaster. And he hated himself even more.

The only thing he loved was his painting class once a week in the basement of Stewart Hall, a class he'd paid for with pocket money he'd saved up for nearly a year. Only there, in that basement room, did he feel like himself. No one knew. Not his parents. Not his friends. He would have died rather than let anyone know he liked to paint. That's the way he thought of it, that he just liked to paint. The idea that he might be an artist seemed ludicrous even to him—but that was because he could never imagine being good enough that he would deserve to be called an artist. His father had been an artist. It would be tempting fate for Vince to aspire to be what his father had been.

The idea of Vince's becoming an artist would have seemed ludicrous to Ted Cunningham for different reasons. Vince didn't want to think what his mother's reaction might be. He enjoyed the classes, but what mattered more was that this was his secret, his very own thing. This at least he was determined to keep to himself.

Along with the Cathies and Debbies, Beaconsfield High School was full of Scotts and Glens in those days. All the Scotts played football, and all the Cathies were cheerleaders bobbing around in tiny pleated skirts and spending their lunch hours on the landing outside the gym practising jumping up in the air and shouting "Yey! yey! Scott YOUNG!" in unison. They were the chosen.

And if you were chosen you'd get a little military-striped ribbon to wear on your navy blue blazer. Good grades would get you a coloured ribbon too, and basketball and wrestling and ski club and even the cacophonous school band. A talent for drawing and painting got you nothing.

Some guys, by the time they got to Grade Eleven, had rows and rows of these multicoloured vertical- and horizontal-striped ribbons. They were the generals and field marshals, and Vince was a foot soldier. Or something. Or—more likely—nothing. He was nothing, a nobody.

The vice-principal, who wore his own hair about as long as the bristles of a toothbrush, used to check the length of the boys' hair. And, too, the length of the girls' regulation grey skirts. The girls had to kneel down in front of him in a long line, and if their skirts didn't touch the floor they were sent home. The very same girls who had to bounce around during lunch hour in colourful pleated skirts that barely covered their buns would be sent home in disgrace if they were caught with a grey skirt an inch above their knees.

Hair longer than an inch on a male meant trouble, too, at least until the day GT (that was his nickname; Gord Turner? Greg Taylor?) sat down in homeroom with his head entirely shaven, and no one seemed to know what to do about him. GT was a big ugly seventeen year old, a rebel, and a pinball wizard. The kind of guy Vince would have loved to be. But of course you had to feel pretty confident to rebel in the first place, and confidence was one of many qualities that Vince lacked. Not to mention that Vince didn't even know where to find a pinball machine, and he didn't dare ask for fear of being laughed at for not knowing.

GT might never have got his mother to sew a single ribbon on his blazer, but he was accepted and liked just for that. For a start, he'd been all through elementary school with the other guys. Vince had landed at Beaconsfield High School part way through Grade Nine, when no one was interested in making a new friend—and certainly not of Vince. And GT was a great party animal, a drinker, a real wild guy. His parents were worried about him, that's what Vince overheard in the halls.

Vince himself went to one party in three years. He smiled and tried to look interested, but he didn't know how he was supposed to behave.

He did go to one school dance in Grade Ten, though he didn't dare ask a girl to go with him.

And just as well. He was taken over by that awful laugh almost as soon as the dancing began, and he spent the rest of the evening leaning against the wall outdoors. He never went to another dance, though he secretly, crazily, hoped to be invited to the Sadie Hawkins dance, that one time a year when the girls got to ask the guys. But he always read the social column in the student newsletter—in which everyone was identified only by their initials—like some sacred document, trying vainly to decipher its meaning. WB was wearing a gown of burgundy satin, he read, and DH spilt Coke down DB's new peau de soie. Who were these people? They inhabited a realm that Vince could only dream of, a dazzling realm of red and blue, silver and gold, while he himself lurked underground like some drab nocturnal creature hiding from the light.

Later, when he was working up north with the Hydro crew, when it no longer mattered and no one was impressed, Vince spent every evening after work playing pinball, loving the flashing lights and the gaudy, metallic colours, getting so good he knew he could take anyone on, even GT. It was the control that delighted him the most, working the little flippers expertly, putting heart and soul into keeping the ball in play, intent on delaying for as long as possible its eventual drop down into the bowels of the machine. He got so good, kept it in play so long, that there was no shame in this. When it did finally drop out of sight, it did so with a thunk he found satisfying, inevitable, necessary.

He sometimes thinks his whole life would have been different if only he'd known where the guys played pinball, and he could have gotten good at it then, when he was thirteen and fourteen and fifteen. The parents of teenagers worry about the wrong things. It isn't the wild kids they should worry about, the ones with a crowd of friends and the nerve to rebel. It's the lonely kids who need to be watched, the ones who don't even know where to begin. Lonely kids like Vince.

It was as if he didn't really exist in that school. GT might have been a rebel against the school's rules, but first he had made sure he had all the other guys on his side, the guys who would never dare to shave their heads, ever. GT had allies. He could afford to buck the system.

Vince could not. Nothing Vince could do at that school would ever improve his situation. He knew that, absolutely. The very most he could hope for was to survive it, grow up, leave it all behind, show them all. He could, of course, have made it even worse. That's why he never spoke to the girl. He liked her so much. Too much. He would have made things even worse if—is there a more anxious age than fifteen?—if he had asked her what she really thought of him.

She seemed as lost as he was, and he was mesmerized. Her family—he'd heard they were from somewhere else—moved in down the street from Vince with a truckload of sculptures, paintings, and furniture unlike any that Vince had ever seen. After school sometimes, and on long summer evenings, he would see her sitting alone on the verandah of her house as still and almost as unmoving as the two marble busts of stern-faced men at the top of the steps. In Latin class she sat across from Vince—what *was* her name?—and he would watch as she pulled out the hairs of her eyebrows one by one with the tips of blunt, pink fingers.

That's the thing about immigrants. They're misfits. Vince got to know a lot of them pretty well back when he was practising law, making his bundle on immigration cases. If they're not pulling out their eyebrows like that girl used to do, they're up to something even crazier. Such easy people to take advantage of. So desperate for papers. Their voices are too loud or too soft, their gutturals too harsh, their views wild, even the ways they choose to cover their heads are offensive. One way or another they have a way of seeming to be insane. Vince's mother knew all about that. She fought against that and won. It was a victory of sorts.

One icy morning, waiting in silence for the school bus, in an almost irresistible fit of pure need, Vince very nearly did ask her—Corky! that's it! they called her Corky—what she thought of him. "Hi," he imagined himself saying. "I was just wondering," he would add, ever so casually, just as though it didn't matter at all. "I was just wondering, what do you think of me?"

Corky.

What could he have been hoping for? Perhaps just to be acknowledged, to have his existence acknowledged. No. He wanted much more than that.

He wanted her to say, "Oh, I think you're so interesting. So different from those others." That was what he thought of her. He wanted her to say, "Oh, I admire you. I like you so much." He wanted her to say, "I think we're kindred spirits, you and I." That was what he felt about her.

At night, alone downstairs after his parents had gone to bed, he would listen to Joan Baez records so quietly that no one knew, writing down the words in a Hilroy exercise book. This was his little rebellion, his first attempt to assert himself, the self that had been dormant. It was much later that he learned to love opera, but it was Joan Baez who first taught him the power and beauty of a woman's voice.

On the back of her album, she had written (it was handwritten on the album cover, and Vince never doubted that it must be in her own hand), "Would it embarrass you very much if I told you I love you?" Vince puzzled over that. No. That was more than puzzling; that was mysterious.

And then—it's coming back to Vince now, thirty years on—his mother came downstairs after midnight and found him straining to hear the songs. She sent him to bed, whispering fiercely so as not to waken Ted Cunningham. And that—yes, that's it exactly—that is when Vince's laugh started, loud enough to waken the dead.

He never did say anything to Corky. Later on, when that icy morning's fit of intensity had passed, had proved resistible after all, Vince climbed onto the school bus behind Corky convinced he would never say anything both true and important to anyone.

And that, come to think of it, is what he loves most about those breathtaking arias and lieder, especially as sung by Jessye Norman. Vince is in love with Jessye Norman. With her face, her vast, majestic body, her rich, passionate, exquisitely controlled voice. She says what he can never say. She expresses what he cannot express.

Vince has fantasies of meeting Jessye Norman one day. He shivers at the very thought.

It was Ted Cunningham who wanted Vince to play football. He himself had never played. He did like drinking beer—never more than two beer—and watching football on television. But he was damn sure that Vince should be on one of the school teams, playing that particular kind of grotesque dress-up game—in an astronaut's helmet and murderous cleats and a padded uniform—and ramming into other armoured adolescents on the field below the school. Football was the only sport for the ambitious English-speaking middle class, for people with names like Cunningham. Playing football meant that you'd succeed in life, in business.

His mother had no particular interest in football. She had no interest in anything much, never—so far as Vince could see—had had any interest in anything other than seeming to belong wherever she found herself. In her mind football served the same purpose as the processed cheese she bought in the IGA, the same purpose as the white summer shoes she wore from May till the end of September, the same purpose as the identical lamps she had placed on identical square tables at each end of the sofa in the living room. When she had another son—Vince was eight years old by this time—she called him Gary. Tiny Gary was what Vince called him. They were still living in NDG then. It was 1963 by the time they moved out to Pointe Claire. Vince was the bane of his mother's existence. Why did he have to laugh like that? Why couldn't he look like other boys? Behave like other boys? Football wouldn't be a bad idea.

And so, at his parents' insistence, Vince signed up for the football team in his final year. Duly he packed his football gear in the morning, and duly returned it to the washing pile well worn. Often it really was well worn, too. Often enough to prevent the coach from phoning his mother. But some of the games coincided with his painting class. That was when he would be glad of the sand traps on the golf course. Which is where he was headed on the afternoon of the accident.

He never did find out what happened to Corky. Did she die? Did she survive?

He never even tried to phone home until he was leaving Constance. His parents were out shopping, and he spoke to Tiny Gary, who must have been watching something extraordinarily good on TV.

It was after that he headed up north with a Hydro construction crew, worked hard, and made good money. That paid his way through a history major and then law school at Laval. No better training could be imagined. If you're going to make a career on the wrong side of the law, the first thing you need is knowledge of the law. Vince knows how to bend and stretch and mold it to suit him. His knowledge has failed him only once—and he spent two years inside paying for that. Never again. He used those two years well, honing his skills, poring over the *Funk & Wagnalls* dictionary, and listening to a man who had the five of dominoes tattooed into the base of his thumb. Call it post-graduate training.

When he came back to Montreal, he dialled his parents' number again, but got some francophone who had never heard of the Cunninghams. It was 1978. Chances were they'd moved down the 401 to Mississauga, like a hundred thousand other refugees from the Parti Québécois. Maybe Vince would look them up when he went to Toronto. If he ever went to Toronto. He'd been to Toronto once, and never could figure out a good reason for going back.

Which, it occurs to him now, makes it all the more surprising that his mother's lawyer ever finally tracked him down. Vince has used enough different names, over the years—A.S. Windle, Tad Wilde, N. Vince Ybl, there are others, too, more than Vince himself can now remember—which must have frustrated the lawyer. A.S. Windle has the appeal of the outrageous, but Vince—probably like the original swindler who first used the name back in Victorian England—is amazed that no one has ever twigged to its meaning. N. Vince Ybl is a favourite. But Ybl, though in fact a real name—the architect of the Budapest Opera House was Miklos Ybl—sounds silly in English and is the more likely to raise questions. Ditto for Tad—Tadeusz—which is in fact Vince's middle name. Immigrant behaviour may seem insane; immigrant names are causes for merriment. And—what is worse—for suspicion.

Vince won't use Wilde again. Wilde is getting overused. Where was it he recently saw an a glossy two-page magazine ad that used the name? The left side showed the fancy pen that was being advertised. The right just had a quotation from Wilde, white text on a black background—very nineties: "No great artist ever sees things as they really are. If he did he would cease to be an artist."

Now that's true decadence, honest-to-goodness look-you-straight-in-the-eye 1990s commercial shit. Luxury items, exquisite taste, and filthy lucre rolled up together in plain black and white. It took someone with even less compunction than Vince to come up with that. Less compunction, and, maybe, less respect. Vince doesn't have a lot of respect, but what respect he does have is reserved for art. It was the 1890s that killed Wilde. And those were the gay nineties; that was a *belle époque*. Which is more than you can say about this whimpering little *fin-de-siècle*. It's the 1990s that will tame him. Tad Wilde has had its day.

And anyway, Vince turned himself into Vince Carlson the day he left home, and he always comes back to that. The others have all been useful enough, and some of them are fun, too, but Vince Carlson is the only name that ever felt right. It did take the lawyer the better part of a year—ever since last summer—to find him and let him know that he and Tiny Gary were to divide the estate equally between them. Trust Thea to do the conventional thing, right to the bitter end.

So Vince still doesn't know what happened to that girl Corky. In his mind, she died. That whole world died.

And that's what's so odd about coming back to Pointe Claire now, and finding it all so wholesome. There are, Vince is finally ready to acknowledge, one or two things about this place that are going to take some getting used to.

Helmet in hand, Madeleine has made it nearly as far as the Edgewater parking lot by the time Vince catches up with her.

"Madeleine, Madeleine," he calls over, his voice breaking with emotion as he pulls up beside her and reaches an arm out towards her, "I didn't want to tell you…"

That has at least succeeded in stopping her. What will it be? Something that would explain his behaviour. Something she's heard of. Something that's bound to create sympathy for him. And something she won't know too much about.

Diabetes? No. Too common.

Epilepsy. That should do it.

"Tell me what?" she asks. And then adds. "Forgive me."

Vince glances at her sharply. She's asking him to forgive her? But there was no trace of irony in her voice. He presses on.

"That I'm—" Vince looks about him anxiously, as though afraid of eavesdroppers, "—that I'm an epileptic."

"An epileptic?" she asks dully, as though not understanding.

"You see! I knew you'd think less of me for it. People get so alarmed by these convulsive disorders. But it's not a disease, really, it isn't a disease—"

He's wheeling the bike along beside her now, across Cartier. He's still not really himself, but he can pull this off, no sweat, he's a fast talker from way back. Just keep uttering words, Vinskie my lad, just keep at it—

"—just a disturbance in the electro-physico-chemical activity of discharging cells of the brain. And it's no big deal, really, *petit mal*, I've never had a *grand mal* seizure, ever. Not once—"

How much longer can Vince keep this up? He's starting to feel sick—

"—So, you see, there's nothing to worry about, just a transient interruption of the stream of consciousness. And rare! Let me tell you! It's so rare! I can't even remember the last time it happened…"

"The last time it happened," she says. Her limp is more pronounced than ever, and she's walking with her head down, repeating what he says with as much understanding as a ventriloquist's dummy.

"Madeleine?"

"Yes." She turns her head but doesn't seem to see him. They're at Cedar Avenue by this time. His performance has been completely lost on her.

"Hello?"

She blinks, connects. "Please forgive me," she's saying now. "It's unlucky. I'm unlucky,…" And her voice drifts away as she stops and stares back through the village.

What kind of New Age nonsense is this? Vince wonders angrily, fighting back waves of nausea. Next she'll be asking him what his sign is.

6

Vince succeeds in waiting until Madeleine has gone on her way before racing up the driveway and—his mouth filling with vomit—abandoning the bike without ceremony outside the garage. He barely makes it to the flower bed before he throws up. Then he retches and retches till there's nothing left. He hasn't thrown up for years, and this feels like the accumulation of a lifetime of bile.

When finally he's done he sits down on the stone patio, rests his head against the cold stone wall, and counts until he thinks he'll never stop counting. He lifts his head, and a small movement catches his eye. Is someone there? Vince turns just in time to see the figure of an old woman disappear behind Carrie's hedge. Janet. Was that Janet? Somewhere nearby, out of sight, a car engine ignites. The blue minivan, Vince realizes. Madame must be heading out. He slides down so that he's lying flat on his back on the patio.

Did Janet see him? Surely not. And what the hell, anyway? Vince is past caring. And who's to say this isn't another symptom of *petit mal*? These women are easily dealt with.

He knows he should get up, go back there. This is like climbing back on a horse after it's thrown you. If you don't, you'll never ride again. Everything depends on getting back in control.

But he can't, he just can't.

Jesus.

What's happening to him?

After succeeding for the better part of his life in forgetting, Vince is now flooded with memories.

He lies there till the shadows have crept over him and he hears Madame pulling up in the driveway again and slamming the door of the minivan. He's recovered sufficiently by this time to have focused on the spider's paradise under the eaves of the house. Now he drags himself to his feet and stumbles indoors and into the shower.

Only there are no towels. Bitch. Where has Sal hidden the towels? And the bedding, for that matter. He dries himself roughly with a pair of jeans. Vince has rented the house furnished, but is supposed to provide his own towels and his own bed linen. He owns neither, and he knows that Sal owns both. He's yanking on his clothes when he remembers what Madeleine said about storage areas.

Ha!

One in the garage, and one in the attic. The attic would be drier. That's the place to start.

His mood begins to lighten.

So he climbs up into the attic and rummages around until—sure enough—he finds a huge box clearly and conveniently marked BEDDING with lilac-coloured magic marker. He rips it open, and finds pure white queen-size sheets, duvet covers and pillow cases interleaved with sachets of lavender.

Next to it is a box marked DUVET and, behind that, one marked TOWELS. What a doll this Sal must be. Other boxes are marked GOOD CHINA, CRYSTAL, LAMPS, and SERVING DISHES. Vince goes through all these boxes methodically, throwing all the ordinary stuff into the now-empty duvet box, putting to one side the things he wants to keep for his own use, and moving the other valuables downstairs into the family room, where he stacks them beside the door to the garage.

It takes him a while to find the box with Sal's CDs. He knows she must have them somewhere—what musician wouldn't?—so he persists, even though there's no marked box to help him. Unless, perhaps, she took them all with her? Surely not. There'd be too many. Eventually, he finds them, dozens of them, at the bottom of a box marked TABLECLOTHS. Sneaky old Sal, trying to hide her music from him. Must mean a lot to her. And sure enough, there's all kinds of material there. Mahler, Elgar, J.S. Bach, Saint-Saëns. Surprisingly little cello, though; probably she took most of those with her. Quite a few operatic works... Yes. Jessye Norman. Richard Strauss's *Vier Letzten Lieder*. Vince studies Jessye's face on the cover for a long time, her proud face, and her regal turban—he's wholly enchanted, she never fails to enchant him—before setting the CD to one side.

Vince lifts out the other tablecloth. There's a little wooden chest at the bottom of the box. Vince lifts it out with some difficulty—it's surprisingly heavy—opens it, and uncovers one paperweight after another, lovingly wrapped in tissue paper. Fancy that, Sal collecting paperweights. They're good ones, too. A very respectable *millefiori*, a green glass doorstop decorated with tiered flowers, a three-coloured miniature that might be a Clichy, even a Saint-Louis weight topped quite spectacularly with a gilt salamander. These will fetch a good price. He wraps them up again carefully.

Vince throws the tablecloths over onto the pile of stuff he neither wants nor needs, sets the wooden chest with the paperweights aside with the other items he'll be selling, and then he carries the bedclothes and the box full of CDs into the bedroom.

There he leaves the box on the floor while he first makes the bed and then moves the sound system into position on the dresser, leaving two of the speakers between the kitchen and the living room. And he *shall* have music wherever he goes.

What *is* that from? It's supposed to be "she" of course, something he remembers from his childhood, something he hasn't even thought of for nearly forty years.

"She shall have music wherever she goes."

It was his grandmother who sang to him and taught him nursery rhymes, Ted Cunningham's mother. The only person in the world who ever called him Vinskie. She would sit him on her lap with a picture book in her hand and read to him in a voice from some other world. He hasn't thought of that in years. She died so long ago, even before Tiny Gary was born. So Vince was her only grandchild, the only one she knew, and she called him her little lamb and treated him as though he were really her own. Why is it coming back to him now? It is all coming back, as though from yesterday.

> Ride a cock horse to Banbury Cross
> To see a fine lady upon a white horse.
> Rings on her fingers and bells on her toes,
> She shall have music wherever she goes.

Is that right? Banbury Cross must be somewhere in England. What's a cock horse? A stallion, presumably. And the white horse must be something else, not a cock horse, so maybe a mare. Rings on her fingers and bells on her toes. He repeats the rhyme in the same kind of sing-song his Granny had always used. There's some kind of magic in the words. But what on earth do they mean? The rhyme itself is mesmerizing, more like music than words. Its meaning is in its sounds and its rhythms. The rings, anyway, make sense.

He's being too literal. Or not literal enough. Just listen. It's erotic, that's what it is. Cock horse indeed. Whatever those bells are on her toes, one thing's crystal clear. She shall have music wherever she goes. Music. Mi-you-zic. Pronounced sex. She shall have it. She shall indeed. She's that kind of lady. A fine lady, somewhere in England.

It's too hot in the bedroom. Vince heads outside to the garage for a fan, sets it up, and then wanders downstairs—upstairs, downstairs, in my lady's chamber!—where the filing cabinet in the family room attracts his attention. He toys with the idea of leaving it till tomorrow—what's his hurry, after all?—but the temptation to have a preliminary look is too great.

It's child's play to pick the lock of the cabinet, packed with documents, photograph albums, and a hat-box full of letters and various odds and ends, including a fat, ruled, spiral-bound notebook filled with small, easily legible handwriting, and marked "Journal 1989-90."

Vince has another look in the cabinet, but there are no other notebooks. Letters in various languages, a substantial stack of newspaper clippings and concert reviews, photographs, school report cards, a deck of old passports—Portuguese, Austrian, Canadian—even a shopping list, with milk, bread, garlic, cabbage and soap followed by a quotation about Schubert, the title of a book about Casals, and a library catalogue number.

Either Sal didn't write a journal before or since, or she didn't bother trying to hide it, and Vince will come across it somewhere else in the house. Anyhow, there's no shortage of material here.

Katarina S. von Friesen. That's the name on her John Abbott College ID card, 1984-85, and on her McGill Faculty of Music ID card, 1985-86. The photograph shows a pale waif of a woman with high cheek bones, a wide mouth, and thick white-blonde hair. She is smiling, and one brown eye, the right one, looks larger than the other. A face remarkable mainly for earnestness and pallor, Vince decides. The pallor accentuated by the hair, and—Vince realizes, peering at the photograph more closely—by dramatically arched, thick, dark eyebrows. What used to be called a striking woman, although the impression she leaves is too anxious to be pleasing. Too anxious, at any rate, to please Vince.

Suddenly Vince knows who it is she reminds him of: the acrobatic female android in *Blade Runner*. The one with raccoon eyes who turns a mean flip. Sal is the spitting image of her. Or at least, she's the spitting image of what that android would have looked like if she'd lived into middle age. That was the point, too, wasn't it, in that film? That the androids, doomed to an early death, were rebelling against their fate. Appearances were deceptive, so you could never be quite sure who was human and who was not. Some vile human had his head mashed at one point. The film was based on a novel, *Do Androids Dream of Electric Sheep?* Clever title.

There's a later McGill card too, 1987-88. In that photograph Sal is less pale, and her face is rounder. And, he almost didn't notice, her name this time is Katarina S. von Friesen Schleiermacher.

Vince is checking out a file marked "Official Documents/Copies." Born in Lisbon in 1939. That makes her fifty-four now. Von Friesen is her maiden name. Her mother's maiden name is Brask. Vince fishes his little book out of his pocket and jots these down inside the back cover. Various schools in Lisbon, Washington, D.C., some place in England. Married Wolfgang Helmut Schleiermacher in 1969 in Paris.

So the Schleiermacher is his. This john got down on bended knee and persuaded a gal named Sal to turn herself into a Mrs. Wolf Schleiermacher. And then he left her, still carrying his name, still, in some real sense, his creature. Schleiermacher's occupations are variously described as administrator, chef, caterer, agricultural consultant, importer, and then finally, perhaps in exhaustion, simply as businessman. Well, that accounts for Sal's anxiety. Maybe the earnestness too. One of them had to be serious.

Daughter, Isabelle Elisabeth, born in Paris in 1970. Son, Nicholas Ferdinand, in 1972, in Vienna. Canadian landed immigrant status, 1976. Canadian citizenship, 1981. A bundle of letters from the elementary schools that Sal herself attended in the States and England with official Quebec certificates entitling Isabelle and Nicholas to English education. Divorce, 1989. The deeds to the house are there too.

So, 1989 was the divorce. Vince checks the dates on the journal. 1989-90. A rant? Maybe. Or a sorry story, stacked with self-righteousness. Boring, either way. But, Vince thinks, setting the journal aside, it just might provide some useful information.

At the back of the file are a torn newspaper clipping and a small envelope. The clipping, dated sometime in 1991, either September or December, he can't be sure, shows a barely recognizable Sal, only her face and arms and knees visible behind a cello, under a headline "West Island Women." He peers at the small, boldface print and deciphers "Katarina von Friesen wins International Music Award" and some reference to the Academy of Music in Bratislava, Slovakia. The rest is illegible.

Vince pulls photographs out of the envelope, some passport photos, some snapshots. An older, rounder, altogether darker Sal, with the anxiety gone from her eyes. The earnestness too, come to think of it. He can't read the expression on her face at all. A long-haired boy in his early twenties with wide brown eyes, and a girl, who looks to be about the same age but must be a couple of years older. Both waifs. Both with their mother's brows. On the back of the photograph Sal has written Nicholas and Elsa, San Diego, May 1991. Two years ago. That must be where her ex lives now.

Vince spends the next hour making a stack of books to sell. A few titles he knows from reading them years ago. *Growing Up Absurd* is one. *Lady Chatterley's Lover. Tropic of Cancer. Catch 22. Zen and the Art of Motorcycle Maintenance.* A whole row of Kurt Vonnegut, Jr. Some of the art books have been inscribed to Sal by their authors, and these go into the growing pile. He knows he'll find a buyer for the *Encyclopædia Britannica*.

There are some books Vince never read but meant to. *The Name of the Rose*. Now that's a title that has always intrigued Vince. Why would a book set out to proclaim its own insignificance? For—the way Vince figures it—if a rose by any other name would smell as sweet, well, then the *name* of the rose doesn't matter, does it? In which case *The Name of the Rose*—this big expensive tome—doesn't matter much either. It sounds like a con to Vince.

He wouldn't mind having a look at some of the volumes on opera. There's nothing to stop him reading about opera, even if he hardly dares listen to it anymore. And he'll hold onto the *Funk & Wagnalls*, his favourite dictionary. He searches the shelves for other material that would interest him. Nothing much in the way of history, though. Nor of biography. Vince has a penchant for the lives of great men. When he's put aside the books he wants for himself, he stops sorting. The dealer will go through the rest and give him a price for the lot.

Upstairs, he pulls the curtain across the open window, plugs in the green-shaded lamp, and climbs into bed. It's been a long day, this first day of the rest of Vince's life. A big day. There was one hitch, he acknowledges. But—he marvels anew at Madeleine apologizing to him—no real harm was done.

Vince flicks on the TV. *Roseanne* is on. He hasn't seen Roseanne in a couple of years. He remembers her large and defiant, at war with the whole shrunken medium. She had been proud, and he had admired that in her, her overweening pride. So often, large women look uncomfortable with themselves, slouching around in nondescript clothing with their shoulders curled in like Madeleine's to protect the unwieldy secrets of their flesh—when instead they should be straightening their backs and swathing themselves in yards of luxurious fabrics. Big, fat men occasionally have the same problem, but less often. A man is more likely to know how to carry it off, more likely to swagger and be admired as Falstaffian. For a woman, it's a life of jokes and scorn, horror and pity. Which is what makes Vince's job so easy.

Too easy. There are so few women he can admire. Only one, really. Jessye Norman is in a class by herself. Opera, which only seems larger than life—it is exactly the size of life at its best and fullest—is the proper medium for such a triumphant woman. No wonder the petty and the immature are impelled to cut it down to size. But no matter how they mock it, no matter how they shriek in imitation, they can no more reduce a Jessye Norman than the smooth-skinned Lilliputians could reduce Gulliver to size.

There isn't a woman alive Vince would compare to Jessye Norman. Where is there another face of such nobility? Who else has the vast, wise, unfathomable quality of her voice? And where is there a woman of such dignity? Such an old-fashioned word, dignity, but that's the word for Jessye, no other. Jessye is a queen. Such bitterness as there has been in Vince's life has been sweetened by her voice. He has never seen her, but he has imagined her. He doesn't know how often in his mind's eye he has conjured up the dance of the seven veils. Sometimes he imagines the veil over her face is the very first to fall, and sometimes he imagines it the last. And he has imagined her with John the Baptist's head. We always kill the thing we love. Such gloating. Such relish. Such a woman.

Even at her grandest, Roseanne was never in the same class as Jessye. And now! Vince stares at Roseanne in disbelief. She's practically thin! She's squeezed herself onto the small screen. Where once she was visibly fighting tooth and nail against the pettiness, the quintessential tininess of television, now she has agreed to its terms. He switches her off in disgust.

The telephone rings, and Vince knocks the remote onto the floor as he reaches for the receiver. It's Carrie. What on earth does Carrie want with him? Not—he glances at his watch—that it's particularly late. But he's packed a lot into this evening already. Carrie he doesn't need.

"I just wanted to thank you for the orchid. You shouldn't have."

"Hey," he says. "There are lots of things I shouldn't have done. But this isn't one of them."

"It's beautiful." She says. And then stops. There's something else. He waits. "I, uh, finished work early, and bumped into Madeleine at the Plaza just now." She is talking too fast. "And Madeleine says you're an artist." This almost accusatory. "That you offered to draw her. That you wanted her to," she takes a quick breath, "sit for you." This isn't a term that Carrie has used ever in her life before.

"Yeah?" he drawls, playing for time. There's no mistaking her tone. What is she accusing him of?

"Well," she wants to know, "is that true?"

"Yup. It's true. Madeleine is telling you no lie." Of course. She's accusing him of not telling *her*. Of telling Madeleine things that he's kept secret from Carrie herself. She's jealous! Ha. And, as he thought, there's no love lost between Carrie and Madeleine. Why not?

"Madeleine said she didn't want to do it, though. She didn't want you to draw her." She's warming up, but she can't quite get used to the terminology. Her voice sounds strangled, unnaturally contained.

"Yup. That's true too."

"I'm calling just in case you'd like, er, just in case you'd be interested in drawing me instead." There. She's said it. A bit bald, a bit brazen maybe, but she's said it.

"Would you like to sit for me, Carrie?"

"Yes!" Such high-pitched eagerness. "I mean, yes, I wouldn't mind." She's making an effort to modulate her voice. "If you need a model, that is. Of course."

"Sure."

"Yes?" There's that high note again.

"Sure, but not right away."

"Oh, no, whenever suits you." And now it's relief he hears in her voice. The temporary relief. God, just listening to her makes him feel tense.

"I'll have to get settled in first. Get myself organized."

"Oh, yes, of course."

"In a couple of weeks, maybe."

"Sure, anytime," she gushes, but she can't quite disguise her disappointment. "I'll be waiting. I mean, I'll be around. Here."

"Yeah, I know."

And Vince had thought he might have to wait a week till he got his first model lined up. Of course, Vince just knew one of them would be willing. Pity it isn't Madeleine. Madeleine is more Vince's type. But Carrie's the one. The consolation is that Carrie's the real estate agent. How con*vee*nient, as the Church Lady used to say on *Saturday Night Live*. Yes, very convenient. Two birds. One stone. Vince is a great believer in combining business with pleasure.

Vince reaches down beside the bed for Sal's journal, which falls open along the spine. He starts reading.

> Gradually—over the last few months—I have found myself feeling the shock less sharply, feeling the rage subside. More and more I am aware mostly of an emptiness—an absence where once there was a man. Words assume meanings they never had before.
>
> Loss. That means that you have lost something. I have lost someone. I have lost Wolf...

Oh Jesus, no, Vince groans. Not a tragedy queen. This is worse even than he imagined. He flips back through the pages to the beginning, wondering how much of this he's going to bother reading.

> I've been sick for the better part of two weeks now, and have lost track even of the days. Wolf has gone. He left before I was awake—and he isn't coming back. I told Elsa and Nicholas that. They didn't know what to say. I haven't felt so alone since they were small.
>
> Oh, why couldn't he have hung on? It would have been all right. We would have been all right—I'm sure of it.
>
> A marriage is rather a dull story, most of the time, except to the man and woman involved. The duller the better, really.

For years Wolf and I were as dull as ditchwater, as happy as larks. I loved him. Oh, I loved him. I wanted to keep him with me—safe—just us. The world seemed to me so full of peril, and our life inside this house, even this house of brick and stone, seemed as fragile and precious as if we lived inside a soap bubble. When he would go away, even if just for a few days, I would find myself stopped in the middle of whatever I was doing—just longing for him to be with me. I don't think I ever quite realized that was what I was doing, it wasn't something I actually thought about at all. I would just long for him with a physical longing that saw me standing in the middle of some room sighing a little, leaning into space, needing him to be there.

And when he would come back to me, I would be shaking. It sounds melodramatic, but it's quite true—I would be shaking when I saw him again, behaving in some more-or-less plausible way, saying ordinary, everyday things, but really I would be all nerve endings and terror, just waiting for the moment when we could be alone. There are couples, I see them all the time, who fondle one another in front of others. We didn't do that. We didn't dare. We hardly even spoke. I would faint if his hand brushed against my hand. When his eyes met mine I would follow him to the ends of the earth.

Can I really wish we had remained that way forever? How can I not? But it was I who put a stop to it. How could I do that? What would I give now for such a love? Oh, I can wish for the delirium. I want it again, now, but not the way it was. I want to be wide awake this time. I want to be me.

Because, while we were happy as a couple, the truth—it took me so many years just to figure this out—was that I, I personally, was not happy. Our happiness as a couple was premised on my personal unhappiness. So—in some way that I never was able to articulate—our happiness was a lie.

"Oh, pu-lease!" Vince says out loud, closing the journal and throwing it onto the floor.

Journals are like nudist colonies. People lay themselves bare, revealing all kinds of disgusting things about themselves that would be better kept hidden. It could be enough to put you off people for good. But great material for an artist. The best. Good thing Vince has a strong stomach. An artist needs a strong stomach. Especially when the nudist colony in question is full of long-suffering suburban matrons.

Vince closes the journal and turns off the light, falling asleep with his mouth open in Sal's queen-size bed, between Sal's sweet-smelling pure white sheets, under Sal's duvet, and with Sal's neatly handwritten private journal on the floor at his side.

PART II

7

Carrie's beige minivan is oozing down her driveway when Vince opens the front door the next morning with a Player's cigarette hanging out of the corner of his mouth, a mug of coffee in one hand, and a raisin square in the other. He waves vaguely in Carrie's direction and sits down. The heat is oppressive today, the lake dark and still.

"Going swimming?" he calls over to her. One end of a wooden easel appears beside the Remillard house, bobs up and down, and then lurches forward, revealing that the man carrying it has a sizable box under his arm as well. Vince watches him struggle.

"I don't have time today," Carrie says, regret lining her face. "But tomorrow I may be going. Or the next day. Want to come?" What a difference a day makes.

"Sure," he says. "Let me know." And she's off down the road.

"Mr. Schleiermacher?" the man queries, setting the easel down and consulting the delivery slip.

"He's inside," Vince lies. "He doesn't get around too easily. But here," Vince finally relieves the man of the box, "let me give you a hand."

"Thank you. Didn't realize you could drive up here."

"Yeah. It's hard to find this house. He should have given you better directions."

Vince opens one box while the man goes back to his truck for the other. The Harley. That's the place to start. He lifts his chair down the steps, sets up the easel, and opens the garage door. Then, Vince wheels the big mother out into full view in the driveway.

It's a very long time since Vince has done any drawing at all, let alone painting. But that's OK. None of these women is any kind of connoisseur of art. None of them will realize quite how much of an amateur he is.

He gets up, rubs the dirt off the mudguard where it got splashed on Monday. Then he sits down again, sips his coffee.

He's staring hard at the Harley now.

It's impossibly beautiful. Impossibly complicated, too. Maybe he should start with something easier. Maybe he's forgotten how to do it—it's so long since last he tried. No. It's like riding a bicycle. And besides, he knows he can do anything he wants. He can do this too.

Clean, creamy white paper. The wide sketchbook up on the easel in front of him, pencil in hand, Vince is poised to begin. For a moment, he registers satisfaction. He is looking at himself, seeing himself as a real artist, and liking what he sees.

That moment gives way to another, a moment of pure terror, for here he is in front of an immaculate sketchpad, and he only looks poised. There's something humbling about this. But Vince has never been a man to be humbled for long. And he isn't banking on starting now.

Easy. Take it easy and just concentrate.

Pencil. The most basic of all. Somehow he has to draw the bike in such a way that it looks as heavy on paper, as substantial, as it feels. Every part of the bike, every line, every curve, every turn, has to have reality and conviction and something else. Necessity. There's nothing accidental about a Harley, and there must be nothing accidental about his drawing.

Of course there will be. His hand is wobbly. He stares at the bike some more, narrows his eyes, ignoring the detail, all those complications. He looks up from the page. No one. He looks over at the Harley.

Don't even look at the page. Not for a second. You know where it is. Just begin.

And he does. Some rough sketches first.

Quick. Quick, before you can even think. The curve of the mudguard. Quicker still. Just get the sense of it. Create the impression. No. Again. No. Keep your eyes on the bike. Draw it without even looking at the paper. Again. No. Again. Better. Again. Again. Right. Now handlebars, wheels. Again. Go over it all again. Don't even look at the paper. Just look at the bike. The wheels. How do they look in relation to each other? In relation to the handlebars? Just that. Nothing more than that. Now, start again. Look at the bike. Look at it. Look.

Vince has never seen the Harley quite like this before. He has never really noticed a lot of things about it before. The way it curves down, dark and oh so sexy. Oh so powerful, too, but female, no mistaking it.

Why isn't that obvious? Harley. Harley's a woman's name. Harley. Carly. Marlee. Merrily. Shirley. Lesley. Brenda Lee. Vivien Leigh. Curly. Girlie. Harley.

A penis car pulls up outside Carrie's house. A black-haired girl throws her arms around the driver's neck and kisses him on the mouth. That must be Carrie's daughter, whatever her name is, just getting home. She climbs out of the car, a flushed, disheveled, slightly pudgy kid, and runs indoors.

Vince takes a look at the driver as he turns his Corvette out onto the Lakeshore Road. A sulky-looking tie guy. Neatly trimmed brown hair and mustache. Wearing a wide-lapelled business suit in a light grey, a dark green shirt, and a green-and-white patterned tie. What's the girl doing with a jerk like that? The jerk catches Vince staring at him, but clearly doesn't care. In fact, judging by the look of scorn on the man's face as he takes in the easel—he can't see the bike from that angle—he clearly doesn't have too high an opinion of artists.

And why expect any different? This is Pointe Claire. Artists are given a hard time here. As that man MacLoon surely knows. This is your average, middle-class, Philistine suburb studded with basement family rooms and gas barbecues sparked by accountants and sales managers and insurance company executives: the kind of place you have to get out of before you can hope to become an artist. Only then can you afford to return. And wreak havoc.

Vince turns back to his drawing, but he's lost it. And, he realizes, glancing at his watch, it's time to get organized. He picks up his easel and carries it into the garage, stashes the supplies. He should be gleeful. This is his kind of day.

He takes the Harley into town, to rue Notre-Dame, where Donald gives him a good price on the paperweights, practically nothing for the paintings. The ID guy is away for a week. Donald will let Vince know when the documents are ready. Vince changes into his city clothes in Donald's back room. The Armani suit, the linen shirt, the tie, all courtesy of Lucette. Vince has never owned more than he can fit into a couple of bags. No. He's owned a thousand things. But has sold them. All he's wanted up to now is a cushion in the bank, and his bike. And now? Vince isn't sure. He knows he's going to need a car. And a garage to keep the bike in. This is how it starts.

"Got any wax?" he asks Donald. He may have no need for it, but he likes to be prepared.

Before he leaves Donald's, there's one last detail he has to take care of. He uses Donald's letterhead and typewriter, scrawls an executive-type signature, and sends the letter through to the Ritz on Donald's fax machine.

He's made his arrangements with the waiter by the time Yolanda drifts in—straight from the beauty salon, judging by the smell of her—on little high heels, lighter than air. Everything that money can do to improve her appearance has been done, but nothing can disguise a face like an old ferret. Her face is overpowered by heavy earrings, her hands by big rings, her frame by shoulder pads. When she drapes her bias-cut linen jacket on the chair behind her, she reveals a cream-coloured linen dress and stringy arms. She's shy, nervous, embarrassed. They always are.

Vince orders Veuve Cliquot. She drinks too quickly. He calls for the menu, suggests the lamb *en croûte*. She's allergic to wheat. So she eats only rice and a salad, while he has the lamb.

But it is still a success! Of course it is a success. This is an old game for Vince.

"How much I prefer mature women to silly girls under the age of forty-five." The timing of that one is important. Too soon and they smell a rat.

It's an hour later when Vince exclaims, "My God! My wallet! I had it this morning, I remember clearly. Stolen! I had everything in that wallet! Everything!"

In apparent consternation, he waves his arms. Which is the signal he agreed on with the waiter who has his fax. The service at the Ritz is second to none. Pity Vince couldn't put the tip on MasterCard. But then—same difference, as they used to say at Beaconsfield High School—he had used some of the proceeds of the morning's sale to tip the waiter. Either way, it's on Sal's tab.

"There's no problem—" Yolanda begins, reaching for her purse.

The waiter is at Vince's side.

"I won't hear of you paying!" Vince tells Yolanda. "I can replace my cards. The American Express office is just down the road."

She glances at her watch. "You won't make it."

"It's true," he agrees, as though in astonishment. "Where has the time gone?"

He lifts the fax off the plate and reads it as the waiter withdraws. Then, in rapture, Vince exclaims, "Oh! Such news!"

"What? What's happened?"

"Just what I hoped!" He waves the fax in front of Yolanda, too fleetingly for her to more than glimpse a letterhead, a typewritten text, an illegible signature. "A breakfast meeting in Manhattan tomorrow!"

"In Manhattan! A deal?"

"Yes! No! Too early to say! Too good to be true!" And he moves as though to stand up, slumps back into his seat.

"Is something wrong?" she asks.

"I can't go." His voice is hopeless as he stares at Yolanda in shocked disbelief. "The banks are closed. Oh! Don't you see? I can't go! It's too, too cruel."

She nods gravely, understanding. "I can help."

"No!" This bravely. "I won't hear of any such thing! Not for an instant."

It works, of course. She not only pays nearly $200 for the meal and lends him the other $250 in her wallet, but—she must be a good customer here—persuades the assistant manager to cash a personal cheque for an extra $500. And she hands that over, too. All to be paid back punctiliously at Vince's lunch with her next week. Which will, of course, be his treat.

She takes her purse when she goes to the washroom, but leaves her jacket draped over the back of her chair, the pocket just under his hand. And there, sure enough, are her car keys. A Mercedes, no less. Vince has time, before she returns, to make an imprint of the car key in Donald's wad of wax.

He won't use it yet. It isn't urgent, anyway, and she'll be too likely to identify him as the thief if the car disappears now. That would be a pity. Her pride won't allow her to make a fuss over the $950. She won't want to tell a soul about that. Sorrowfully, she will just chalk the loss, and the lunch, up to experience. The car is a different kind of crime altogether. The car will be straight theft. She will have no compunction about reporting that. And she may have ways of tracking him down. So he'll wait until long after she's expunged A.S. Windle from her memory to steal the car.

He should be elated, Vince thinks as he pulls back into Sal's driveway early that evening. He has stopped off to have the car key made. And his pocket is full of cash. Another successful day.

But he'd rather not have gone into town at all. He'd rather have stayed home and finished a drawing.

Is this how it starts? he wonders idly. Is he going to become a suburban couch potato—resisting the idea of going into town, settling for West Island mediocrity, losing touch with his contacts downtown?

Vince snorts. Never. He could never become a West Islander like that. On the contrary. He's inspired by MacLoon. Vince too is an artist. That's what this is all about. And he would have preferred drawing—spending his day doing something new to him, something exciting—to more of the same old thing.

He thinks of Yolanda. It's too easy, this game. Probably, if he were practical, he should be checking out this week's Personals ads, setting up yet another win. But why? He doesn't really need the money. He doesn't need to be quite so practical anymore. And he can't be bothered with Yolanda types. You can do that for a certain length of time. For years. Decades. But not for ever.

He's sitting on the top step, his morning's work on his knees. The roughest sketches of the Harley at least have life, even if it's all but impossible to know what it is that they are supposed to represent. Maybe he should have continued with the rough drawings, done more of those, worked with them.

As soon as he had tried for any more recognizable image, the drawings lost their spark. The feeble little pencil markings on the paper are now all too obviously attempts at drawing a bike, but there's not enough movement in them. Vince is far from ready for Carrie, that much is clear. He really should set up his easel and get going again. But he can't. He just doesn't have the energy.

That's the other problem. When he spends his day generating a thousand dollars, he just doesn't have a lot left over for anything else.

He catches a glimpse of a pale, bespectacled man in a lightweight suit turning into Carrie's driveway. That must be the husband. What was it that Janet called him? The White Rabbit. He reemerges a short while later wearing droopy shorts and white running shoes, with sandy-coloured tufts of hair sprouting from his chest. A minor character, no doubt about it, and looking every inch the part. Either he's forgotten or he sees no need to change out of his beige executive socks. No calf muscles. What a loser.

Vince listens to him mow the lawn and then fiddle around with the barbecue. Steak, no doubt. Such a male ritual, searing raw flesh out of doors. Barbecuing is the perfect way for a man to maximize both his manliness and his domestic self-righteousness with minimum effort.

Vince sits out there on the step until the light has faded. He loves the Harley even more in the dark, gleaming in the dark. Vince loves the Harley the way the camera loves Liz Taylor.

A movement next door on the garage roof catches his eye. Raccoons the size of pigs, marauders outlined against the moonlit sky. Vince heads indoors to bed. It's time for the tragedy queen. Vince hasn't often had such a good opportunity to see the way a woman's mind works. Know thine enemy as thyself. Is that a quote from something? Or has Vince just coined a phrase?

> Who was it? Some woman I read recently said that the only question you need to ask is, What are you going through now? It was someone surprising, the kind of person you couldn't imagine would ever care. But she's right about that question, if only you can think to ask it, and if only you're able to answer it. For the answer to that question says it all.
>
> There are times when you realize only long after the fact what you were going through. Oh, in a sense you know. Like when you're expecting your first baby—you know full well that this is a time of change. But—if you're like me, at any rate—you want to deny that it'll really change you. Why did I do that? Why deny something so obvious? It seems so silly now, but I suppose I wanted to remain unchanged. My body unchanged,

my thoughts, myself. I suppose I must have known that it's impossible, really, to give birth to a child and remain untouched by the experience, but perhaps I hoped that denial would minimise the change.

It's sure that nothing at all prepared me for the effect of the baby herself—it was cataclysmic—like a bomb going off in the middle of my life. There is nothing like it, not even love, though love comes close. Never, ever have I been so desperate as when Elsa was born—so ecstatic—swinging so wildly between desperation and ecstasy. Why is it no one tells you all that? Is it because no one would ever dare to have a child if they knew what it was really like? Perhaps it doesn't hit everyone this way. I don't think it does. There are women who claim to take it in stride. I distrust women like that.

I've been thinking a lot about those days—funny the way life wheels around in circles. How friendless I was here at first, how much I felt a stranger, all cooped up, desperate for company, going stir-crazy. And ashamed, too. Ashamed of not being happy. A husband, a big house, two beautiful children. What more could I ask for? I was convinced no one else could feel as I did, with so few real complaints.

So I went out this afternoon. It was too beautiful a day to miss. Not far—just up Cedar to the school, around the circle and back home. It was enough. It was exhausting, actually. I've slept now for a couple of hours, and still I'm tired.

But it was lunchtime, and when I reached the school, the mothers—they all looked like such young mothers—were waiting for their children. The mothers had one in a stroller, as often as not, sometimes a three-year-old walking alongside as well. And they'd edge up the street and home in a small, slow procession. Those women. How are they managing? They look so competent, so able. Some of them even look happy. Are they really? I wonder. I have always wondered that. Always.

I didn't manage very well. Not well at all. But no one knew. I looked just the way those women look now. My clothes careless, my hair loose, always a bit rushed, never enough hands—but smiling through it all, my voice calm with the children, almost always calm. On my way home, Elsa trotting alongside, Nicholas in the stroller at first, and then stumbling along with his hand in mine, I used to see the same women once in a while, on fine days, sitting alone on the porch for a few moments while the baby slept, watching young children on the swings before dinner, sipping tea in back gardens while their children played. I used to watch them and wonder, how are they managing? And I was sure they were doing much better than I. I wasn't fit for company. There were times I wouldn't dare even sit out in public view. I was too likely to burst into tears.

But then—who knows?—perhaps they were too. How many of them were staying indoors, out of sight? How many of them really did burst into tears while their children played? On the surface, women's lives can seem so idyllic. And be so desperate.

Well, that explains the big eyes, Vince decides. And the errant husband. This Sal is wallowing in self-pity.

And with so few real complaints. You said it, sister. Well, if you want real complaints, just wait till yours truly is through with you. You'll have more real complaints than you ever bargained for. And, after years of groundless dissatisfaction, won't it be a treat to have a good reason for bitching.

The details have changed—the hair, the amount of makeup, the type of shoe. The shorts are wider now, and the T-shirts baggier than anything I would have worn. Everything these women wear looks more comfortable than anything I think I ever owned. I can hardly even remember what I would have worn, but I know it's not the same as what these women are wearing. I know that because I vividly remember—about six months after Nicholas was born— looking around in the shops and realizing that the styles had changed entirely when I wasn't looking.

What hasn't changed, though, is that these women spend most of their waking lives alone, indoors, out of sight: more alone, more cut off than any Turkish woman ever was in a Sultan's harem. In some essential respect, these women in their twenties and thirties are indistinguishable from the way I was, the way my own mother was, the way women have always been. This village is still full of women whose lives are tangential, in most ways, to the world of men.

On the way home, in one of those gardens behind the retirement home, there were two women sitting outside on some of those white plastic chairs that archaeologists of the future will use to identify the remains of the dying years of the twentieth century. They were leaning in towards each other, whispering—as though the stories they have to tell are any different from the stories that women everywhere have to tell. It could have been Carrie and me, twenty years ago. Or Madeleine and me. For I did eventually make friends, and we would get together from time to time in one another's kitchens, on one another's porches, where, crazed by isolation and neglect, we would blurt out confidences we would live to regret.

But always with other women. Never with men. That would have been a scandal. Young mothers cannot spend time respectably in the company of men other than their own husbands. And as the husbands escape to the city early every morning and get home only when they're exhausted, young mothers cannot spend time respectably in the company of men with anything left over to give them.

THE TRAGEDY QUEEN

Some women do hold on to paying jobs, even when their children are small. I used to envy those women. But that was before I knew any of them well enough to understand what it was really like. That was before I learned how they would work as close to their homes as possible, in offices, in schools, at the hospital. How they were still the ones to get home in time for the children, to take them to the doctor, arrange for a sitter, buy the present for the birthday party, ration the video games, hollow out the pumpkins, tie on the skates.

But, even then, I thought that these women—the ones with paying jobs—must have some time, at least, to spend with men in their places of work. Lunches, perhaps. Coffees. Chitchat of one kind and another. In practice they're spending their lunch hours doing the grocery shopping, picking up the repaired vacuum cleaner, phoning home during their breaks to check up on the ten year old who's been home from school all week with stomach flu. And besides, the men they work with choose to spend their time with the other men in the office or flirting with the single women—anything rather than be reminded of domestic duties they have succeeded in delegating to their own wives.

Is it any wonder that it is rare to encounter a woman who is both sane and respectable? And is it any wonder that, in daytime, the only men who are normally in the village keep themselves well hidden behind a cash register or the wheel of a truck—or race through at dangerous speeds en route to the golf club or the yacht club: the company of other men.

I've sometimes thought that the shortage of men here in the village gives it the air of a wartime community. Within the village lives a population of grass widows and their children. Beyond it are armies of uniformed men and single women who know little about the matrons' daily struggle to keep the home fires burning.

But how did this happen? The home begins, in the early days of marriage, as a refuge for the men after a day in the trenches. Why does that change? For it does. By six o'clock the wives are anxious for adult company, adult conversation, a man. But by six o'clock the husbands are anxious for quiet. They look for it in front of the TV, in the garden, in the garage, with work they couldn't finish at the office, calculations about taxes, pension contributions, car mileage, oil consumption—anything to avoid their demanding wives and obstreperous children. And if they fail to find a clever way of ducking them at home, then they take to missing the train, working late, hanging out in the bars downtown until the wife and children are asleep.

Is that why people treat suburban life with such disdain? I've heard the snide tone in which city dwellers dismiss people who live in the suburbs. What do people have against the suburbs? I used to think it was a prejudice against the middle class—against people who can't afford to raise their kids in Westmount, and who prefer not to live in the inner city. But maybe it isn't that. Maybe it's not just a prejudice against the middle class, but a prejudice against women. For it's women who live in the suburbs—women and children. There are few singles in the suburbs. And the men are hidden away more carefully than a forbidden language.

What a whiner this Sal is. But that's what a journal's for, isn't it? All the whining that no one in their right mind would listen to. And no risk of being challenged, either. With a journal there's no danger of contradiction.

Vince himself wouldn't be caught dead keeping a journal. That's not true. He wouldn't be caught dead keeping a journal like Sal's, an overwrought journal reeking of earnestness and introspection. If Vince kept a journal, he would write it in the full knowledge that it would be read by prying eyes. So it would be a deliberately dishonest journal, a journal designed to throw his readers off the scent.

He can see himself doing that, tricking his readers into thinking they were privy to his secrets. Writing a journal, as it were, of a man who is not himself, a made-up character that everyone will confuse with Vince Carlson. That's the only way he'd ever write a journal. The more he thinks about it, in fact, the more the idea appeals to him. One day maybe he'll give it a try.

Vince tosses the journal aside and flicks on the television just in time to see that John Demjaniuk—the alleged Ivan the Terrible of Treblinka—has been acquitted by an Israeli Court of Appeal after spending eight years in detention.

And there Demjaniuk is, sitting with earphones around his big bald round head in court, hardly believing what he hears. Beside him an Israeli guard with the darkest eyes Vince has ever seen watches with something that might be sympathy.

"I miss my vife," says the pasty-faced old man. "I miss my family. My grandchilds. I vant to go home."

Only no one wants him. The United States has stripped him of his citizenship for lying about his past. Maybe Ukraine will allow him to return. There is his family now, a pretty daughter, her pleasant-faced husband, their three children—what have they all had to contend with over the past ten years since their father and grandfather transmogrified into a monster?—outside their home in Ohio, looking forward to having him home again. And now, before Vince's very eyes, the monster, a man charged with crimes against humanity, is turning back into a loving suburban grandfather. Is this what they mean when they talk about the banality of evil?

Who is evil? Not even Demjaniuk, apparently. And certainly not Vince.

Admittedly, Vince is a bit of a trickster. But that's a long way from evil. What would life be without play? Vince is a man who has taken his play seriously. That's what makes life worth living, turns an ordinary, messy life into a work of art. And Vince is an artist first and foremost. Is it his fault if the world is full of stupid people? Why should he take their little feelings into account? That would be to compromise his integrity as an artist. The very idea makes his flesh crawl. He'd go to jail first.

He has gone to jail first.

So he's callous. Careless of other people. Sometimes even cruel. So what? The only thing that holds other people back from behaving as he does is that they care more for the opinion of others. They are slaves to their neighbours, and freedom belongs to those, like Vince, who acknowledge no allegiance to community. And besides, every artist mines the landscape for his material. And if the results aren't pretty? Too damn bad. That's a very different thing from evil.

Some Toronto artist has been charged under the Public Morality Act for showing pre-pubescent children engaged in various sex acts with adults. What a fool. He'll end up in jail—unless he has a very good lawyer.

Art always causes an uproar. The artist is society's natural enemy, always challenging convention, morality, rules, prohibitions, laws, forever dabbling with the forbidden. A criminal, in short.

The Public Morality Act is a direct descendent of the law that banned an English translation of *Salome* from the London theatre. So it played instead in the French in which Wilde had had the foresight to write it. And that same Public Morality Act is a kissing cousin to the law that put Wilde in jail for sodomy. He was a fool, too. Flouting convention in broad daylight. A fool and an outlaw. But evil? No.

Besides, it isn't really a question of right and wrong. It's really a question of what you can get away with. And of circumstances. There's *grand mal* and there's *petit mal*.

But what did that guy in Toronto expect? You can't just throw yourself on the mercy of the authorities, oh no. That's MacLoon's problem too. He's daring enough, but he won't get away with it. Not for much longer. It isn't the neighbours; the neighbours matter only to people interested in winning a popularity contest. But only a fool would take on City Hall. Daylight is unforgiving; even the daring need the cover of darkness. You can get away with anything, but only if you're cunning.

And one thing is clear. There's one law for the lion, and one for the lamb.

Feeling sleepy, Vince sends Peter Mansbridge spinning into oblivion. What's that sound? Vince imagines he can hear singing. He listens more closely. He checks, but the radio's off. He gets up and shuts off the ceiling fan. Yes, it's definitely singing, and a woman's voice. Getting louder as he goes towards the open bedroom window. It's coming from next door. And now silence. One song has ended. Vince stands perfectly still, waiting. And in another moment Janet's wavery soprano begins again.

> There is a tavern in the town, in the town,
> And there my true love sits him down, sits him down
> And drinks his wine 'mid laughter free
> And never, never thinks of me.
>
> Fare thee well, for I must leave thee
> Do not let this parting grieve thee,
> But remember that the best of friends must part, must part.
> Adieu, adieu, kind friends, adieu adieu adieu
> I can no longer stay with you, stay with you
> I'll hang my harp on the weeping willow tree
> And may this world go well with thee.

Wavery, but sprightly. With a sprightliness that's quite at odds with the sense of the song. That's no light-hearted tavern song. A suicide note set to music, more like. What has Janet's life been that she can sing that song so blithely? That she can sing at all?

Is he there now, her gentleman friend? Surely not. This has the ring of solitary singing, pure and unselfconscious. What a dame. No self-pity there.

Sal could learn a thing or two from Janet.

Vince likes Sal less and less.

8

A car pulls into the driveway the next morning, and the driver serves Vince with a court summons. Working at his easel, Vince is irritated by the interruption. That's the forty-second summons he's been handed. All criminal charges—fraud, theft, possession of stolen goods, breach of contract. And all lodged by companies.

He glances at the summons cursorily at first, then more closely. This is no company. This one is Laila's doing.

Laila. That's a name that takes him back—a year and a half? longer?

She was a demanding one. Determined, too, with an unshakable sense of how Vince should look when she took him out. And of how much he should drink. That last Jessye evening of his put an end to his affair with Laila. She had a nice collection of gold jewellery, though. On the day when he left her house in Town of Mount Royal, he took all her jewellery with him and sold it for $6,000.

Vince lights himself a cigarette. He may have underestimated Laila. The women don't often go to the police. By the time Vince has discarded them they're too embarrassed to lay charges. But here's Laila spending a small fortune on her lawyer—and for what? Does she really think she can win? Vince will be acquitted of every one of the charges against him. He has his friends in the legal system, and charm has always been his ticket. Nothing sticks to him. The authorities know it and Vince knows it.

The more worrying surprise is the speed with which the law has tracked him down here. How did they know he'd moved into this house? There's only one way. The real estate office must have told on him. That means Carrie.

So she ratted on him. Well, she's just going to have to make amends. And there is one thing he needs from her. Just the one. Time to make some moves to get her on his side.

What he wants from her is simple. He wants her to keep Sal at bay when the first of August comes and goes without a rent cheque from Vince.

The best strategy will be for Vince to play hard to get. He wants her chasing him. And she's the type to go for a sparring partner. Well, that should be easy.

He'll need to know more about her. It's a difficult time for a woman Carrie's age. All the more so for a woman who makes a point of looking after herself. Talk about losing battles. With a nymphette for a daughter, too, just to complicate matters further. An extraordinary mother. A husband who has lost whatever interest he ever had in her. Not too good for the self-esteem.

Carrie's going to be so grateful to him, she's sure to play. Yup. She's going to be eating out of Vince's hand.

By the time Carrie is at the door, Vince is changed and ready to soak his aesthetic sensibilities in chlorinated water, Pointe Claire's sunlit answer to a Turkish bath. She takes one look at him, and then slams the door of the minivan shut and heads off at considerable speed up Cedar Avenue. He follows on his bike, clad only in helmet, shades, sandals, and black silk bikini underwear bulging with the pack of Player's tucked in the side.

Zigzagging at an invigorating pace up leafy streets, they skim past Cedar Park with its soccer field barely visible behind the elementary school, and past the tennis courts and playground on Clearpoint Park, before rounding a corner past the blackened shell of what a sign still proclaims as the Anglican Church of St. John the Baptist.

St. John the Baptist. *St-Jean Baptiste.* That's not at all the same saint. Not at all the same church. A different world altogether.

Vince pulls up by the baseball diamond at the entrance to Kinsmen Park. A teenaged boy wearing wide pants cut off at midcalf is skateboarding on the road, and two or three others are playing hackysack nearby. And there, in the corner under the trees, is the Lakeshore Swim Club.

Vince had come here a couple of times as a kid. His family had never joined, probably his parents never even knew the pool existed, but in the afternoons non-members could pay—what?—fifty cents or a buck to swim, and on the hottest summer days Vince would cycle over for an hour or two. One day he'd got caught in the middle of a water polo game, and as they were short one player, Vince had been invited to join in. He went back the following day, and the one after that, but it never happened again.

It's noon, now, and the pool is emptying of children, who are being wrapped in thick towels and shepherded home for lunch by crisply dressed mums. One or two young mothers, instead of heading out to minivans and bikes and tricycles and candy-coloured strollers, are getting themselves organized around the picnic tables by the evergreens sheltering the baby pool. The lifeguards, finished with their morning's work, are retreating with their umbrellas into the velvety shade of the white clapboard shack. Still shimmering in the sunlight as Vince and Carrie arrive, the turquoise water soon settles into an inviting mirror calm.

Vince pulls out a cigarette and watches Carrie step self-consciously out of her sundress and sandals. Her body is small and tidy in a pale bikini. Too many carrot sticks, too few dirty weekends.

"Want some beer?" he asks, revealing the half-litre can of Labatt Blue he has wrapped up in his towel.

From the look on Carrie's face, he might have just emptied one of Madeleine's little plastic bags under her nose. Carrie glances around anxiously—hoping no one has seen Vince with her—before shaking her head. She needn't have worried: there isn't another soul in sight. She stuffs her hair into a pink bathing cap encrusted with white rubber flowers, and then turns and dives into the shallow end, spritzing Vince's cigarette.

He watches her efficient breaststroke for a minute before throwing his head back and taking a long, cold guzzle of Blue. Where was it he read that article about Jessye Norman's daily regime of swimming? So many laps of breaststroke, so many of butterfly—a great way to develop her lung power, no doubt, but the thought of Jessye barrelling through the water, the thought of Jessye in a bathing suit, almost defies the imagination.

Almost but not quite.

Vince pictures Jessye's vast brown body in the vast brown bathing suit described in the article. She'd need a bigger pool than this one.

The heat is ferocious, the air heavy, the sky suspiciously lurid. Vince ambles over to the baby pool and sets his Blue and his towel down in the shade, heedless of the consternation his presence causes among the young mothers unwrapping whole-grain bread and plain yoghurt for their children. Then, feeling like a hippopotamus, he does his best to submerge himself in six inches of water.

"I'm sorry, sir. The baby pool is only for the little kids." The voice belongs to a boy of sixteen or seventeen, one of the lifeguards. Vince wonders if he's been waiting to pounce.

Vince looks the boy up and down. A perfect taut body. Six feet of sinew and muscle. The tense face comically like a photographic negative, brittle white hair, eyebrows and lashes against a sun-reddened face. Vince sweeps his arm around the pool area. "There aren't any little kids in the water at the moment. I just wanted to get wet for a moment."

"No, well, that's the rule."

"Is that a fact?" Vince stands up. The water is lukewarm anyway, a tepid urine soup.

"Are you a member of the club, sir?"

"Well, actually, no," he answers, stepping over the concrete lip of the baby pool and onto the grass. He's taller than the boy, but not by much. "But I'm planning to join. I will be a member soon. Scouts' honour."

"There's a charge of five dollars per day for the use of the pool by non-members. The public swim is from two to four on weekdays."

"So, you're telling me I owe you five dollars?"

"I am, sir. The cash is in the chalet. And, until you're a member, you are restricted to the two afternoon hours." And, without so much as a blink, he turns on his heel and leaves.

They're everywhere, the cops. Even in paradise.

And the way to deal with cops is to bend over backwards being cooperative. Appearing to be cooperative. Appearance is all that matters. The right appearance inspires trust. It's as simple as that.

This little control freak has hardly made it back to the chalet when a deferential Vince is shoving a cheque under his nose. "I'm not sure of the amount yet," he explains apologetically. "That's why I wanted to speak to the membership person first, but here, you can fill in the amount yourself. And, hey, just be sure to add on an extra five dollars for today, eh? Whatever I owe you…"

He doesn't bother adding that he's post-dated the cheque.

Carrie is lying on her front beside the pool when Vince pads back towards her. Has she not overheard the exchange with the lifeguard? Nor even felt Vince's footsteps drawing near? Perhaps she really doesn't know he's there. He stands over her, studying her body. Her buns look so inviting that Vince makes a point of reminding himself not to give them a friendly little pat. She wouldn't mind one bit if they were safely out of sight, but she'd have kittens if he touched her here in the open where anyone could see.

"Cute little bathing suit," is all he says, sitting down beside her. From this angle the curve of her back is quite fetching. Hm. He's starting to see with new eyes. Starting to see lines and curves and angles and shadows. Good sign, that.

Carrie has nice, elastic skin, lightly tanned to the colour of buttery caramel. How much longer before he's ready to start painting? Skin interests Vince a lot. The colour of skin, the texture of skin, the surface that's more or less smooth, more or less sandpapery, more or less cool, dry, taut. He's fascinated by what lies behind the skin, too, by what lies under the surface. Fascinated and, this may be the one thing he's ashamed to admit, repelled. Vince figures that skin is the only reason we can bear to look at ourselves in the mirror. There is a limit to our tolerance of colour.

Once he saw Cronenberg, his all-time favourite director, interviewed on TV, saying how odd it is that we have such a horror of what lies inside our own skin. Vince has thought about that a lot. There's a Montreal artist called Mark Prent Vince finds pretty impressive too, a misleadingly mild-mannered little sculptor who seems to be utterly devoid of squeamishness. That's the kind of artist Vince would like to be. He aspires to that. Even as he knows he himself would flinch.

Vince lies down flat on his back, stretches his arms up behind his head, and arches his back for maximum attention-getting. The way Carrie's tensing up, he knows she's checking out the fruit basket in his silk bikini. Now there's a thought: one that might give Fruit of the Loom underpants an entirely new lease on life. Someone in their advertising department should pay him a fortune for the idea. Just so long as they don't give him a lifetime supply of their underwear. Vince has more expensive tastes. The bikini he's wearing now could easily have cost fifty dollars, plus tax, on the Main. Culotte, that was the name of the store. Well protected, though. Vince had wanted a one-piece cotton tank suit in black, as well, but there was no way of getting that out the door without setting off the alarm system.

"I'll be ready for you soon, Carrie." He puts just enough emphasis on the word "ready" to titillate her.

"Oh?" Then, realizing what he means, she collects herself, says, "Oh, good. When?"

"Soon. Got myself some supplies already. Just getting warmed up. It may be this weekend. Is the weekend good for you?"

"Sure!" she says, too quickly. "Yes, I mean," she says more calmly. "That would be fine." And she turns over, sits up, and folds her arms over her chest in one smooth move so that he catches only a glimpse of her neatly organized little breasts. Her face, unfortunately, is one of her less interesting features. Standard-issue pretty. Small, undistinguished nose, the kind that many a better-looking woman would pay a king's ransom for. Unremarkable blue eyes. Dimpled chin. It would be easier to make a little Hummel figurine out of Carrie than a work of art.

A woman's streaming face appears at the end of the pool, gasps, and disappears. In its place her ass comes up out of the water flaunting a big red and white maple leaf. She completes the somersault and pushes off—it's the athletic shrew from Wilton—and when she surfaces again she's practically half way up the pool, churning her way towards another somersault.

"Is she on a national team or something?" Vince asks, gesturing towards the woman.

"Who?" Carrie turns to look just as the woman somersaults back again towards them. "Oh, Iris. Not so far as I know."

"Then why is she wrapped in the Canadian flag?"

Carrie laughs. "Anyone can wear those bathing suits! There's nothing official about that. They make them for men too. You could wear one."

"Why? Don't you like what I'm wearing now?"

Carrie looks the other way. "Most men," she says prudishly, "wear real bathing suits. Not just underwear."

"Yeah, well, I'm not most men."

"So I've noticed."

"And besides, it covers the same parts of the body. Of course, it is silk, and it can be a little revealing when it's wet. But so what? I'd rather wear this than hide my equipment behind a maple leaf."

Carrie shows no sign of having heard. She's still in Doris Day mode, watching Iris, thinking God knows what.

"Is she in training, or what?" Vince asks.

"Oh, she's always in training. She never stops."

"How come? What's she training for?"

Carrie looks over at Vince, makes some kind of decision, as though to tell part of the story. "She always liked to be fit, but now it's become an obsession. She's nearly fifty, but you'd never know it. Of course, in most ways, she has the body of a woman of thirty."

"So what? What's it for? Does she have a lover?"

"A lover!" Carrie nearly yelps the word. It must have been on the tip of her tongue for years. "Of course not! She's working to keep her body healthy."

"And?"

"And... and to keep herself sane."

And failing miserably, Vince thinks to himself. He decides against telling Carrie about his exchange with Iris.

"Does she have a husband, then?"

"She's married, of course." Carrie says this as though it's obvious to the whole world. Come to think of it, Carrie says a lot of things as though they're obvious to the whole world. Amazing how little she learned from her mother.

"Of course? Why is everything so obvious? It isn't obvious to me. That's why I'm asking."

"We're all married. When we stop being married," Carrie goes on, in an exaggeratedly patient manner, "we stop being here. It's very nearly as simple as that. There are exceptions. Sal is an exception, I guess. She's divorced."

"And she isn't here." The exception that proves the rule. There's that Ted Cunningham shorthand again. At least Vince is becoming aware of how often he uses it. Maybe that's some kind of improvement. He has more and more the feeling he'd be a better man if he managed to wean himself of that kind of shorthand. He can't seem to break the habit, though. Most of the time he doesn't even notice he's doing it.

"Right. But she was here. We can be here for a year or two after a divorce. It takes time to sell a house, see the kids through whatever school they have to be seen through."

"We? You include yourself in this?"

"It has nearly happened to most of us. It should have happened to some of us, only we chickened out."

He waits. There are times when questions help, but this isn't one of them.

Carrie sighs. "First you say it's because of the kids. But then you realize it's because you're scared."

"You. Yourself."

"I. Myself. I guess I'm talking about myself."

"Scared of what?"

"Of the unknown. Of jumping off into the unknown. The devil you know is better than the devil you don't know."

"And your husband is the devil you know."

"Actually, that makes him sound a lot more interesting than he really is. He gave himself gum disease last year, for Christ's sake, by overflossing—" she explains, her voice rising.

"He must have interested you once..."

"We were high school sweethearts. Inseparable since Grade Eight. Since we were thirteen years old. We got married a year after we left high school. There seemed no reason not to. His parents and mine bought the house for us, that was their wedding present. We've been here ever since. Three kids in four years. Colleen is the youngest."

"Uhuh. The messy room. I think I caught a glimpse of her this morning."

"This morning? Oh yes, she'd been sleeping over with her friend Tanya." Vince is watching closely. She believes what she just said. Of course, that jerk just *might* have been Tanya's dad in the Corvette... But if it was, then what was Colleen doing kissing him on the lips?

"...does that sometimes." Carrie has not stopped talking. "At least I know where she is. That's so important."

Vince says nothing.

"You're a good listener."

Vince meets her eyes with his own, switches on his patented kind, gentle, modest little smile, says nothing.

"Maybe we'd have had less trouble, Reed and I, if he knew how to listen." Still Vince says nothing. "We've had our ups and downs. More downs than ups… Sal was my best buddy in those days. She had her own problems. Reed and I nearly split up, in fact. And then… well, we blinked. Edged back, somehow, to a way of getting on. We don't expect too much of each other anymore. But at least we don't pick on each other the way we used to. We don't fight anymore. Ever. We don't do much of anything anymore."

"And Sal? Was she still married at that time?"

"Yes, she was." Carrie looks at him with a flash of resentment. She wants to tell her own story. She doesn't want to talk about Sal. "Her husband left later on, of course, when she thought their problems were behind them."

"Of course." Vince mimics her little-girl voice.

A beat. She sits perfectly still.

Then, "Yes." Another beat. "Of course," she repeats in a suddenly deep voice. She is leaning heavily on the consonants as though for an imbecile. "A lot of things *are* in fact obvious. Maybe not to you, but they're obvious all the same. *Of course*"—the sibilant is stronger now than the guttural sound—"women out here are married. Haven't you noticed that? Men too. Men and women who live out here are married. You move here when you get married and want to have kids. That's the kind of place this is. *Of course* Iris doesn't have a lover. She wouldn't dare. Everyone would know. Someone would tell her husband, and that would be that. And *of course*"—more and more sibilant—"there are problems in every marriage. All the time. Most of the time we choose to ignore them, but they're there all the same."

In her anger, Carrie has forgotten to look pretty. With her lower lip, her jaw, the muscles in her neck tensed, Vince for the first time sees a face he'd be interested in drawing. He dips his feet into the water and wiggles his toes. "I seem to have pissed you off. I didn't mean to. Let me take those one at a time and explain why it isn't obvious to me. Will you let me do that?"

Carrie nods briefly.

"First off. Of course people out here are married. Let's start there. I'm not married. Sal isn't. And even if she's gone, she's coming back. She hasn't sold the house. She's just rented it. And I'll bet there are more than two of us. Your mother isn't married. There's another. Which brings me to the lovers. In a colony of women, married or not, there are in fact going to be one or two, or even three, who take a lover. Someone may know, granted, but not necessarily the husband. And by the way, it isn't completely wild to suggest that he might have a lover of his own somewhere else. OK. Iris may not have a lover, but it was not a stupid question. The women I'd wonder about are the ones who are busy running and swimming and bouncing around doing aerobic exercise programs and parading around outdoor pools in cute little bikinis."

He puts his hand up as she begins to retort. The line of the lower lip. If he can capture that, he'll have her. "Let me finish first. And, what was the third? Marriage. Yeah. Well, you'd know a lot more about marriage than I would. But, if you don't mind my saying so, you don't make it sound like much fun. If that's the way you think, maybe you made the wrong decision when you decided to stay married. You're a young woman. Why don't you just get out and start again?"

"But I'd be dirt poor. I can't make a proper living for myself, selling real estate, not in this market. There's nothing I can do that will pay me enough to make it worthwhile. For what? For the probability of being lonely for the rest of my life? For the virtual certainty of being worse off financially than I am now? Reed isn't exciting, but he does have two great qualities. One, he's a good provider. A notary with a good, steady income. And two, we're used to each other. We can sit by the TV in the evening and understand each other's comments."

Jesus. Vince contents himself with saying, "There's more to life."

"Yeah, like romance." She pronounces the word the way she might pronounce the name of a vegetable she has seen advertised but never tasted. The mouth has changed again. There are deep new lines at its corners now. Which might make a good drawing too, but it would be so unflattering that she'd never come back for another sitting. Vince catches himself. There's something not quite right about that way of thinking. What is it? Why is he worried about whether the drawing is flattering or not? He's an artist. He's interested in truth, warts and all. Isn't he?

There's time enough to figure that out later on. Right now he has to concentrate on what Carrie is saying. What matters for now is just this: that the trick will be to get her angry for long enough to get that mouth right.

"Like being swept off my feet," Carrie is continuing. "Like making a brilliant new career for myself. We can't all do that." She must mean Sal. Aha. So she's jealous of Sal? That's good to know. "Like starting all over again. Dreamland."

Which, Vince thinks, but does not say, brings him back to the subject of a lover.

Carrie shrugs. She's winding down. Back to being pretty again. Vince's eyes leave her face. She has nice shoulders. What a waste, really, if there's no one to appreciate the time and effort she devotes to looking good.

Iris is climbing out of the pool like a teenager, lifting herself with her arms just high enough to plant a foot on the concrete lip. An ass like a rubber ball. And skin like an old boot. As Vince watches, she rubs herself quickly with her towel.

Iris isn't sexy. Not at all. Funny how in real life the fittest bodies are pretty sexless. That, at least, is the way Vince sees it. Sexless and deceptive. Looking at Iris, you'd never guess what a shrew she really is. Vince much prefers the physical flaws that are evidence of human weakness. That's why he's always wondered at the fuss made over movie stars with the perfection and the armed, sexless impermeability of androids.

The movies come a pretty poor second to opera anyway, so far as Vince is concerned. He'd choose the big screen any day over TV, of course, but no movie he has ever seen has had the extravagance of grand opera. Some of them try. Vince's been to movie epics that have aspired to the quality of opera. No matter how hard they try, though, and no matter how much money they spend and what kind of technical wizardry they use, they lack the kind of opulence that the opera conjures up effortlessly out of the faded costumes and dusty chestnut trees that have been pulled out of storage for yet another season of Puccini. And the reason—Vince has thought about this, has felt sorry from time to time for movie directors who are doomed from the start—is that the opera maintains distance. That's its overwhelming power. And that's where the movies fail: in close-up. As soon as you show the faces of the stars in close-up, you're sitting around the kitchen table with them, drowning your sorrows in Labatt Blue.

And movie stars, even the best of them, come a pretty poor second to the *grandes dames* of the opera. Elizabeth Taylor is the movie star Vince admires more than any other—puffy face, chins, corsets and all. Even Liz is a long way from Jessye. But, then, Jessye is pure magnificence, reserved for very special occasions. Liz is small beer, just the best of a bad lot. A lot more interesting than Roseanne, admittedly. Good enough for daily use. Whenever Liz shows herself in public after her latest facelift with her latest husband, Vince waits with relish for the tabloids to track her down in disarray, as they inevitably do. He imagines her throwing furious scenes in the night with this new, unsuspecting husband, imagines the remorseful aftermath. How much more exciting, that, than the sound of androids clashing by night.

Carrie glances shyly at Vince, considers whether she's said anything she'll regret. He smiles the smile of a man who knows that life is not always easy, that it takes courage just to carry on.

"Excuse me, Mr. Carlson, sir." It's the lifeguard with the white eyebrows again. He's more polite than the last time. Which may have something to do with the fact that he has Vince's cheque in his hand. Or it may have something to do with Carrie's presence. He's smiled at her.

"Hi, Mrs. Vale."

"Bobby is the assistant manager now," Carrie tells Vince. "He's an old friend of my son Richard's."

"Mr. Carlson,"—the muscle-bound negative waves the cheque in front of Vince—"there must be some mistake. I just noticed that the cheque is dated August first…"

"Oh, yeah." Vince speaks mildly, looks honest and concerned. But what an observant little martinet this Bobbie turned out to be. And in front of Carrie, too. "Is that a problem?"

"I'm afraid, sir, we aren't supposed to accept post-dated cheques."

"Oh, well, I didn't know that. Nobody told me that." He's debating with himself. His cash-flow's good right now, though he will have to pay for the electronic equipment next week. He got his inheritance in the morning's mail too, but that's his nest egg. This post-dated cheque will be for such a small amount. Should he offer just to write another? No. They'd wonder why he post-dated the other one to begin with. Besides, old habits die hard. Vince resents paying for anything he can get for free. "I'm so sorry about this. The thing is that I'm expecting a big cheque early in August," he lies, "and I was kind of trying to put off some payments until then. Don't want to run short, eh? I just hate having to borrow money. Neither a borrower nor a lender be. That's what I always say."

The negative looks uncertainly at Carrie.

"We're not supposed to…" he repeats.

"Oh, I don't think it'll be a big problem," Carrie interjects. "Tell them I said it was OK."

Vince tries to look grateful.

"I must run," she adds, pulling her dress over her bathing suit. And she's gone.

As Vince charges down Cedar Avenue, scarcely looking where he's going—his head is buzzing with irritation—he nearly runs down a scruffy-looking man crossing the road. He would have hit him, too, if the man hadn't jumped out of the way in the nick of time.

Without giving the matter a moment's thought, Vince accelerates, aware vaguely of the man's stare—and the Harley is rounding the bend by the time Vince gets an uncomfortable feeling in the back of his neck.

No, couldn't be. That couldn't have been one of Carrie's kids. Too old. But the feeling won't go away, and Vince turns to look behind him just in time to see the man put his hand out and open Carrie's evidently unlocked door. It's MacLoon.

Shit.

MacLoon and Janet. MacLoon must be the gentleman friend. Well, whaddyaknow. It makes a kind of sense. That Janet's a free-thinker if ever there was one. Not a bit like her daughter. More like the chunky kid, whatever her name is. Janet probably wouldn't bat a carefully made-up eyelash at that girl's carrying on with tie guys. That girl is the apple of Janet's eye. Probably she could get away with murder.

Yes, Vince can see why Janet and MacLoon get on.

But what's MacLoon doing with a woman with one foot in the grave? Most men are not too interested in women of seventy-six. But then, MacLoon is not exactly your average suburban matron's fantasy lover. MacLoon is hardly Fabio. And beggars can't be choosers.

That's what Ted Cunningham would have said. The saying has come to mind entirely unbidden, like a reflex. No matter how Vince tries, no matter how many perfectly good, precise words Vince keeps in his head for every eventuality that life presents, he can't seem to keep that stale, moronic shorthand at bay, not even when its meaning runs counter to everything he holds dear.

It's that foul-up with the lifeguard that's bothering him. It was just a little slip, really. It doesn't matter. Nothing matters. Vince is sitting pretty. It's all a question of blitheness, the priceless gift of not caring, not giving a good goddam. All these years Vince has been blessed with that gift in abundance. There is no reason why it should fail him now. So why does he feel like breaking something?

When in doubt, make a sale. There's something cheering about making money, Vince has always found. Should he head down to rue Notre-Dame right now? How about it? No. It's too hot an afternoon for a trip into town.

The electronic equipment won't be arriving till Wednesday. Which is OK. It'll take Vince another week to sort through Sal's stuff. He fishes his phone book out of his jacket pocket, finds the number he's looking for, dials, and makes an appointment with the dealer for the following week.

Stashing the court summons out of sight in a drawer in the kitchen reminds him of another little duty. He phones Le Tulipier again—where the woman is a lot more cordial to him than she was the last time they spoke—and orders French long-stemmed yellow tulips to be delivered to the Château Nasso on Sherbrooke Street.

"How many?"

"A dozen will do," he says. If he's excessive Judy will know he wants something.

The message this time will just read For Judy the Judge. There isn't another soul on earth with the nerve to call her that.

What next? Where else can he build up a few credits for himself?

Madeleine.

Hm.

Another one for the Yellow Pages. Le Chocolatier Belge. The biggest box. No card at all. Delivery before five o'clock. Guaranteed.

That'll give her time to hide them before Pierre steps off the train.

Vince turns on the radio just in time for the four o'clock news. There's still time to get some real work done. He picks up his drawings and studies them. He's improving.

It's time Vince had a living model. That's what he really has to work on, that's what he's got to be able to do. And soon, too—he needs to have some practise before any of the local ladies come over to sit for him.

A child would do, although children are the most difficult of all to get right. They have so few lines, they are so unformed. All you get is an impression, wide, open, smooth: a face lying in wait for life to put its stamp on it.

Would it work to draw from a photograph? Vince eyes the morning's *Gazette* doubtfully. There's the new Prime Minister, Kim Campbell, in a navy blue suit at the Big Seven conference, looking thoroughly intimidated in a row of stalwart presidents and a well-kempt prime minister or two. Short hair, short legs, a woman in a man's world, trying too hard. Could Vince draw her? No. All the decisions have already been taken, by the photographer, the light, the camera itself, and by all the cartoons he has seen over the past several months. What Vince needs is a real, live human face that no one else has drawn.

Of course. *Of course.* He hears Carrie's voice.

But this really is obvious. He can model for himself. A self-portrait. *Of course.* All the great artists did it. Rembrandt, for example. Van Gogh. Why didn't he think of that before?

Where? The only mirror is in the bathroom. Vince brings in the radio to listen to a Hank Williams special on Oldies 990, sets himself up with the smaller sketchbook on a stool in front of the mirror, and studies his face, its features, its lines, its light, its deep shadows.

A big face. Not a great face. Pudgy, pockmarked, guarded. Good thing you don't need to be Robert Redford to attract the ladies. And you don't. Charm is what it takes.

Brutally short, straight hair. Vince doesn't know what to make of his eyes. They're not always quite so intense, or he doesn't think so. The ears are much more polite: small and neat. Not very interesting, having ears as your best feature. But he could make himself look handsome in the drawing. It would be a lie, but he could do it, that's within his power. Getting it right, though, that's another story.

Think of your face the way you think of a fern, or a bowl of apples. A subject. Just that. Vince tries to see himself as a stranger might, as if he'd never seen the face before. The mouth is tilted. That's where to start, with the line of the lips: that line there, the slightly skewed curve of the lower lip in the shadow of the upper. Sneak up on it quickly, now, before you let yourself think for another second. Dash something off, as rough as can be. Just get going. Get started.

And he's off.

And that's when the phone rings. Is he never going to be left in peace? He peers at the display. An unfamiliar number. An unfamiliar name. Vince lifts the receiver.

"Yeah?" he says impatiently.

"Win?"

Vince freezes. He knows that voice. And who it that called him Win? Win is A.S. Windle. But there's only one woman who ever thought of calling him Win.

Laila.

"Vot?" he answers. A name like Schleiermacher calls for a German accent.

"I'm looking for a Mr. A.S. Windle," she persists. Her voice is cold. Did she recognize his voice when he first answered?

"No Vindle here. Vas tenant, but he not pay. I kick him out."

"Yeah." She doesn't sound convinced. There's a pause. "Then I guess you must be interested in tracking this crook down, too." Nice move, Laila. Clever. "May I ask your name, please?"

"Schleiermacher. I am Schleiermacher."

"Well, Mr. Schleiermacher, I'll let you know if I find him."

"Ja," Vince answers, resisting the temptation to add, Und vot gut vill zat do you?

It's midnight when Vince puts aside his work. He looks out the bedroom window. Black night. Not a soul in sight. Vince picks up the sturdiest of Sal's kitchen knives and heads outdoors and down the driveway, where he first snaps the antenna off the blue minivan and then hunkers down and slashes its tires.

An upstairs light is still burning in Carrie's house, he notices when he turns back up the driveway. A bedroom window. Vince stares up at it. Is that Carrie's room? What's she doing? He knows Carrie hardly at all, he realizes, closing the front door behind him. Far too little to allow him to judge how she'll react when he makes his move. And he wants to be sure he doesn't miscalculate with Carrie.

There's a pretty long section in Sal's journal about Carrie, he remembers, pulling off his jeans and climbing into bed. Sal's take on Carrie should be right on target. Sal, to give credit where credit is due, is a woman who has her uses.

Feeling vulnerable. Very much the victim—hateful and resentful—and unable to make things better in any way.

Thinking about the Adult Learner party in Baie d'Urfé I went to with Carrie. Carrie and I were no longer as close as we once were, but we'd signed up for the Adult Learner program at Abbott together, both needing to take that first big step out of the house. Perhaps, too, we both hoped—I know I hoped—to rediscover the intimacy we had felt in the early years, when the children were small and we seemed to have the same difficulties. Like wartime camaraderie, the closeness of mothers is intense and temporary. Anyway, there we were at this party, Carrie and I and about twenty other women who had started at the same time.

Things were not at their lowest-ever ebb then between Carrie and Reed. The worst time had been over the previous winter. Carrie could talk of nothing else for months, and I learned more than I really wanted to know about Reed and his limitations. I must have thought I knew him pretty well, in fact, because I was taken completely by surprise when he led me into his bedroom during a dinner party one night and kissed me full on the mouth. Then he let me go, and neither he nor I ever mentioned the incident. Soon he was too busy banging drums out in the woods with his men's group to give me another moment's thought. By that time, he and Carrie were picking their way through to a new tolerance of each other. She tolerates his drums, he tolerates her career. They will stay married for ever. They are terrified at the merest possibility that they might be even worse off without each other than they are together.

Becoming students again had been a big step for all of us, but especially for Carrie. Or maybe I just knew her best. It was difficult for all of us to get out of the house, to dare to assert ourselves when we had never in our lives felt less assertive. And each of us was more or less racked by worry and guilt over abandoning the life of housewife and mother in order to answer this selfish need to go to college, to take a step out of our little domestic worlds and into—what? None of us knew. All of us feared. And dreamt.

I was one of the lucky ones: I knew what I wanted out of it all. Abbott was just the first step for me—I was pretty sure of that. I already had my sights set on McGill. And beyond. I was heading out. Carrie was painfully unsure of herself, of what she was doing, why she was doing it, where it would lead her. She was desperate to find room to study. Emotional room, for a start: room in her own life, in the life of the family. But physical room too—in that huge house, not a single corner was hers.

And was a single corner of it Reed's? Vince wonders, but half-heartedly. How did Carrie manage to saddle herself with such a specimen in the first place? Imagining the White Rabbit in his glory is more than Vince is capable of.

There's a scuffling outside the bedroom window. The raccoons, probably, foraging for food. They're welcome to whatever they can find. Vince certainly isn't going out there after them. They can be vicious, for all their woebegone eyes.

Vince closes the journal. Vas not so useful as he hoped. Not so gut. Too much Sal, not enough Carrie.

9

By Sunday morning, Vince is feeling pretty sure he won't betray himself, at least not with Carrie, who probably wouldn't know a Rembrandt from a Carlson. Actually, she would, he decides on cheerful second thought. Carrie would prefer the Carlson. And besides, if things work out the way he wants, he won't get much on paper before she molests him. How far she gets depends on how cooperative she is.

Vince pads around the hedge and into Carrie's back yard, which he has not seen before. Against the stone wall are sunflowers as tall as Vince, and a vegetable garden is laid out with mathematical precision along the edge of a goldfish pond studded with coloured glass and pebbles. He finds Carrie on her knees, weeding.

"This is all your work?" he asks.

"Yes," she says. "Well," she adds with obvious reluctance, "Reed helps me with some of the heavy jobs."

Vince watches goldfish weave patterns in the water of the pond. "You know, the last time I saw bits of coloured glass and stones was in that black garden—" he nearly said MacLoon's garden; what is his real name, anyway? "—on Wilton…"

"Oh, Scott's garden." She hesitates, but then becomes animated, unable to resist commenting. "His isn't a real garden at all. His is a *creepy* garden, all black rubber and bits of garbage."

"He recycles materials, doesn't he?" Vince ventures. How will she deal with that?

"That's twisting words," she says impatiently.

"You think so?" Vince asks mildly, wondering how to change the subject. This is obviously the wrong one to raise with Carrie.

"I certainly do," she says, getting to her feet. "A garden recycles the products of the garden, mulches them, mixes them back into the soil to enrich it. The point isn't just to reuse any old materials—plastic and rubber and God knows what." Her voice is charged with self-righteousness. "We're talking about a garden, here. The whole point about a garden is that things grow in it. That's what a garden is. A little corner of the world full of light and hope and growth." At this she looks up at Vince innocently. Oh, let the world beware. "Nothing grows in that garden except moss and mould. A black garden! It's sick! I'd rather see sunflowers."

"But why should it bother anyone? Why does it bother you? You can't even see it behind all that hedge."

"So what? It's a sick secret garden. And all the hedge does is keep it dark even in midday."

There are sick secrets, Carrie, he thinks of saying. But she doesn't want to hear that.

"Hey, Pollyanna," he says lightly, "how about today? You ready for me today?"

She looks as though she is about to say "I thought you'd never ask." "Today's fine," is what she says, and in an almost normal voice, too. "Reed has gone off to his brain gym. Colleen is God knows where."

"Anytime, then."

She's so pleased. He turns to go. But why not now? Now when he can spend the rest of the afternoon buttering her up.

"There's something I have to ask you." He looks at her anxiously, winningly. Carrie smiles back. "A favour."

"Sure!"

"Well, I don't want to alarm Sal or anything..." he watches her smile fade. That's to be expected. "But the money I've been waiting for is late. I've had a word with the guy, and there's no problem, of course, but it's coming in a bit later than I hoped. So, I thought, well, if I were overseas, I wouldn't want to start worrying over nothing. So, maybe, you know, as a favour to Sal, I know you're friends, I thought maybe I'd ask you not to worry her unnecessarily."

"You mean," she asks, her voice rising a good octave, "you don't have the money to cover the August rent cheque?"

"Yeah, like I explained. But it's no big deal. You know how it is. Sometimes people let you down, and there's nothing much you can do about it. Just a slight delay. It won't make any difference, really, but I know Sal will worry. I know I would worry if I were in her position. Especially now that she's on her own, for whatever reason." He throws that last phrase in just for good measure; it won't hurt to remind Carrie that she has her own reservations about Sal. "She won't know it's no big deal and she'll get all frantic about it."

"When *will* you have the money?" she demands.

"Oh, it's a matter of days, just a few days."

"A few days?"

"Oh sure. There's no problem. It's just that I know you're handling all the details of the rental for her, so I figured you were the one to speak to. Never having met Sal, and all…"

He pauses. That should do it.

She's thinking it over.

"Of course, I don't want to put you in a bad spot." He smiles at Carrie apologetically. "I was just thinking about Sal. You know. Imagine yourself in her situation. But if you don't like the idea, I'll understand. *Of course.*"

That raises a faint smile.

"It's a bit tricky," she says hesitantly. "I'd like to help you out, you know."

"I know that, Carrie. Don't say anything now. Think it over." And Vince fixes her with his eyes. She blushes. It's going to be all right. He's sure of it. "For now, all you have to do is concentrate on looking good for your first sitting."

"What should I wear?"

He says nothing. Actually he hadn't thought of this at all.

"Does it matter what I wear?" she tries again, tossing her head prettily.

"Hm." He stops and turns briefly. "I'll be doing head and shoulders. So the only thing that matters, I guess, is that it not be something too high-necked."

"Dark? Light?"

"Light," he says quickly, without hesitation. He hasn't a clue what difference it'll make, or if indeed it'll make any difference at all.

"Ten minutes."

"Where do you want me?" Carrie startles him. She hasn't knocked. And the lawyer's cheque, the big one, is lying on the dresser in the bedroom. He cuts into the bedroom to hide the cheque inside one of the dresser drawers. The last thing Vince wants is for Carrie to see the cheque. He'd better remember to lock the front door from now on, he decides. Or even—he has to grimace at the absurdity—to set the alarm.

Carrie has changed into a white cotton shirt and a matching skirt with a wide navy blue belt and navy blue espadrilles. White clip-on earrings and beads. Very much the superannuated girl-next-door, and this a woman who fancies herself a bit of a *femme fatale*.

"Great. That's perfect," he says unctuously, steering her back towards the front door, and then he can't resist adding. "I'm surprised you don't have white lipstick."

She laughs. She's so unused to insults, here in this polite little suburb, that she doesn't even recognize one when she gets one. "I don't think they make white lipstick anymore. That's a very sixties idea."

Vince hadn't thought of that.

"Let's do it out here," and he gestures to the chair on the corner of the porch that's visible not only from the upstairs of Carrie's own house, but also from the Remillards'.

"Here?" She's checking out the sight lines too. What is that tone in her voice?

She sits down, but hesitantly. "Wouldn't it be better to do this indoors?" she asks.

Disappointment. That's it, unmistakably so. She's disappointed she won't be sitting for him indoors. Naughty, naughty.

"It's summer. Let's enjoy the great outdoors while we can." Then he relents, just a bit. "We'll have to do a whole bunch of sittings. Maybe we'll do some indoors later on. OK, now," he's looking her over with what looks like a professional eye, "sit facing that tree over there. Right. And now turn your head to face me."

The result is bland. Barbie at the beach. The thought reminds Vince of Klaus Barbie, and Klaus Barbie reminds him of Ivan the Terrible. But that's Barbie Doll he had in mind, not the Butcher of Lyon. Not that they're quite so far apart as people choose to think. Vince read somewhere that the Barbie doll was partly based on a German streetwalker doll named Lilli. Some woman at Mattel had bought a few Lilli dolls in Europe way back in the late fifties and had told her people back in the U.S. to make them look wholesome. So Lilli, every frustrated Kraut's wet-dream, turned into Barbie—and the rest is history.

Carrie's sitting there prettily. And expectantly. This lady is ready for Vince. All he has to do is sit tight and she'll take matters into her own hands. Right now she's basking in the attention she's getting. This is the kind of service that hairdressers perform for their customers, Vince thinks, studying her.

"Haven't done a lot of work in pen and wash for quite a while," he says. "But I figure that with features as delicate as yours, that's the best medium."

She smiles radiantly. Features as delicate as hers. Oh, she's a sitting duck.

There's one way Vince knows he'll get her raging. But he's keeping that in reserve, just in case he feels like it later on. Right now he needs a model, a respectable drawing, and an ally. So, he needs some subject that will get her just riled up enough to start looking interesting. The White Rabbit should do the trick.

Vince walks over to her—and sees her stiffen; is this it? He cups a hand on each side of her head—she holds her breath—and pulls off her earrings. These he drops into her lap, adding, "Take the beads off too. Cheap."

Her face clouds.

"That's better. Sexier, too. I like that expression. There's something sultry about that." He picks up his pen. "So, Carrie, tell me about this men's group of Reed's."

Vince is on his way.

It's mid-morning when Madeleine limps up the stone steps after a breathless Mitsou. Madeleine looks at Vince quizzically. Can the chocolates be from him? She doesn't dare ask. And Vince doesn't let on. Not in front of Carrie. Mitsou nuzzles his balls, and gets the quarter pound of Genoa salami Vince lifted from the Marché Seaubois for this very reason. You always have to have a treat on hand. That's rule number one. Having resolved not to alarm Madeleine any further than he did the other day, he's non-communicative, intent on what he's doing. You have to know when to play hard to get. That's rule number two.

Madeleine smiles encouragingly at Carrie. "Nice," she says, standing behind Vince and watching him work.

Nice?

Vince stares critically at his drawing. She's right, too. There is something nice about it. Carrie is just too pretty. Even when she's sultry, she's no more than pretty.

It's up to him to make her more interesting, he's the artist here. Only he has to flatter her too. He has to be able to use her. And she wants to look pretty.

Vince frowns. That's the problem. He should have realized it before. He did, in a way. He had a sense there was something not quite right about this.

Carrie purrs. "Is it a good likeness?" she asks after a while. "I can't wait to see it."

"It's not ready for viewing yet," he says firmly.

"Oh, no?"

"It'll be days before it looks like anything."

"But Madeleine says…"

"I know. But nice is just a stage we go through. Like pretty. What we need is true. The true you." And he stares intently at Carrie, as though she mattered. As though it goes without saying that Carrie will like the true Carrie.

And that does not go without saying. Will it be the true Carrie? Or will it be a pretty Carrie? But surely, Vince muses in some dismay, he doesn't have to choose between these. Surely not. He's just going to have to be devious, that's all. That's what art is all about. The use of devious means. There's nothing devious about a pathetically serious little journal like Sal's. Or about a nudist colony. It's art that's devious. Vince who's devious.

"Oh," breathes Carrie.

"Oh," breathes Madeleine. And then, fanning herself with her hand, she asks, "Wouldn't you be more comfortable in the shade?"

The sun has moved around, and Vince is now standing in full sunlight. "A little sunshine won't hurt me. Even vampires can come out in daylight. They just need to wear a sun block of 15 or higher." The women exchange looks. Madeleine is uncertain, but Carrie laughs. "That's according to some Vampire Research Center in upstate New York."

"So, are you some kind of vampire?" Carrie teases.

He shakes his head. "Blood I have no interest in." It's true. Vince is a relatively harmless kind of guy, a vampire only in the secondary, metaphoric sense. Which reminds him. "Any news from Sal?" he asks.

"I had a letter this morning." Madeleine is relieved to be back in known territory.

"Oh, yeah?" Carrie is trying not to look put out. Madeleine, evidently, is now the closer friend. Carrie has been displaced. "What does she have to say?"

"It's mostly about the teacher, the academy of music, politics even. She's loving it over there. Of course, she still misses Wolf."

"Sal *misses* Wolf! That's a laugh," Carrie sniffs. "She practically *drove* him out!"

"How can you say that?" Madeleine asks.

"It's true. I know. I knew her long before you knew her, Madeleine. She's the one who was responsible for that divorce. She didn't know when she had it good. God! When I think of it! He used to make her coffee every morning before she even got out of bed. And still she was dissatisfied." Carrie's voice is bitter. "She wanted things her way. Her way or the highway. He didn't know what hit him. I'm glad he found someone else."

Madeleine hesitates. She's one of the meek.

"She should have been satisfied with a cup of coffee?" Vince can't resist asking.

"That's just an example," Carrie says impatiently. "That's what marriage is all about, little things. A man who knows how to make coffee in the morning exactly the way you like it, just so strong and no stronger, with just that amount of milk—that's a lot." And a lot more than Carrie has, by the sound of it.

Vince can't resist. "The best cup of coffee I ever had," he offers, "was at a little place on Jean Talon I can't remember the name of."

"You're not married," Carrie retorts. "You don't know what it's like." She looks over at Madeleine for support, but Madeleine is unused to argument. "That cup of coffee in the morning means that you have a husband who knows you, accepts you, and cares about you. That cup of coffee says it all."

"Hold me back!"

"It may not be very spectacular, but then," Carrie adds piously, "the good things about a marriage are not too spectacular." She pauses. "In comparison with… with…"

"With a passionate romance?" he suggests mischievously.

"Yeah," Carrie says uncomfortably, "I guess. A marriage *is* going to look rather pale in comparison. There'll be some strong colours here and there," she gestures towards her garden, "a flash of red, some strong greens, a streak of purple, but these bold colours will stand out all the more because they're set in a paler background. There'll be pale lemon, too, and lilac and cream."

In his mind's eye Vince pictures vomit splashed over a flower bed. An unwelcome reminder.

"And a pond, too," he says. "With more than one fish in it."

Carrie blushes furiously.

"I'm going away for a bit," Madeleine says, glad of the opportunity to change the subject.

"Away?" Carrie asks.

"To Maine."

"So you'd like Colleen to look after Mitsou?" Carrie finishes the thought.

"She's willing. I already spoke to her. But she seemed to think you might object."

Carrie looks cross, as if Colleen has been washing her mother's dirty linen in public. "No. No problem. It isn't Mitsou that's the problem. It's Colleen. When are you leaving?"

"Tonight. Pierre wants to leave after dinner, after the rush. There's no one at home now, is there?"

Carrie shakes her head.

"Well, I'll bring Mitsou back later in the afternoon when you're finished here, then," she says, smiling tentatively at Vince as she turns to leave. "I have to bring her food over anyway."

Vince flashes a winning smile back at Madeleine and brushes her upper arm with his fingertips delicately, sufficiently, as he accompanies her down the steps. And there, out of Carrie's sight, he whispers, "Did you like the chocolates?"

"Oh! It *was* you!"

He kisses her lightly on the lips, bids her goodbye, and turns back to Carrie. Madeleine will have time to think about him now as she lies awake in a strange bed. And she'll have ripened nicely by the time she returns.

It's noon when Carrie leaves. Vince gives Judy the Judge a call.

"There you are!" she exclaims. "What beautiful flowers!"

"This is just a social call," he insists. "Just to see how you're doing," he explains.

He asks for nothing. Not yet. Tells her nothing about the summonses. She is duly charmed.

Vince still has most of the day in front of him.

He's doing just fine, getting nicely into his stride, and there's only one little item of unfinished business that needs to be taken care of. He grits his teeth. He isn't looking forward to this, but there won't be a better opportunity than this very afternoon. And it has to be done.

Golf Avenue. It's time he checked out Golf Avenue.

Feeling purposeful—there'll be no nonsense this time—Vince pulls on his helmet, heads out to the garage, and cruises onto the Lakeshore Road. Why is the Edgewater parking lot full? Vince wonders. And then, as he cruises past, the owners of the cars begin to emerge, unmistakably a congregation. Parishioners, obviously. But why here, of all places? What are the God-fearing doing in an old sin salon?

He makes it around the corner of Golf without incident. No surprise there. It was the other day that was the oddity, he thinks, picking up speed as he nears the fieldstone gates to the golf course itself. You've already keeled over. You've already thrown up. Nothing like that will happen again. Just take it easy. See it through, all the way. And then it's going to be OK.

There used to be a sign on the stone gate that said Beaconsfield Golf Course, Speed Limit 19 mph. That sign's gone, now, and a saner, soberer sign now proclaims: Club de Golf Beaconsfield. Propriété Privée. No Admittance.

Off limits, the whole street is off limits, and Vince is—always was—an interloper here. This was the setting for his wretchedness.

It's OK. He's doing OK. Just keep going.

Beaconsfield Golf Club. That's a mystery, right there. Why did they call it that? This is Pointe Claire; the border with Beaconsfield is several streets west of here. How could they not know that? Or—as Vince suspects, on no evidence whatsoever—did they think the name Pointe Claire sounded too French, the name Beaconsfield reassuringly English, to the Anglo-Scottish business types the club wanted to attract as its members?

With the fairway, the pond, the copse on his right and, on the left, house after house flicking past him like images in an old Kinetoscope, Golf Avenue seems much as he remembers it. If anything—he can't help feeling, slowing his pace—it's more stately and more beautiful than memory would allow. The ancient maples and poplars are taller than they were, the willows more langorous, and the fruit is burgeoning on the apple and crabapple trees; here and there are the stumps of dead beeches and elms. The fieldstone wall that divides the gardens from the strip of lawn that belongs to the club all the way up the avenue is overgrown with vines. Beyond this wall slope the lawns leading up to the old houses with their old wooden verandahs. Vince doesn't remember those weathered shingles. But the house beside it was always white and green. And those two, stained dark brown, look familiar. One even has the crossed golf clubs carved into its wooden shutters and, next to it—still! are they living here still?—the sign "Cross Patch," home of the Cross family, one of the few families on the street that belonged to the Golf Club.

It is pretty, Vince has to admit. This street has coloured his memories more than he has ever wanted to acknowledge. Perhaps he should have come back at some other time, some time when the grass was yellowed and the ground caked. Some time when it was looking less fresh, less glossy.

But it's OK. So it's pretty. Perfectly manageable, though. Just think it through, tame it, rob it of its mystery. You can do it.

He's rolling downhill now, and the garden and driveway in the gully are awash as they always were, the road itself is wet, and the golf course pumps are working to drain the enormous puddle around the trees on the other side of the road.

The Harley lurches slightly over the dip in the road—had Vince forgotten about that? Vince has forgotten nothing—and up past the parking lot and the club house on the right, checking, as he always did on his bicycle, to see if he's lined up the wet tire marks behind him. He's not looking at the houses at all now. Over the crest of the hill, he edges past the eleventh hole, drinking in the view of the fairway sweeping down and curving around the trees towards the highway and the railway tracks.

There are only three more houses up here on top of the world. He remembers the middle one, the white one, too well.

He pauses, refuses to look at the house. He needs some time, some peace, a chance to take the scene in, absorb it, tame it.

Vince moves on, past the white house, and pulls up beside the silver BMW in the parking area—what do they call these things? there's room for half a dozen full-sized cars to park here—outside the next house, the very last one on the street. It has changed almost beyond recognition. The change wasn't obvious at first, for the wooden cottage set back from the road under the trees on the very edge of the hill is stained the same deep brown as in the days when the Innis family lived here, and its chocolate-coloured roof and its white-trimmed verandah have the same slope as ever. But the house itself is two or three times the size it used to be. Instead of being built up, though, or out, it's been built *down*: down the side of the hill. Judging by the windows and the door right down at the bottom of the hill, there are three substantial brown-stained storeys now that didn't exist the last time Vince saw the house.

Vince has turned off the engine and pulled off his helmet. He is stunned by the silence of the afternoon. He turns not towards the white house, his parents' house—but out over the fairway.

This hillside used to have two separate and conflicting lives. Probably it still does. From May to November, it was the exclusive preserve of the golfers in dazzling summer cottons, who whined up the hill, most of them, in their little electric golf carts, and surveyed the world beneath them with suspicious, proprietary eyes.

A few of the houses belonged to club members, but most of the golfers lived elsewhere and came out to the club on the weekend or in the evening after work. So this was a street divided, for the most part, into golfers and non-golfers, and there was a natural enmity between the club and the residents. And a sharper enmity between the club and the residents' children, who were told to be quiet, get lost, shut up, fuck off, all summer long by surly-faced putters.

But when November came, and the club closed, the golf course turned into a park. The dogs ran loose around the edge of the pond and up and down the fairway. When the snows came, the pond became a skating rink, the golf course a series of *pistes* for cross-country skiers, and the hill a playground for shouting children from all over the West Island with sleds and toboggans and flying saucers. Dodging one another and the tentative little skiers in the YMCA beginners' classes on Saturday mornings, they skimmed down, and then chugged awkwardly back up the slope like Michelin men in their bulky, garish snowsuits, wearing down the snow, ruining the fairway, screaming with hilarity and excitement and eventual exhaustion.

So there was no doubt whose side the snow was on. One year, though, the snow came so sparsely and so late that the golf course was a smudge of moss and icy dirt on New Year's Day. When Vince looked out of his bedroom window, there were four golfers in mud-stained clothes trudging cheerfully up the hill with their bags slung over their arms. Those were always the best kind of golfers, the tolerable kind, the ones who insisted on carrying their own bags, the ones wearing beiges and browns and tans and greys. In his mind Vince long ago decided they were the only serious golfers, the only ones who played for the sake of the game.

Which, for all he knew, was a good game. Even during his short-lived career as a lawyer, Vince had never been a golfer. As a kid he used to detest the golfers themselves. But there was something appealing about the sounds of the game—the crack of the wood, the tap of putters, the thunk of the ball dropping. It might well be satisfying to be a skillful golfer, to have that kind of control.

Truces were rare in the war of attrition between the golfers and the residents. More common were forays—bold on the part of the golfers, subversive on the part of the residents—into enemy territory.

When the Club was hosting a championship, it closed the street to traffic, and residents couldn't even get home without carrying a specially issued pass. The hissing for silence was never as insistent as on those occasions. Which was pretty cheeky, given the amount of noise the golfers regularly made during their drunken Saturday night revels. Sometimes Vince could fall asleep in spite of their smarmy band, but then he'd be woken in the early morning by crashes and tinkles as the revellers played bumper cars in the parking lot with one another's Oldsmobiles, Buicks and Cadillacs.

The residents left most of their retaliation to their animals and their children. When the last light faded—and the last of the golfers had retired to the clubhouse for their rye-and-gingers, Pink Ladys and Bloody Marys—back doors would open up and down Golf Avenue, and the dogs would trot over the road to snuffle the smells of the night and of one another.

Daytime raids during the summer were risky, but the children on the street were practised at following the path of golf balls that had whizzed past them and into one of the gardens. One summer, Vince collected more than twenty brand new golf balls, and sold them to a boy who lived down the road. This guy spent every summer day caddying, and then, as if he hadn't had enough of the golf course, he'd go out onto the fairway to collect worms for the owner of the corner store.

Best of all, though, was the expedition of small children from the house at the crest of the hill—the bored offspring of lunchtime visitors—who set off in broad daylight on tricycles one Sunday afternoon across the green opposite Vince's house. They left tracks all over grass as fine and as precious as green velvet, and then they made their escape before the golfers sitting under the yellow umbrellas at the back of the club house recovered sufficiently from their consternation—and from their anxiety over exactly whose children these might be: what if these were the children of an influential club member?—to defend their territory.

Why didn't the residents complain more? Vince wonders now. But of course the war was undeclared. And most of the residents, Vince's parents included, were grateful, in the end, for the existence of the club: the spectre of the course being sold to developers was never far from their minds. A nuisance the club might be, but it was great for the value of their property.

And no matter how rough they were with the children on the street, the golfers were careful to maintain a veneer of civility with the parents. Even an occasional rogue tricycle was more tolerable than any number of possible hazards from openly hostile residents.

The loyalty shown around here to the devil you know is quite breathtaking. Even if grudging, Vince decides, reminded of Carrie. And that is the secret of his own success.

With that encouraging thought, Vince finally turns his attention to the house itself, 52 Golf Avenue, with the little path winding up the hill from the driveway. It's still the same white cottage—though the white, he notices, is no longer painted clapboard. That's all been covered over with aluminum siding designed to look like wood. But it has the very same green wooden shutters and a new green roof, the same sash windows, the same fieldstone steps and patio—now festooned with flowers, which his own mother would have considered too showy, a waste of money—the same almond bushes on either side of the steps, and the same monumental fieldstone chimney.

The bedroom upstairs at the right was Vince's. There are white venetian blinds on all three of the windows—the two facing out across the golf course, and the one looking over to the Innis's—so that he can see nothing of what the room has become, whose it might be. Behind it is Tiny Gary's old room, and to the left, facing out over the golf course, is the big room, Thea and Ted Cunningham's room.

The main floor looks unchanged. Dining room, entrance, living room, and the addition that became the family room. Because—he'd almost forgotten this—of course there's no basement in the house. Or only the smallest basement space, hardly big enough for the furnace and the water heater. None of these houses up here on top of the hill have a proper basement. They're built on pure, sheer, ancient rock.

Vince drives down towards the clubhouse, all around the rose garden, and then turns left onto the road that curves over the top of the hill, and down past the escarpment towards Cartier.

He pauses at the top of the hill, where the red and white maple leaf hangs limply from the flagpole. Some days, in the spring before the season started, when the fairways were too wet and still too fragile to play on—or else in fall, after the first snow—Vince would come up here alone and stare out towards the silver spire of the village church, the low roofs of the houses and shops, and beyond, to the trembling expanse of Lake St. Louis. The snow around him would glow orange, blue, grey, anything but white. Behind him, the golf course swept downhill and away to the railway tracks, where it would funnel itself into a narrow path before opening up again. Several—Vince doesn't know how many—of the holes were on the other side of the tracks. When he used to stand up there, a train would be trundling past, as often as not, a train so long that he would wait and wait for the caboose.

At night from his bedroom he would hear the trains moaning. They'd be crossing the railway bridge in Ste. Anne de Bellevue, on their way onto the island of Montreal. He's heard those same moans in other towns too, and he's never heard them without again becoming, for a fleeting instant of confusion, the boy who slept upstairs at 52 Golf Avenue.

How's he doing? Vince tests his reactions gingerly as he continues on his way down the hill and past the escarpment. Vince used to find fossils over there, on the lip of the escarpment. He'd climb out as far as it would hold him and then, hanging on with his fingertips, he'd scramble among stones and roots fifteen meters above the paved road to find perfect, minuscule fish-like creatures protected from damage for all eternity in shards of Precambrian rock.

Vince is pleased with himself. He is hardly aware of any reaction at all to these scenes from his adolescence. An unaccustomed emptiness, perhaps. And just a slight headache, and that could be because of the storm that seems to be gathering over on the lake. Only the faintest sense of—what?—uncertainty maybe. Something ever so slightly unsteady. Nothing compared to his reaction earlier, nothing at all dramatic like that. But that's enough for one day. Quite enough.

The road curves down around the escarpment, past a tee on the right side, another hole on the left, a parking lot, the driving ranges, and finally the gates out of this little Eden onto Cartier. So named, Vince learned as a kid, because the foundations of the Jacques Cartier Bridge were built with the stone from the quarry. The quarry owned by Frank diPietro's father.

Vince turns off Cartier onto Salisbury, and then to Waverley. When not inspired by the most banal sense of physical geography, most of the street names in Pointe Claire respect the two solitudes. And only the two. Is there anyone who knows what the Indians called Pointe Claire? The place names now are either Anglo-Scottish or French, in the main, honouring Presbyterian or Catholic heroes, explorers, saints, shrines, and cathedrals.

It's just then that Vince notices for the first time a little street running down towards what is now Kinsmen Park. DiPietro Avenue. That must have been the access road to the old quarry. Given the importance of the diPietros in Pointe Claire, the wonder is only that the street is so small. Admittedly, the bar trade did give them a bad name. There were complaints to the Minimum Wage Commission. And what did happen to the Edgewater Hotel? One way or another, rightly or wrongly, there were always rumours about the diPietros. With a name like that, of course there were rumours about them. They could have been saints, and still people would have wondered. Their only hope would have been to change their name to something like Henderson, or Legault. That's what Vince would have done.

When he gets back to the house, Vince sits outside the front door and smokes cigarette after cigarette, staring out over the lake, counting interminably to himself, one thousand four hundred and twenty three, one thousand four hundred and twenty four, one thousand four hundred and twenty five, until he loses count and starts all over again, one, two, three, four, five, six, seven, eight…

He would love a glass of red wine. Just a glass or two to steady him. It's about time, he can see—oh, he trembles at the thought—for a little bit of Jessye, too. Oh, yes yes yes. Vince hasn't had a Jessye evening since— when?—since that night at Laila's. That night nearly killed him, and he hadn't even had much cheese. Laila had packed her daughter off for the evening and had made a Lebanese meal. The main course was spring lamb cooked in its mother's milk. He never did find out where she got the mother's milk.

No. No wine. If he starts on the wine now, he'll drown. He just knows it. It's getting worse every time. He really is going to kill himself one of these days. One, two, three, four, five…

A voice. "Will you join me?"

10

Vince whirls. Who spoke? Janet! She's sitting alone in the dark on the screened porch, her rings catching the light from inside Carrie's house.

"Join you?" he asks stupidly.

"Yes. I'm the only one at home. Won't you come over for a chat?"

"Well," he hesitates, "I was just about to head out to the shops."

"For what?"

"For, er, for a bottle of wine." He's trying, without much success, to think fast. He's been wanting to talk to her. About herself. About MacLoon. About himself, Vince—and about how different his own life would have been if he'd had Janet for his mother. But then again, maybe his own grandmother was a bit like Janet. That's a thought.

It can wait. What's urgent is his need for wine.

"I've a bottle here we could open," she stands up and turns the porch light on. "Is white all right with you?"

Oh, sweet heaven. Vince is already on the steps of the porch. "Sure. Anything."

"Anything?" She looks at him more closely. She's caught the desperation in his voice.

He doesn't give the bottle more than a glance when she produces it, and, even though it is white, it's not a bad wine. At least it's nicely chilled.

Janet says nothing. He's pouring himself a second glass almost before she's tasted her first, and offering her a Player's.

"No. I prefer my own." She allows him to light her Sobranie.

They sit in silence, for which he is grateful. So grateful that he doesn't even find the silence surprising.

Eventually, he speaks again.

"I went back today to the house I lived in as a kid."

She waits.

"Just that," he says. "Nothing more." Then, after another minute, he tries shrugging. "No big deal, really."

She smiles gently at Vince. When she smiles, her face and her chin fold up in unexpected ways, and she looks her age: she looks like a woman who has smiled a lot over a period of nearly eighty years. There are secrets hidden in the shadows of her skin. How do you end up smiling at seventy-six? That's quite something. Vince would like to feel he'll be smiling at seventy-six. He would like to feel he'll still be in one piece at seventy-six. Looking at Janet, Vince wonders about those secrets.

"I guess that's one reason I came back here. But I didn't know what I'd find."

"What did you find?"

He doesn't answer at once. "I don't know yet. It was beautiful, more beautiful than I remembered. And... oh, I guess it brought a lot of things back to me, things I haven't thought about in decades."

"How old were you when you left?"

"Fifteen." Then—is it her smile? the darkness? the wine? he's reacting powerfully to the wine, he can feel it taking effect—he feels like talking. He feels sure she'll understand. "I ran away. It sometimes seems as though I've been on the run ever since... That that's where things started to go wrong. And if only I could get back there, somehow I could turn everything around, make it all different."

"Different in what way? What do you want that you don't have now?"

"Just different. Better." There's another long silence. "I don't want to be alone anymore."

"Who do you want to be with?"

"I don't know." It's true. He really doesn't. But then suddenly he's adding, "A woman I can love. Someone who'll be on my side. Who'll accept me as I am." *In vino.*

"Have you ever been in love? Really in love?"

"I'm in love now. In a way."

"In a way?"

"Yes. It's hopeless."

"Why hopeless?"

"We haven't even met. I just love her from afar. But I love her madly in my own way. I would do anything for her."

"Is this," Janet is feeling her way with some care, "someone who lives near here?"

"Oh no! If only she did. No." Then, recklessly, insanely—he's never told anyone this, ever—he adds, "She's an American, but she lives somewhere in England. She's a singer, an opera singer called Jessye Norman."

There. He's done it. He pours himself more wine, listens to the silence, feels pretty sure it's OK.

"Yes," she says. "I've heard her." And then, eventually she asks, "And what do you love about her?"

"She's magnificent, beyond compare. There's no other woman like her. She's wise, warm, powerful."

"Is she gentle?"

"Oh yes, she's gentle." He thinks, corrects himself, really he hasn't thought of her in quite this way, "She can be gentle, I guess." He looks at Janet. "I don't really know."

"She's alarming too, don't you find? Isn't there something rather alarming about her? I think I'd be afraid of her."

"Yes," he agrees slowly. "There's a risk. I guess I feel that's a risk I have to take. I would die for her. And I guess I feel I would die happy. The very thought…" He's babbling. He hardly knows what he's saying.

"And what do you dream of?"

"That I will meet her, finally. That I will be alone with her. Alone, in private, no one else around…"

"And can you imagine that?"

"Not quite," he admits. Such a sad admission, really. This is his great sorrow. He has never been able to imagine them actually touching. He can imagine meeting her—oh, he's had lots of scenes of meetings. But then, just when he is reaching for her—or could it be that she is reaching for him? he's never even got that far—his imagination fails him and the scene fades. "Almost, but not quite."

"You're not afraid you'd be disappointed? What human being can live up to the kind of expectations you have of her?"

"Jessye can." He knows this. He pauses. Days of wine and Jessye. Vince is feeling shakier and shakier. It can't be the wine. It must be the day. His day is catching up with him. He concentrates on breathing until he can trust himself to speak again. "I'm not afraid of disappointment. Not at all. To be disappointed would in some ways be a relief, in fact." He believes every word he's saying. "I would no longer have to live—as I do now—with the certainty that I'm missing out on the best that life has to offer. I could resign myself to making do with other women—all of whom now pale in comparison."

The wine is gone. And just as well. Vince has talked more than enough already. He's said too much, he now realizes. Far too much. He eyes Janet warily. She still has the half glass of wine in front of her.

And, knowing there's to be no more wine here, he can feel his mood darken. He's still thirsty, and there's no more wine. Janet probably won't even finish the first glass she poured herself. How could she pour more than she'd want? He looks at her with resentment, angry with her for having only one bottle of wine, for having only white wine, for not offering him her own glass, for drawing him out, for his loose tongue. What did he say to her? How much did he actually say? How much was just in his head?

How can he salvage something out of this? His mind is a muddle, but he knows he went too far, that somehow he has to fix things, yet—not even knowing what exactly has to be fixed—not really caring, even.

"I like intimacy," he says, leaning forward and taking Janet's hand. This has always worked like a charm, and a seventy-six year old should be a piece of cake.

Janet has felt his change of mood. She pulls her hand away impatiently and lights herself another Sobranie.

"What's wrong?" he asks with feigned innocence. "Have I done something to annoy you?"

"You've chosen the wrong person to bullshit." she says. He should have guessed she would be quick to anger.

"I would like us to be friends." Surely she won't turn that down.

She pulls on her cigarette. "I'm starting to see why the woman you claim to love is a woman you've never even met. Intimacy! Let me tell you, I know a fair bit about intimacy. And about false intimacy. I know your type. In my day I came across all types. And I don't have any more patience for you now than I would have had then."

What is she talking about?

Of course. Janet was a stripper. He hadn't forgotten, but he's been too busy thinking about himself to give her much thought. And that is the kind of mistake Vince doesn't make. At least not when he's in full control. He takes a long drag on his cigarette, tries to pull himself together.

"False intimacy!" He laughs, but hoarsely. She has spoken more truly than she can possibly know! "Oh, if you only knew."

"I do. I know exactly what I'm talking about. You've been lying to me. You don't want intimacy with me. You don't want intimacy with anyone. What's going on? What are you doing here?"

"What are you talking about?" What a dumb thing to say. He knows it as soon as the words are out of his mouth. Did she see him throwing up the other day? If so, he would be a fool to deny it. He hates her for getting him to say a dumb thing. For making a fool of him.

"You're not what you pretend to be. I don't know what you are, but you're not what you pretend to be. I don't know what kind of game you think you're playing—"

But Vince is charging through the door and down the porch steps long before she's finished speaking.

It's no big deal, he figures when he calms down. He can make up with Janet later on, if he feels like it. Nothing, ever, is irrevocable. People forget. And even when they can't forget, they're so anxious to think well of others that they forgive them their trespasses.

But maybe he won't bother making up with Janet. What does he need Janet for? A little amusement was the most he ever expected from Janet. And, when it comes to amusement, Vince knows there are bigger fish in the sea. Bigger fish, even, in this little suburban pond. Madeleine will be back soon. Madeleine, his favourite. Not to mention Carrie. She hasn't refused him yet. And she won't.

More wine.

Vince wants more wine, and there's none. The liquor store is closed. He drinks wine so seldom, he's always insisted on good wine. That's part of the ritual, part of the pleasure. There has to be pleasure, oh such pleasure, to justify such inevitable pain. It has to be Jessye, it has to be good wine, and he has to drink it with the very best of food. If a job is worth doing, it's worth doing well. It's not even worth thinking about doing it with—whom?—Madonna? The very thought. And cheap *dépanneur* wine holds such paltry pleasures. And so much more pain. Unnecessary pain.

Vince picks up his wallet and keys and then, fear edging into his consciousness, he puts them down again.

It's early. What to do? How to distract himself?

Focus on the good stuff. There's been so much good stuff. So many wins. So many victims in his wake. Sal. Maybe the journal will distract him. He picks up where he left off last time.

> We were aged from about twenty-eight to sixty, all women who had at some point thought they would spend their lives caring for others, now trying—with so much trepidation and so little confidence in their own abilities—to make their way back into the world. It was hard. Doubly hard, since so many of us were in the throes of a crisis in our marriages. Several would drop out of the program, drop back out of sight.
>
> We knew one another by our maiden names. There was some bureaucratic reason for that—something about the computer recognizing us only by the names we used during our long-ago schooldays. But it was curiously appropriate too. You can lead one kind of life for decades as an adult and then suddenly—I've seen it happen so often—find yourself thrown back into the past, to a self you haven't been since you were a teenager. I'm convinced we all felt more like our old schoolgirl selves at Abbott than we ever had at home. I know I did.
>
> Sometimes you'd think modern feminists were the first to agonize over the difficulties of combining the care that women lavish on their children

with the care they need to lavish on themselves, their creativity, their careers. In a lot of what I've read, women in the past—though they certainly had other problems—seem so much better off in the support they had with child-rearing: history comes down to us women as a long procession of nannies, grannies, aunts, maidservants, cooks, and governesses. Our problem, though, in our tightly budgeted little nuclear families, is that we are left to do it all on our own, singlehandedly. It's too much, really, for any woman to cope with. And, at the same time, it's too little to satisfy her. It's so hard to bridge that gap. I was charmed in my first-ever English course at college, to find that Speranza, who was an Irish writer as well as Oscar Wilde's mother—that's the only thing most people know about her—once wrote:

Alas but the fates are cruel
Behold Speranza making gruel!

I laughed at that. I remember copying that out in my little notebook. We read far better poems than that one, real poems, serious poems, but that's the one I remember. It mattered so much to me, wrenched as it was out of the muscular jaws of motherhood. I was never Speranza. I have yet to meet a woman with as grand a sense of herself as I think she must have had. But I knew everything there was to know about making gruel. And I suppose I, too, had found the fates cruel—aching to burst out of confinement even as I lovingly stirred the bowl of Pablum, Canada's gift to madonna and child. But at John Abbott I hoped to inch my way towards becoming Speranza.

Elsa and Nicholas were both in school, but my day still revolved around them because Nicholas came home for lunch every day and Elsa was finished for the day by mid-afternoon. I wasn't happy at all. Nothing was right, all of a sudden. Wolf and I couldn't seem to agree on anything. I put it down to a kind of marriage fatigue, something as mysteriously unpredictable and as dangerous as metal fatigue in an aircraft.

The fairy tale had got it all wrong. What really happens when Prince Charming kisses the princess is that she falls into a kind of waking sleep, and in this trance, locked away from the world in a fug of her own, she allows herself to have baby after baby, wash dish after dish, and clean house uncomplainingly. She turns into a creature barely recognizable even to herself, a kind of caricatured mother figure with a mother's voice and a mother's peculiar certainties and multiple anxieties.

Some women never really emerge out of this fug. In most cases, though, there comes a time when the princess does awaken. Her youngest child may be only two years old, or five, or even twelve: it doesn't matter. When she does awaken, she looks around her with the eyes of the adolescent girl she was once. She is astonished to see what she has done with her life. She is appalled to discover all her adolescent confidence—she was confident as a girl—has been destroyed. She is convinced for a time, such a terrible time, that she will never be able to do anything ever again other than wash dishes and provide tea and sympathy.

It's a mixed blessing, this awakening. Sometimes I think I'm worse off than before. For now I have awakened, and I have decided the life I had been leading is not enough. There's no going back into the fug now. And so Wolf and I stumble about, calling out to each other desperately in unfamiliar languages, waving our arms around blindly in the hope that we'll somehow find each other again.

The journal entry ends there. Vince closes the volume, lies back and stares at the ceiling.

Such a luxury, this kind of introspection. The navel-gazing of a privileged suburbanite with more money than sense. And by what right? To *each* according to his needs. Vince has never even tried to shake off the conviction that the haves are evil incarnate. And Sal, in his book—in anyone's book—is a have. Why shouldn't Sal's house, and Sal's belongings, be of benefit to others as well? Such as Vince himself.

Naive and self-indulgent as the journal is, he can make the effort to conceive of it as a step in the right direction, really, this search of Sal's for the self, for the real person inside those clothes, behind that veil. And he will give her credit for quoting Speranza. And for knowing who Speranza was making gruel for. There aren't too many people who've figured out that Wilde was a human being made of flesh and blood rather than just some monstrous fop with a sunflower in his hand. Sal might yet turn out to be his favourite victim.

When Vince awakens in the morning, the storm has come and gone in the night without clearing the air. The lake is menacingly dark and still. The moisture that rises off its flat, shimmering surface drifts around in air already saturated with heat and humidity. By lunchtime it is impossible to swim, so crowded is the pool, and the lifeguards are on full alert not only up on high in their tall chairs, but pacing around the concrete lip, too, peering into the depths, matching waving arms and legs with breathless children's faces.

"So, are you ready for me?" Vince asks, peering over the hedge into Carrie's garden. She is sitting in the shade wearing an oversized shirt over her bikini and reading *The Gazette*.

"Sure." Suddenly self-conscious, she closes her shirt over her bikini. Vince is watching her closely. He's hoping for some good news from her today. "When do you want to start?"

"No time like the present."

"Now? Right now?" She looks around quickly, but no one's around.

"Why not? You don't look too busy."

"Well, I'm not, right now, that's true. I came home early. There was nothing much to do. But what... I mean, I do have to get some dinner organized..."

"Can't Reed do that?"

"I don't know."

"Ask him. What're husbands for, anyway?"

She doesn't answer that. She's uneasy. He doesn't like that one little bit.

"I'll need a couple of hours at least," he says blithely enough, "just to get the sketching finished. But if this isn't a good time..."

"Oh, it'll be OK. I'll just leave a note for Reed. I'll be there in a few minutes." And then, as if it's an afterthought, "Oh, by the way, I spoke to my boss today. I really wanted to do what you asked, but I just can't. I'm going to have to tell Sal if the rent isn't paid on the first of the August."

"I hear you." He shrugs, keeps his voice light. "I'll have the money soon after, like I said. Pity that Sal has to worry about it, though."

"Mmm, I guess so..."

"Oh, well. No big deal."

A fat lot of use Carrie has turned out to be. Vince walks back to Sal's house pursing his lips. The Remillards have left a budgie outdoors in its cage on the other side of the fence. Vince sits down outside the front door and listens to its chatter. Suddenly his mood is sour.

Carrie is really asking for it.

"How do you want me today?" Carrie asks when she joins him on the front porch ten minutes later. Does she listen to herself?

"Indoors, my dear, sheltered from the sun and prying eyes." At this she does blush. His voice may be solemn, but that's OK. She's in a mood to put the best construction on anything he does, and she'll attribute his solemnity to the depth of his desire for her. He steers Carrie into the dining room and perches her on the stool he's positioned in front of the drapes. He hardly even glances at the drawing he's been working on. It irks him. Nice. It's far too nice. Far too flattering. And to think that he sacrificed his integrity as an artist. And for what?

"The line of your neck is good, very good," he says in the little artist voice he's been practising. "Actually," he's more and more distracted now, all professional, all business, "could you just pull the collar of your shirt up? It'll give me just a hint more, just to see the collarbone."

She undoes a button, pulls her shirt neck apart a bit. It isn't going to make such a big difference that Sal knows he's late with the rent. She's going to find out sooner or later. How she reacts matters more. How long till she tries blowing the whistle on him. And how loudly she blows it when she does. Carrie could have played a big part in that. Well, she's chosen which side she's on. She's made her bed, so to speak. Let her lie on it. Vince watches a crow swoop down from the maple on the far corner of the Remillards' garden and knock the lid from the cage. The budgie squawks only once.

"Beautiful. Beautiful," Vince says. "Such skin. The skin tones, well, I won't get those till I work in oils, but the shadows, those I can do. There's this wonderful dip just under the collarbone." And, "You know, I haven't done a nude for some time." No kidding. That's really what he says. "There's something very important about a nude. Do you know anyone who might be willing to model for me?"

"A woman? In the nude?" She has trouble controlling her voice.

"Oh, that hardly matters. A man or a woman. The kind of body hardly matters. All are true." And he allows himself a little sigh. "It isn't possible to be an artist in this society without giving the gossips a field day. No one seems ready to believe in the purity of art. Especially out here. Small minds. Provincial minds. People who would blush just to hear the word 'body.' But then most of them have bodies they might well recoil from…"

Goaded by the challenge, she swallows air, succeeds in lowering her voice, and asks, "And what kind of body would you like to draw?"

"An interesting body. A body that interests *me*, you understand, a body that excites me in some way. Not too athletic, not too big"—what a convincing liar he is, he could make a fortune writing novels—"but cared for. A body that tells a story."

Concentrating all his attention on the light bouncing off her collarbone, he makes her wait a full minute before looking up at her face briefly and adding matter-of-factly, as if the thought has only just this instant occurred to him, "Your body, now. I'd love to draw your body."

"Oh."

"This very drawing here," he stares disconsolately at the head and shoulders he's been sketching; it is almost as if he has forgotten she is even there, "would be so much more interesting if I didn't have to fight against all that white cotton, all that starch." He makes an impatient gesture with his hand. "That's an alien structure. Alien to the lines of the body. My pen wants to follow the line of the neck, the shoulders, the arms, the breasts." He looks up at her. "And if we lived somewhere else, well, I would propose it to you. If we lived in Montmartre, say. Or in New Guinea." He glances over to see if he's overdoing it. But no. She's lapping it all up. "But I wouldn't dream of it in Pointe Claire. I couldn't do that to you."

"But who would know?" she almost gasps.

He just looks at her, and sets about cleaning the nib of his pen.

When he glances over at her again, she is unbuttoning her shirt.

"*Ca*-rrie," he says, and the tone of his voice conveys an affectionate-sounding reproach in the syllables of her name. "I shouldn't have started complaining."

"But you're right," she insists, dropping her shirt on the floor. "Is that better?"

"Yes, oh yes."

"And shall I take off my bra too?" She reaches behind her to unhook it.

"There's no need to take it off," he says in an appraising voice, as if deciding between cabbage and cauliflower at the supermarket. "If you just loosen it, that would be wonderful. That way I can see the natural line of the breasts, but I won't actually be drawing them. It'll just be head and shoulders, the classic bust. You can tell everyone you were wearing one of those little suntops."

She has taken her bra off completely. Her small breasts quiver and tighten around nipples that are like underripe strawberries.

"I said that there's no need to take it off," he says irritably. "I can't draw you like that, you know that. People will talk, especially these people,"—this with a wave of his brush hand, taking in all of Pointe Claire, all of Canada. "And you're just distracting me."

"I would like you to draw me like this."

"But then you won't be able to show it to anyone."

"No. But I would like to have it anyway." She has a thought. "You could keep it."

He goes over to her, and she is startled, wondering what he is about to do. But he just touches her elbow in a perfectly business-like fashion, and gets her to stand up. "You know, if you're willing to go as far as this, it would really be better to have you standing. Then I could do the whole body. And, if you were to stand like this," here he turns her to the side, and gets her to incline her head in such a way that her dark curls fall across her face, "I could do a nude and no one would even know who the model was. No one except your husband of course," he adds with a hint of uncertainty. "What do you think of that idea?"

She steps out of her espadrilles and begins to undo her belt.

"No," he says firmly, brushing the side of her breast lightly as he reaches out his hand gently to stop her from undressing further. "No. I couldn't start on this today. I'd need to think about it first." He turns back to his drawing of her face and neck and studies it thoughtfully. When he looks up, she is still standing there, half naked and barefoot and uncertain.

"You are a wonderful model. You have just the kind of body I love," he says, looking her over from top to toe, pausing deliberately before finishing his sentence, "to draw. Put your hands on your waist. Yes. Now lean back slightly."

As she does so, he gets up and goes over to her again. "No. More like that. It's the angle I'm interested in, the line of the breast." He moves her right shoulder, and stands back to study the effect. "Yes." He walks to the far side of the room, and stands quietly and just looks at her. "Try moving your right foot forward, towards me, about two inches. And now to the right a bit. A bit more." He shakes his head. "Would you mind, actually, taking your skirt off? I need to see how that leg position works. Might as well go the whole hog, so to speak. At least let's get the position organized today. Then we can begin work tomorrow."

She steps out of her skirt and panties in one move. He seems not to have noticed.

"Yes." He is leaning against the back wall. "That will be good. Will you be able to remember? I tell you what. At least let's mark where your feet are so that you can find your position more easily tomorrow."

He picks up a piece of charcoal, and goes over to draw around her feet on the wooden floor. "Perfect." He smiles as he stands up. "OK, you can move again now." He lifts her chin. Her eyes search his imploringly. Yup. This is it.

The silence is oppressive. Vince isn't about to break it. And then, sure enough, Carrie puts a hand on his. Still he says nothing. Just meets her eyes, looks pretty neutral, and waits some more.

And then, when he thinks she's chickening out, she puts one hand on his cheek, and with the other begins undoing his jeans, while her lips meet his.

He lingers just long enough to give her a good taste. Then he pulls back. "What are you doing, Carrie?" he asks, wide-eyed, all innocence.

"Oh, I've been waiting for this," she says, leaning into him, still not realizing. "I can't wait any more." Her hands are around his chest, kneading the flesh of his back. Not unpleasant. But resistible. Easily resistible.

He puts up his hand to push her away. "No, Carrie."

She stops, but she can't believe her ears.

"I think you've misunderstood." His voice is firm, matter-of-fact. There's no mistaking it.

She recoils as though he's slapped her. "Misunderstood?" Her voice is a squeak, and she's hunching up, backing off.

"Yeah, I like you as a friend, Carrie. I don't want this."

She's lost her voice completely now. Her hands are on her cheeks. Her eyes and her mouth are perfectly round.

"How embarrassing for you. Really. What a shame. Maybe I should have seen this coming. But I have to tell you, Carrie, that I'm not attracted to you." He smiles at her kindly, apologetically. Then he moves towards her awkwardly, as though to comfort her.

She backs away from him, gathers her belongings. In the doorway, she pulls on her clothes. And then she is gone, holding the shirt together with one hand.

Some *femme fatale*.

11

Vince catches a glimpse of Carrie pulling into her driveway two days later. Vaguely convinced that his victims cease to exist once he's lost interest in them, Vince is irritated to see her. And she, evidently, to see him. She marches straight into the house. He listens for her to slam the door. And sure enough, she does. He laughs.

Later that morning, the telephone rings. He doesn't recognize the number at once from the display, but the name he knows. Yolanda. She will have been wondering why he hasn't called her back before now. And since he hasn't, she may be suspecting he never will. If he doesn't answer, she will just persist in calling. While she'll be too embarrassed to file charges against him, she just might have some way—who knows what connections she has?—of tracking him down from the phone number alone. Or even—although it's unlikely she'd think this one through— through Le Tulipier and Sal's MasterCard number. Which means that this is the end of the road for A.S. Windle.

Vince clears his throat and picks up the receiver.

"Gut mornink," he says.

"Hello?" Her voice is uncertain. "I would like to speak to Mr. Windle."

"Mr. Vindle? Not here, lady."

"Not there? Where is he?"

"Gone avay."

"Still? We were supposed to have lunch this week. When will he be back?"

"Von't be back, lady. Moved avay. Vas here only short time. Not pay rent. I kick him out."

"Where did he go? Where is he?" she asks shrilly.

"Amerika."

"Where, though?" This is a wail. "New York? Is he in New York? Do you have a forwarding number for him? I have to find him. He owes me money."

"Ach, no. No number. Sorry, lady."

That takes care of one irritant.

The truck with the hot electronic equipment that Vince has been expecting pulls up the driveway just before noon. Vince opens the garage door and, with the help of the driver, stacks the boxes neatly along the back wall. They'll be safe there. They don't have "stolen goods" written all over them. And, besides, they'll be in the garage only a short time. The dealer will be here in a matter of days.

July is edging into August, and Vince has time on his hands. He tries working on his drawing. An unexpected side effect of his sessions with Carrie, though, is that he's finding himself working with less enthusiasm than before, with more of a sense of duty. And he's starting to understand why. It's that problem with the prettiness. He never did resolve that. And in some way he's disappointed with himself.

So he's relieved when Donald Rimmer calls early on Monday afternoon asking for W…W…Wincenty. Vince's fake ID is ready, and he heads into town to pick it up. The banks have closed by the time he's ready to prove he really is Wincenty Tadeusz Cunningham, so it's Tuesday morning when he sets off again with his big cheque and his ID tucked away neatly in his hip pocket. Vince is feeling particularly business-like, his thoughts as crisp as newly minted banknotes. He figures the Bank of Montreal in Place Ville Marie should be the best place, the least likely to question a deposit of $186,000.23. It's just before ten o'clock, and the dealer said he'd come by sometime after eleven. Vince is cutting it fine. He's hardly onto St. John's when he changes his mind—Place Ville Marie is too far to go just to do one item of business—and heads north to the Fairview branch instead.

There's no sign of the dealer when he gets back to the house. Vince could do a bit more on the drawing… No. It's too hot. And he'll hardly have got himself set up when he'll be interrupted. Later on, maybe. Or tomorrow. So where is he going to direct his energies?

That pretty oak niche in the hall is portable, if only he can prise it off the wall. Vince goes to the pantry, where he's seen a selection of tools. Maybe the screwdriver and the hammer will do the trick, he is thinking when the doorbell finally rings.

The man at the door, shiny-faced, looks as though he's about to collapse from heat prostration. It's a new guy—business must be brisk in the underworld—and as he backs his unmarked truck up towards the garage, he hurls invective at Vince about the blue minivan blocking half the driveway. Being the kind of Québécois who has learned to have contempt for the linguistic abilities of Anglos, he speaks a fast idiomatic French in the hope of forcing Vince to beg him to slow down and repeat what he's said. This kind of one-upmanship is a breach of linguistic etiquette, and the dealer knows it. But it's a hot day, and he's in a lousy mood—in a mood to resent Vince, the West Island, English Canada, the English language. Not all Anglos make good victims, but some of the middle-class mice who live on the Lakeshore are prepared to wallow in borrowed guilt over the way that Montrealers with nothing in common with them other than some version of the English language took advantage, once upon a time—not of *les Québécois*, for they didn't call themselves *Québécois* in those days—but of *les Canadiens*. Few Anglos—few French from France, for that matter, few francophones from anywhere outside of Quebec—can play this game and win. But it's only fun with Anglos, for only they can be depended upon to be sufficiently abject in defeat.

    Vince smiles. He knows this game well and can give as good as he gets when it comes to *joual*. The dealer, who has fully expected to triumph in this little skirmish, is so nonplussed when Vince answers in kind that he looks ready to reconsider not only his in-your-face attitude but an entire nationalist mythology. No surprise there, at least not for Vince. All you ever had to do to take the wind out of the *indépendantiste* cause is speak French.

    Vince scans the neighbourhood for prying eyes. Next door, Colleen, in the uniform of hip punko decadence—black cut-offs, Doc Martens boots, and a blue Hawaiian shirt that looks as though she pulled it out of someone's garbage—is licking a gaudy red popsicle and talking to a short, thick-set man Vince has never seen before. She's bursting out of her shorts and shirt, with the boots half way up her stumpy little legs. Radiant, too. A natural beauty with beestung lips shaped like a cupid's bow, messy black hair, skin like milk. And, Vince notices, what looks from this distance like a tattoo on her upper thigh.

    The popsicle is going to last precisely ten more seconds. She tips it to prevent it falling off the stick and takes a huge bite. She's the spitting image, Vince decides, of Snow White in the Disney movie—winsome as all get out, and quietly collecting dwarfs. She laps up the last of the dripping popsicle in the nick of time, and then tilts her head cheekily to the side. Her guy—Happy, Sneezy, Dopey, is anyone keeping track?—kisses her goodbye, climbs into his Rabbit, and is gone. Neither of them has noticed Vince or the truck.

    Vince walks into the garage behind the truck, closing the door from the inside the second the truck is all the way in. The dealer climbs down to check out the goods. And this is where it becomes clear that Vince's surprise advantage in the linguistic skirmish outside was, in truth, a small, unimportant victory. The dealer isn't prepared to pay as much as Vince hoped. Vince decides against selling him any of Sal's loot.

Vince walks all the way down to the end of the driveway to see the dealer on his way. No one in sight, in either direction. As the truck accelerates towards St. John's, Vince turns and notices Colleen again, this time with Mitsou on the leash, walking down Cedar. Mitsou's head is wrapped in a bandage that covers her right ear completely, so that she looks crazily lopsided, almost human, like that self-portrait of Vincent Van Gogh.

Vince watches as the dog pees under the hedge. Neither he nor, evidently, Colleen notices the owner of the hedge until a short, round man clambers into his car, slams the door, and backs onto the street, where he stops behind Colleen and Mitsou as they proceed on their leisurely way. The man is peering out his car window at the ground by the hedge. Chagrined to discover that Mitsou's only legacy is a slight dampness, he glares at the girl anyway as he drives away slowly. As luck would have it, though, Mitsou chooses this very moment to take a dump. Vince watches to see if the man will notice. He does. Three houses away, he stops and moves his car into reverse. Colleen isn't waiting around to be harangued, though. The second Mitsou is done, Colleen sets off at a bound across the back garden of the next house, a reluctant dog in tow. No wonder Janet has a soft spot for Colleen. That kid has all the right instincts. In a couple of decades she might even be interesting.

The first of the month comes and goes, and Vince is screening his calls. They'll be after him soon enough. And, sure enough, there's a call from the real estate agency. It's unlikely to be Carrie herself, although she's sure to be behind it. He lets it ring and ring.

Later, there's a long-distance call. That'll be Sal herself. Well, he's ready for her. He's ready to face the music. What kind of music, he wonders? What will she do? What will she say to him? He feels a kind of elation, really. The thrill of the chase. He doesn't answer.

The next call is from the Banque Nationale. That's Sal's bank. Vince hesitates, and then decides to brazen it out rather than have them turn up at the door.

"Mrs. Schleiermacher, please." A man's voice.

"This is Mr. Schleiermacher."

There's a moment's hesitation. This isn't what he expected. "I'm calling with regard to a MasterCard issued in the name of Sal Schleiermacher." Aha! Sal must have got her new statement. And either she herself or—more likely—Carrie has phoned MasterCard. It can't be Madeleine. She doesn't get back until tomorrow. Any one of the stores Vince has ordered from would have had this phone number.

"Yes. I am he. How can I help you?"

"My understanding, sir," the voice persists, "is that Sal Schleiermacher is a woman."

"A misunderstanding, I assure you. I am Sal. Salvador Schleiermacher."

"I see." He's not convinced. But he figures he has an ace up his sleeve. "In that case," he continues smoothly, "I wonder, sir, if you would mind, for your own protection, of course, telling me your mother's maiden name."

Vince smiles. He's a pro. He's already turned to the back of his little book. He's ready for them. "Brask."

"Thank you, Mr. Schleiermacher, sir." The man can't keep the surprise out of his voice.

The next call is Sal again. Vince lets it ring.

He catches sight of Madeleine the very next morning, picking up Mitsou next door, hugging her, and exclaiming over her mutilated ear.

There being no sign of Carrie, Vince sidles over towards the hedge to speak to Madeleine.

She's looking quite fetching, with her mouse-coloured hair piled loosely on top of her head. She's wearing a long denim dress belted just a little bit too tightly at the waist. Hardly a fashion plate, mind you—she's too short to carry off a long skirt—but quite sexy in spite of her brown socks and scuffed shoes. He contents himself with saying, "Why don't you come over later on and see my etchings?" He's been dying to say that, but has been biding his time, not wanting to encourage Carrie in her already vivid imaginings. Madeleine is such an innocent, though, that she probably has no idea what it means.

But she does. She gives him one look, and Vince knows what's been on her mind. In the afternoon, when she comes over to visit, she's nervous when he moves close to kiss her. Of course, he has moved in too close. You're not supposed to stand that close, not unless you're lovers, not unless you're married, and there he is, *that* close. She looks up at him, surprised, alarmed. Her relief is palpable—and so, too, is her disappointment—when it looks as though he's just going to greet her with the usual kiss on both cheeks.

Only he kisses her more than he's supposed to. He kisses her right near her neck, nuzzles her—and she wants more, he's sure of it, almost sure—and kisses her more acceptably on the other cheek.

He steps back. She's leaning forward, towards him. On full alert. She could close her eyes and know if he blinked. One beat. Another. He waits until he can hear her sighing. Yes. And only then, when he hears her sigh, does he himself move.

At first it's as though he's just shifting a bit, perhaps he was standing in an uncomfortable position, perhaps he's getting a cramp. You can't blame a guy for moving if he's getting a cramp.

And then he sighs too. Just a little, barely audible sigh. He nuzzles her again, whispers in her ear, puts a hand on her waist. She's keen. Oh, yes, she's very, very keen. She's dying for this.

Vince was right about this one. And why shouldn't he be? He's the pinball wizard from way back. You lose one or two, that's to be expected. There's no shame in letting a ball drop down into the bowels of the machine. It happens. It's no big deal. There's always another ball, always another game. But a setback is no more than that, a setback. He's in control.

Now she's starting to sway. Any second now she's going to keel over. Tightening his grip on her waist, he pulls her towards him until her lips touch his. Lightly at first. Then not lightly at all.

He takes her hand. She doesn't demur when he leads her into the bedroom. Doesn't demur when he unbuckles her belt and drops it on the floor. She doesn't demur at all. Just keeps her head down. He lifts her chin to kiss her again, kisses her cheeks, her eyes, her brow. Then, reaching up under her voluminous denim skirt, he tears down her lacy panties as he backs her onto the bed. Her knees buckle against the bedframe and she falls back easily, all spread out. Except she's still completely dressed, with only that twist of lace around her ankles and those little brown socks and shoes somehow still on.

"*Vincent*," she whispers, her eyes opening wide, "I've never done this before."

"Well, then, it's about time."

"*Ah, oui*," she breathes, and then bursts into tears.

Tears have never stopped Vince.

Madeleine has hardly dried her eyes when Carrie starts ringing the front doorbell.

"Well, well, well," Carrie says, her face red and skewed, as Madeleine plumps herself down on the stone lip of the fireplace and tries to look as though nothing has happened. She's rearranged her clothes plausibly enough and her hair looks fine. There's something odd about her face though. What is it? Her eyebrows. That's it. He must have smudged her eyebrow pencil when he was kissing her. "Fancy finding you over here, Madeleine. I'd have thought you'd have had more sense, Madeleine. You've always been such a sensible woman. At least that's what they say, Madeleine. They say you're such a sensible woman." With each repetition of Madeleine's name Carrie loads more sarcasm into her enunciation. She sounds strung out, and she looks a wreck.

Vince puts himself between Madeleine and Carrie as though to protect Madeleine.

"What can I do for you, Carrie?" he asks. He manages to keep his voice friendly. He doesn't want to give her any credibility at all.

"Do for me? Ha! We won't go into that! Oh no."

"Is something wrong?"

"Nothing's wrong at all, no. Nothing at all." Dismay is written all over her face. She obviously hoped to find Vince on his own. Certainly Vince can think of a thing or two that she might say to him that she would not particularly want Madeleine to hear. "Nothing as far as I'm concerned, anyway." Another moment, and then she decides on the tack she has to take, faces Vince squarely. "But Sal is a different matter."

"Sal?"

"The rent." She turns to Madeleine. "Maybe you haven't heard," she says acidly. "He hasn't paid the rent."

"That's not true, Carrie," Vince says calmly, reasonably. "You don't know what you're talking about." He touches Madeleine lightly, but doesn't look at her now. Madeleine and Sal are friends. He's going to have to make this very convincing.

"Oh yes, I do. I spoke to Sal this morning. She's been trying to reach you for days, but you seem not to be answering the phone. No money had been deposited in her account as of this morning. And that's a fact." This last is triumphant. Her anger is so obviously fuelled with bitterness, and of course—*of course*—the last thing she can talk about is the real reason for her bitterness.

Vince steals a glance at Madeleine. She's looking shell-shocked, but that isn't only because of what Carrie is saying. Even if Madeleine is taking Carrie's accusations in, surely she would be more shocked by Carrie herself than by the accusations. Yes. Carrie is her own worst enemy. She's ruining her credibility every time she opens her mouth about Vince. Off with his head, she insists to anyone who'll listen. Off with his head. As crazy as the Red Queen. And her fury intensifies as she realizes how little attention Madeleine is paying to her diatribe against Vince.

"Carrie, Carrie, Carrie," Vince says sadly. What an idiotic name she has. Carry. Carry-on baggage. *Carillon*. Carrion. Vince likes carrion best, its echoes of putrefaction, its evocation of flesh that's unfit for food. "Don't do this," he pleads with her, as though for her own sake. "Please calm down. You know I explained this to you. There's no surprise here. I told you I would be a few days late with the August cheque…"

"A few days! It's the tenth!"

"A few days," he repeats, eyeing her distastefully, his voice brooking no disagreement. "She has her money. All is well, Carrie. There's no problem. Sal has no reason to be worried. I told you I would be getting my money a little later than I'd originally thought. Just a few days. Well, it arrived, and I transferred the rent money into Sal's account at noon today," he lies. Then, his eyes swimming with sympathy, he looks at Madeleine. "I thought it would be a pity to alarm her. Poor woman. She's a friend of yours, isn't she? I feel so badly about this. So far away, and now probably frantic. And," he turns back to Carrie with more than a hint of self-righteousness—he's getting good at the self-righteousness; it must be something in the air out here in Pointe Claire—and a whole lot of reproach in his voice, "for no good reason." He shrugs, as though helplessly, just as the telephone rings, and he hurries to answer it.

"Hello?" the voice is faint, cool, and accented. It's Sal.

"Yes, hello."

"Is that Wincenty Carlson?" Her voice surprises him. He has started imagining that he knows her well, and this is the voice of a perfect stranger. Not at all overwrought. Downright calm, in fact.

"Speaking." There is an element of curiosity in his continuing the conversation. He could, after all, rattle off something plausible enough to convince Carrie and Madeleine not to give the phone call a second's thought, and ignore Sal altogether. He doesn't want to let them know who's on the other end of the line, but at the same time, he can't now resist hearing what Sal will say.

Of course, it's possible that Sal may have told Carrie she'd phone him this afternoon.

She may have told Madeleine, too, for all he knows.

The thought sticks in Vince's throat. And suddenly he feels convinced the women are all in cahoots. Can they be that devious? No. Carrie might be. But there isn't a devious bone in Madeleine's body. Nor, surely, in Sal's. Vince would bet his life on it.

"I have been informed by the bank that no funds have been transferred to cover the rent for August."

"Yes," he says cheerfully, "I believe that is correct."

"I have tried repeatedly to reach you by telephone, without success until now. I would like to know when the rent will be paid."

"Today is what I have in mind."

"I will expect it and will phone the bank for confirmation tomorrow afternoon. Unless I receive that confirmation, I will be instituting proceedings against you immediately with the Rental Control Board. Given the delay, I would also ask you to give the real estate agent post-dated cheques for the rest of the year."

"No problem. Ciao, baby."

Carrie is still fuming. "Your money arrived?" she repeats, ignoring the interruption. She can't have known who it was.

"Yes, Carrie, just like I said it would. The money arrived, and I transferred the rent money into Sal's account."

"Prove it!" she orders.

"Prove it!" Vince is incredulous.

"Prove it?" Even Madeleine is outraged. "*Carrie!*" she says, pronouncing it like the French word *carie*. A cavity. Now *that's* good, Vince likes that a lot. That way the name conjures up a mouthful of decay.

"Yes. Prove it!" Carrie insists. She is beside herself, way beyond caring what either of them think of her. "I want to see some proof. I'm not leaving here till you show me some."

"Really, Carrie, don't you think you're going a bit far?" Vince laughs. If it were only Carrie, he'd play up the outrage. But he's anxious to reassure Madeleine. So he goes into the kitchen and comes back with a bank book from the Bank of Montreal at Fairview. "Hmm. I'm not sure I kept the deposit slip." He smiles. "I didn't realize I would be facing the Spanish Inquisition. But—" he waves his bank book in front of the two women, "—there's the proof that my money arrived, just like I said."

"186,000!" Carrie breathes. She stares at Vince. As he figured, she's too preoccupied with the amount to bother checking the date he made his deposit. And so what if she did? He'd have a story about how long it took to clear an amount of that size. He's got all the answers. "Where did you get that kind of money?"

"Actually, it's 186,000.23," Vince says. "If I were as rude as some people around here, I would tell you to mind your own business. As I am not in the habit of being rude to anyone, I don't mind telling you that this is an inheritance." He pauses for effect. Then, ignoring Carrie, he looks deep into Madeleine's worried eyes. He didn't really want to tell them this, but he sees no alternative, and he might as well milk it for all it's worth. "My mother died a short while ago, and my brother arranged for her house in Toronto to be sold. He and I share the estate. I had good reason to believe the money would have arrived well in time for the August rent, but it was held up. Here is your proof, Carrie. Are you satisfied?"

How could she not be?

She leaves without another word.

Vince is a man who likes to play his cards close to his chest, and Carrie has forced his hand. Her persistence has succeeded in getting him to let her—and Madeleine, and Sal, and the whole of Pointe Claire village, for that matter—know that he has inherited money. Not that that knowledge will do anyone any good. And she'll find out all too soon that he has not, in fact, made any deposit at all into Sal's account. And then, all too soon, as soon as Madeleine hears from Sal, Carrie will be vindicated, and Madeleine too will turn against Vince. So he has no real reason to destroy whatever shred of credibility Carrie still has left. But he can't resist. He can't resist squashing mosquitoes, either, after they've drawn blood.

"Hell hath no fury…" Vince shrugs at Madeleine, as though reluctant to speak ill of Carrie.

Madeleine says nothing. She has no love for Carrie, but she's too gentle a soul to join in an attack. She stoops to the floor to lift a charcoal drawing off Vince's sketch pad and reveal the drawing of Carrie—from the neck up—that Vince finished on his own a day or two ago, "I didn't know if you'd want her to see this, so I covered it up when she arrived."

"Hey." Another take-charge type. It seems to happen to all these women. Even the ones who look as though they'd roll over and die if you so much as said boo. Leave dewy-eyed damsels alone for long enough out here and they metamorphose into managers. Bossiness as the last refuge of the lovelorn. She may look like Vince's type. And he'll make hay happily enough with her while the sun shines. But he won't be heartbroken when she, too, turns her back on him.

"Are you going to give it to her?" Madeleine wants to know, gesturing towards it. Madeleine now has her arms wrapped around her chubby little legs, which she has drawn up under her skirt. Her chin is resting on her knee.

Vince picks up his sketchpad and pencil. Could he draw Madeleine? Last night Vince felt confident that he was ready to try more than just a bust, but now, face to face with the possibility of fitting this entire woman onto a sheet of paper, he is much less sure. It would be tricky getting the proportions of her body right. This is where his lack of training would really show through.

Vince has a history of biting off rather more than he can chew. Also, he hastens to add, a history of taking giant strides. The two tend to go together. Nothing ventured, nothing gained. There's another Ted Cunningham saying. They're coming fast and furious.

You just have to be prepared to land flat on your face some of the time. Or in jail. But even jail sentences come to an end, and there's always another chance somewhere down the road. When one door is closed, another one is opened. Just so long as you haven't lost your nerve.

"Do you think she'd want it?" he asks.

"Why not? She looks great. You've made her look better than she looks in real life."

Vince knows that all too well. "It isn't finished. And, besides, she's in no mood to accept a present from me."

"Maybe you could wait a bit, until she's calmed down, and then give it to her."

"*If* she calms down," he says darkly. "She may not."

Indeed she will not. For several reasons, all of which Vince knows well.

Vince laughs as though at a great joke, and Madeleine laughs too. That's one way of flirting. By laughing just a little bit too much.

She wants more, he suddenly realizes.

He looks at her, at the sheet of paper in front of him. Oh, he has no patience for this. Enough! Madeleine's right here, panting for more. She has no interest in sitting for him. He can take another run at the art another day. He throws the pencil in the air, takes Madeleine's hand, and pulls her to her feet.

"Madeleine," he says, in his deepest and most serious voice. He leads her back to the bed. Oh, Madeleine, what big tits you have. He's N. Vince Ybl, after all, don't let anyone tell you otherwise. N. Vince Ybl. She moans as he reaches up to her neck and starts unbuttoning her dress.

"*Non!*" she says suddenly.

He stops. "Eh?"

"Don't do that... I don't want you to see me. Can't we do it just the same way again?"

"How come?"

"I'm shy," she says, folding her arms across her breasts.

"Don't be shy," he cajoles.

"But I am. I always have been... I..."

"Is something wrong?"

"Yes. I had an accident as a kid. A collision... I was lucky to get out of it alive, I guess. But my side,"—she runs her left hand down her right arm—"and my right leg never fully recovered."

Vince sits bolt upright. "Where?" he asks quietly. "Where did this happen?"

And even as he asks, he already knows the answer. He can feel himself shrinking from her.

"On Golf Avenue. That was why I was so upset the other day when we fell. That's where it happened. That's where I lived when I was a kid. I'm sorry. I—" she tries to say more, but emits only a small, anxious sound.

Vince is speechless.

He stands up, stares at her. Why didn't he realize this before? She's the one. He searches her face, looking for clues, signs that might have helped him realize who she is. But this is the face of a middle-aged woman. He can't see that girl in it anywhere. The eyebrows? The hair? No. The body? Completely unrecognizable.

Vince backs away from Madeleine.

Corky.

Tell her the truth. Tell her the truth. All you have to do is explain, tell her you're the one. That's all. It's so long ago, what does it matter now? And, besides, it wasn't your fault. She's the one who came barrelling out onto the road without looking. You have to tell her the truth. You have to. It's important. Just tell her the truth.

He can't.

He just can't do it.

He's lost his voice.

Well, do something. Touch her. Smile understandingly. Kiss her. Show her it's OK. Get on with it.

And he can't do that either. He just stands there with his back to the wall and stares at her as if he's seen a ghost. He has. She has brought him face to face with a ghost. A sad, hopeless, desperate ghost. The ghost of his own fifteen-year-old self.

Madeleine gets up off the bed and goes quietly into the bathroom. And it's only then that Vince notices that Sal's journal is lying on the floor in full view. Did Madeleine see it? Probably not. She was lying on the other side of the bed. But Madeleine would recognize Sal's handwriting. He pushes it under the bed.

"I thought Sal was going to put that lamp away," she says when she comes back into the bedroom. Her voice is resigned. She's trying to reestablish some kind of normalcy. She hardly dared hope for love, and she's not surprised to find it so soon denied.

Vince looks at her blankly; he doesn't know what she's talking about.

"The Tiffany lamp," she explains. "That lamp over there, on the dresser."

"What?"

"Did Sal leave it out for you?"

"How else would it get there?"

Madeleine shrugs. She doesn't really care. "I guess she must have changed her mind. Or maybe she just ran out of time at the end. She was going crazy, trying to get ready."

Vince nods dumbly, looks at her as if she's speaking a language he has forgotten.

Standing in the doorway, she loosens her hair, shakes it out, and then ties it back again neatly.

"I'm going," is all she says.

It takes Vince a long time just to sit down on the side of the bed and put his head in his hands. And a long time after that before he raises his head and stares blankly at the doorway where he last saw Madeleine.

Then, at some point, his brain kicks into gear again, and it occurs to him that it's a good thing he didn't go so far as to prise that oak niche off the wall. Madeleine would have noticed that.

And, he thinks dully, so what if she did? What would she make of it anyway? She has other things on her mind.

The very idea that he nearly did something so obviously damaging to the house is giving him pause, though. He's getting careless. Maybe it's just as well that this is the end of the ladies' visits.

Vince hasn't lost his talent for finding a silver lining.

But this is some cloud. Alienating Carrie was one thing. But he wanted Madeleine.

Things are going wrong. They'll take another turn for the worse, too, when Sal gets the Rental Board involved. Not that any of it would matter if Vince were in control. But he isn't. And he knows it. That's what is really worrying. Vince is out of control.

12

Jessye. It's time for Jessye. Oh, God, yes. Jessye. Vince hasn't had a Jessye evening in so long. And it's time, really it's high time. He needs a Jessye evening.

Vince hesitates, fear tickling the short hairs on the back of his neck. He banishes it. The day's a write-off anyway. A little wine won't do him any harm. Probably it'll do him a power of good. He needs steadying. And, besides, maybe it's time to live dangerously again. Dare he? Oh, yes. In any case, he can't now stop himself.

Oh, Jessye. A loaf of bread, a glass of wine, and thou beside me.

Vince could die happy.

And, mounting the Harley, setting off to the village, Vince slides into a curious state of relaxation, now that he knows the die is cast.

His first stop is the Marché Seaubois, where he throws a couple of fat endives and a small jar of Dijon mustard into his shopping basket, pockets a nice roll of *chèvre* and a little bag of pine nuts while Mike is looking the other way. He's feeling more himself. It always perks him up to pull a fast one. And there are unforeseen advantages to solitude. Now that he has no further reason to cosy up to the local ladies, Vince finds himself able to look around him at the village streets with an almost philosophical detachment.

Next stop is the liquor store, where he picks up three bottles of Mouton Noir—oh, it will be to die, this meal, it will indeed—

Vince is moving faster and faster by this time, breathing more and more shallowly.

And then back on the bike again, and over the highway to the Swiss Vienna Delicatessen. Vince goes inside and buys a pound of almond crescents and four poppyseed squares. The day after, he knows from bitter experience, he will crave sweetness.

Back in the house, Vince sets Jessye down gently on the player and turns her on.

His evening has begun.

He uncorks all three bottles of Mouton Noir, pours himself a big glass and, after one slow, appreciative sip, drains the glass and refills it. He sets half a dozen rashers of bacon under the broiler, and finds a bowl for the vinaigrette. A heaping tablespoon of dijon, olive oil, garlic, vinegar, salt, a grinding of pepper; he stirs quietly, ever so quietly—nothing must get between him and Jessye—quietly and deliberately, till it's properly combined, and then sets it aside. He turns the bacon, sets a small cast-iron pan gently on the stove and roasts the pine nuts.

A pause.

Another glass of wine.

He has never heard her quite like this. "September Song." Such sadness, such wistfulness. How has he lived without knowing of this recording?

He waits for the end of the first song before lining a dinner plate with a fan of endive leaves.

The bacon is crisp, and he transfers it to another paper towel to drain and cool while he sets four fat rounds of the *chèvre* under the broiler. A minute and it's hot, soft. He slides it onto the endives, crumbles the bacon over the plate, sprinkles the hot pine nuts on top and then, with trembling hands—his industry has masked the enormity of his need but it has not entirely disguised the terror in his heart—he pours the vinaigrette over everything. And this is the meal he takes to the table with his fourth glass of Mouton Noir—he's already into the second bottle—and his Jessye.

It is as he hoped—as he knew—it would be.

He takes his time, savouring the taste—all those powerful, delicious flavours—and the perfect texture of every single mouthful before helping himself to more.

Giggling a little at the thought that you might as well be hanged for a sheep as for a lamb, he's almost through the second bottle by the time the music draws to an end, and then he slumps in his chair and allows the wine to take effect.

In due course, the plate clear, the final lied sung, the third bottle half gone, Vince lifts his head.

What now?

Vince is getting sleepy, and it's not even ten o'clock. He pours himself another glass, drains it quickly.

No more. He pushes the bottle away. If he has more he'll fall into coma.

The euphoria is already fading, the terror closing in.

How to keep himself awake? If he goes to bed now, he'll be awake by one in the morning. Even another hour will help. With every hour he inches closer to sobriety, reduces the agony of the inevitable headache. Oh, the *chèvre* salad was wicked good. The Mouton Noir too. And Jessye was incomparable. But what a deadly combination. Why does he do this to himself? After the last time, he swore he never would again. The punishment is more and more severe. He thought he would die the last time. And he's going longer and longer without succumbing. He's been pretty pleased with himself, in fact.

But he couldn't help himself today. The need so far outweighed the terror that he couldn't help himself. It's as though he's been working up to this evening ever since he arrived. How was he to know how strongly it would affect him, coming back here? And not only that. He hadn't really reacted at all, either, to the news of his mother's death. It isn't as though he was close to her. Not for decades. Maybe not ever.

But that's it, now, he consoles himself. That'll be it. Nothing but the occasional piss-poor beer from here on in. And it shouldn't be too hard to stick to that. There's nothing else left, really. Nothing can touch him anymore. This really will be the last time.

Like a zombie he was, flitting from shop to shop, picking up the cheese, the wine, like there was no tomorrow. And now tomorrow is nearly upon him. Oh, Jesus.

He'll just sit on the bed and watch the television news. That should keep him up. He stares at the little world inside the box, concentrates. A hole in the ozone layer has opened up over Central Europe, adding to the woes of a region already devastated by the second year of drought and the first plague of locusts in more than half a century. Meanwhile, Hurricane Calvin is wreaking havoc in the Pacific, and there's flooding in south-east Asia. The UN is hoping to evacuate desperate civilians out of Srebernice in Bosnia. The Americans are getting shit for having bombed Baghdad. And, as if that isn't enough, there's a special feature on the warlords in Somalia. It really should be enough to keep Vince awake all night.

He yawns and stretches out his long legs. The world is never in any danger of running out of evil. That seems to be one infinitely renewable resource. And most of the time, Canadians, English Canadians, that is—this is just one of several good reasons Vince has always felt closer to the Québécois—seem pretty capable of convincing themselves it has nothing to do with them. Like some exotic import—figs, say, or rubber—evil is thought to flourish elsewhere, in far-flung corners of the globe, even in the big, bad United States. It does not flourish in Canada.

English Canadians have an infinite capacity for amazement when confronted with irrefutable evidence of evil in their midst. For evil does admittedly—and regrettably—have a toe-hold even in English Canada, though it's all too easy for most Canadians to convince themselves that that's the fault almost entirely of native people and black people and francophones and immigrants from God knows where. Just look at the people who have attempted assassinations recently: one was a crazed Hungarian. And then there were some Armenians, too, weren't there? What was their beef? Quebec separatists are one of English Canada's favourite enemies. And then there are the native people, the First Nations of these *quelques arpents de neige*. Of course, the smallest speck is seen on snow.

A quick jab at the remote and Peter Mansbridge is sucked up into the ether. Vince picks up Sal's journal, and then lets it drop again. He can't be bothered with Sal now. He lies back, fully dressed, and falls into a heavy sleep.

> And wakens, as he dreaded, in agony.
> Oh, God have mercy. This is unbelievable.
> He went to bed too soon. He should have stayed up longer. Why did he have to buy the *chèvre*? He knew what effect it would have. He should have allowed himself wine, but no cheese. He should have bought only the one bottle. One would have done nicely, and maybe he wouldn't have woken like this. He should…
> Oh, God in Heaven, he shouldn't have done this to himself.
> Never again. Never ever again.
> Vince turns his head slightly, ever so slightly, opens his eyes. Oh, Jesus it hurts. Vince fights against nausea and dizziness to the kitchen, downs three 222s, gets back to bed he doesn't know how, sinks back into coma.

It's six o'clock when he stirs again, wakened by corpulent grey squirrels chasing one another over the roof. He does a quick check of his wounds. There's an improvement, slight but merciful. The light hurts now, though, filtering through the thin cotton of the curtains, and when he gets up to piss he pulls the blind down as well.

It's the doorbell that wakens him next, in the early afternoon, and he kicks off the duvet and lies flat on his back before staggering to his feet and pulling on his jeans. Two swarthy men are silhouetted against the glare of the sky.

"Win?" the taller of the two asks.

"Yeah?" Vince begins. He's squinting, trying to make out their features.

They have turned and are walking away.

Win. They called him Win. And he answered. Shit.

"Whaddyawant?" he says, too loudly. The sound of his own voice is painful.

They're gone.

Vince closes the door gently, downs another couple of 222s, and falls back into bed in his jeans.

At five o'clock he lifts the blind, winces, and steals a look at the day. Crows the size of cats are flapping their wings in the branches of the tallest pine in the Remillards' garden. The lake is sullen, the skies overcast. Overcast! It feels blinding to Vince.

He gets up and gets as far as making coffee before he gives up and returns to bed. The philosophical detachment of yesterday afternoon has gone. Vince feels empty, limp. Maybe he's come to the end of this little ride. Maybe it's time to move on. But where? For what? And why? Why should he? What happened yesterday? Something happened. Golf Avenue. No. That was before. What happened yesterday? The effort is too great.

Madeleine. Yes, that's it. Oh, Jesus. Madeleine is Corky. Was Corky. And... And he was taken aback. He was shocked. After all these years he was face to face with the past he had locked away forever.

Sal's on his case... But so what? What can she do, anyway? Vince is still sitting pretty. Isn't he? What now, though?

He shouldn't give questions like these a moment's thought. Not now. He's in no state to plan his next five minutes, let alone the rest of his life.

There was something else. Something else happened. What was it? Vince shrugs. He can't remember. If it matters, it'll come back to him.

This is punishment indeed. He must never, ever do this again. This will be the death of him.

Vince spends the evening hiding indoors, watching television silently—he can't bear even the thought of sound—until the incomprehensible gesticulations of anonymous souls, a whole world that excludes Vince, finally goads him into turning up the volume half way through *Prime Time News*. There's a disaster story from the American Midwest, where the Mississippi has flooded its banks, and smiling residents of communities from Des Moines to St. Louis are shown pitching energetically in to build up barriers against nature. "All I want," laughs a bouncy woman with tawny hair, "is water for a shower."

Life should be so simple, Vince thinks, biting into a poppyseed square and switching to MuchMusic. And he watches just enough of some video called "Runaway Train" to realize it's about runaway kids—and then he's quickly changing channels again.

Musique Plus is where he stops this time, and there's that cute little buxom blonde singer—what's her name?—gabbing about something or other. The same name as that woman's dog. Madeleine's dog. What does it matter? What does anything matter?

Vince has no heart for any of this.

Get your thoughts back on track, kid. Enough of the wallowing in self-pity. What happened happened thirty fucking years ago. So let it go. Enough.

Back to the journals. Every time he dips into them they irk him more than the last time. Why is that? Vince always has been able to convince himself that his victims deserve what they're getting. Interesting, in a way. But not the kind of thing Vince's about to give a lot of thought to. That might interfere with the process. He's superstitious about that too. He knows what he has to do and he figures he'd better just do it without subjecting it to too much of an examination. All Vince is sure of is that Sal's journal irritates the hell out of him. And that's just the kind of fix he needs right now. He flips through it till he comes to the very first entry he read. How sappy she seemed. He needs a reminder of that.

There it is—

Our happiness as a couple was premised on my personal unhappiness. So—in some way that I was never able to articulate—our happiness was a lie. And the only way it could become something else, become a true kind of happiness, was for me to say, no, this isn't working for me anymore. There are so many reasons just to keep going, keep pretending. So many reasons not to say anything. Because as soon as I said that, everything was in jeopardy, the marriage, the children, Wolf, me, the past, the future, everything.

So we had some bad years. We were badly out of sync with each other. Really we had led such different lives. When you have children, it's as though you've lived in different countries for a period of several years. At some point you wake up one morning and look at your husband—while he, quite likely, is looking at you the very same way—and you wonder why on earth you are sleeping with a stranger. That's when divorces happen.

It could have happened to us then. But it didn't. We were making it back. I had already reached the point when I knew—when this rather surprising new person that I had become knew—that I wanted to be with Wolf. At that point Wolf's very strangeness was what was most attractive to me about him. No, that's not quite right. It was the combination. His strangeness and his familiarity. And for a while it seemed he was getting used to this unexpected new wife who was so determined to go to college, get into McGill, play the cello. He wasn't entirely sure about her, I knew that. There was some part of him that still hankered after the young woman he'd married. Or that couldn't quite understand why that young woman couldn't play the cello. But I thought—oh, I wish, I wish—he'd gone past that.

Learning a musical instrument is like learning another language. It changes you for ever. It takes so much time—endless practising, endless repetition—and talent and, most especially, desire. You have to want it with all your heart, and once you succeed, you can't, you just can't be the person you were beforehand. So I was no longer the young woman he married. In so many ways I was quite a different person. We were still discovering each other, exploring these new selves of ours. That was exciting. It was all so much better. Not only better than in the bad times, but better than ever. That's how it seemed to me.

But I was wrong. Maybe I was deluding myself. Maybe he really didn't want me to be wide awake. Maybe he was too old to change as much as I thought he had changed. Maybe he just went crazy at the thought of growing old.

What could I have done differently? What should I have done differently?

Thank God I had started something new before this happened. I cannot regret the fact that I said what I had to say, did what I had to do.

Oh, but the emptiness. I feel the emptiness more and more keenly as the shock and slowly even the anger wear off. I can only hope I have found something new that will fill the void. Sometimes I feel certain that I have. I wish it so fiercely. At other times I fear I will turn out to be no more than a dilettante, that my talent will never equal my ambition, and my playing will never be more than competent.

But can I take the loneliness? The feeling of abandonment? It doesn't help to know that for a while I did my share of abandoning him. I had to. I had to find myself before anything else would ever be right. I never really went away. I always wanted us to find each other again. And we were, too, we were finding each other again. And then he left. He left me for ever and ever.

How could he do that? How?

In some moods I am afraid for him. What a cliché he has become, after all. And how long will it last, with this girl who's a year younger than Elsa? So many men seem to need this, the girl, the young woman, the last bulwark against time. It does make one wonder how women are supposed to cope. How often is a woman's love life doomed to an early death?

Maybe I too am going crazy at the thought of growing old. Nearly fifty-one. That's old enough. Too old, the sceptics would say—have said—to be trying to establish a career in music. Too old, they would say, for love. Not that I have any hankerings after younger men. I leave that to Janet. Who knows what I will feel like when I'm in my seventies, but the face and body of a man decades younger than I will not now cause me to rediscover my youth. I rather imagine, on the contrary, that he would make me feel my age the more. But, besides, my desire is not so much to rediscover my youth. I am anxious to learn what life now has to offer.

It is evening. And I am alone. This is my wedding anniversary. The anniversary of a wedding between some other me, a twenty-year-old me, and some other Wolf. A 20th anniversary on August 20th at 20:00 hours. It sounds like the end of some world war. The end of something, surely. The beginning of something else? What? That remains to be seen. I know what I would like. The sounds of the cello fill my being. I love the sensuousness of the instrument, its music. That much I can say. But I don't dare to articulate what I wish for, what I want from this music. I hope too much for my wishes to come true. And I fear too much the ridicule of the sceptics.

I am looking at the last photograph ever taken of Wolf and me. Nicholas took it last September, almost a year ago. I've been staring and staring at it, sure that somewhere it must hold some hint of what was to come. It must. He'd known her for a year already by then, he'd already arranged to take early retirement, he must have made his plans. In the photograph, Wolf looks better than he does in our wedding picture. Less fresh, admittedly, but more solid, handsomer, better. It's his eyes. That's where I can see it. His eyes are still kind, but there's something evasive about them. His hair is better cut. His clothes fit him better. He is less anxious than he was, and less brash. I can't see any sign of worry, but he was always good at hiding that. He doesn't look like the kind of man who's about to pack his belongings and walk out. And he doesn't look like the kind of man who's panicking. He just looks like the kind of man who knows he is loved by some woman. But does he know that the woman who truly loves him is me?

It isn't working. Vince isn't feeling irritated by the journal at all. Admittedly, her story is pretty pathetic, but... Vince may have been underestimating Sal. Or maybe she just has an attractive voice.

He's kept reading, hoping for the moment when he could toss the journal onto the floor in exasperation. Or disgust. And that moment hasn't come.

What's going on here? The exasperation Vince feels is exasperation with his own failings. The disgust he feels is disgust at himself.

PART III

13

The cold wind blowing in across the lake the next morning is the beginning of the end of summer. Vince watches dispiritedly as a couple of dozen sailboats race straight for him, running before the wind. It's ten o'clock, and the gaudiness of the spinnakers mocks Vince's dullness. He stops to stare at an unfamiliar pale grey-and-cream coloured creature in the lake. What is it? Only when it moves does he realize it's a duck with its ass up in the air like hands at prayer.

The wind has been taken out of Vince's sails. There's no gainsaying that. What he has to do now is chart a new course. And here he is, flapping around in the doldrums, going nowhere fast.

Inspiration. That what he needs now: inspiration.

Vince sighs deeply, drawing the fresh air off the lake into his lungs before heading back indoors. It'll take more than that to get him moving again.

The car. Yolanda's car. Patience and good weather are what the job will require. So this will be as good a time as any, Vince decides. Not that he needs the car just yet, but he'll need it for when the snow flies and the Harley has to go into hibernation. And, Vince decides, knotting his grey silk tie, a win will do him a power of good right now. He reaches into the drawer for the little envelope with the car key.

The body shop in Pierrefonds will cost Vince a pretty penny. There's no messing with those guys. They do a thorough job, though. Filing off the serial numbers and replacing them with the numbers of smashed cars that are no longer being driven. Changing the description of the vehicle that appears inside the door. And processing brand new identification stickers right there on their computer. No wonder they're busy.

It's inconsiderate of Yolanda to live so far out of the way when Vince can't take his own wheels. Public transport is not for him. He grimaces, pulling on his pigskin shoes. It's a fifteen-minute walk to the 211 bus stop, a thirty-minute ride to Lionel Groulx. Then it's the *métro* to Verdun. And another bus. An hour and a half at least.

And a cab? He picks up the phone—how about a cab that accepts MasterCard? A cabbie who will pick Vince up in five minutes at Cedar Park School—for the last thing Vince wants is to have the man know where to find him. A cabbie who will trustingly whisk Vince off to Ile des Soeurs and—when they're sitting outside the condo next door to the pyramid—who will figure the MasterCard number that Vince reads off his June statement is better than no payment at all. And who will be so sad to learn he's wrong. The only hitch would be if the cabbie were to phone in for an approval code—and discover that the account has been closed. But with the fare amounting to—what?—about forty bucks, there'll be no need for an approval code.

When he does get to Ile des Soeurs, Vince has to hang around without arousing suspicion for nearly twenty minutes before a glossy black-haired woman pulls up outside the parking garage, opens the door, and drives in with Vince striding in purposefully behind her. There are four Mercedes in the garage. The clean white one is Vince's bet. He fishes the key out of his pants pocket and tries it in the door. It works. In seconds he's nosing up the ramp and on his way to Pierrefonds. He makes it look easy, but it isn't. Vince has earned this car.

Word is getting around about Vince. He watches his neighbours meeting in the street and glancing his way. Up and down the Lakeshore Road he sees the women talking, comparing notes, opening their eyes wide in disbelief and then narrowing them in anger. Vince meets their eyes boldly, stares them down. He is a bit of a crook, of course, and he does have a mean streak, but he's quite sophisticated and basically harmless. There are a lot of men around here with respectable, well-paid executive positions—the husbands of many of these same women—who cause a lot more harm in the world than Vince.

Not to mention the political crazies, like those *têtes carrées* making speeches just last week about violence in Quebec if the English aren't treated right—and threatening to dismember Quebec if Quebec dismembers Canada.

And who are the hoodlums who are torching cars in driveway after driveway between the village and Cedar Avenue? "Oh, it's just kids." That's what people are saying. What horror will it take for them to change their tune?

But who is it who's being denounced around the kitchen tables of the neighbourhood? Not the crazies. Not the hoods. Not the white-collar villains. Upstanding citizens like that get off scot-free. And meanwhile, Vince—who is practically a saint by comparison—is painted an axe murderer.

No one waves across the hedge. No one who knows who Vince is will even speak to him. And certainly no one will sit for him. Not that it matters. He is spending less time drawing, anyway, and then, deciding it's time finally to move into paints, gets stuck for an entire week because he has no gesso for the canvas. Yet this is his opportunity. He knows it. Now, finally, he could be getting down to work without interference, without ulterior motive. And he will. One of these days he will. Just as soon as he's finished with this new bit of business that he'll have to see to tomorrow.

At least, with fewer distractions, fewer visitors, he can consolidate his position, set himself up for a long siege. He spends two days sorting out the garage to make room for the Mercedes. It's another week before the body shop in Pierrefonds calls to tell him it's ready. Vince drives it around the neighbourhood all weekend just showing it off. He negotiates a pretty fair price for Sal's loot, including the dining table and chairs he found in the storage area. On the strength of a morning on the telephone, a promise of quick turnover, and prompt payment of only $5,000, he has leather coats worth $50,000 delivered to his door one day, and a computer, a laser printer, and a state-of-the-art photocopier the next. Demonstration models for the showroom, he had explained. As sales grow, his $186,000.23 edges up over the $200,000 mark. He has less and less desire to head into town, less and less need.

And with any luck at all, he'll be wintering over in Sal's house. When the summons from the Rental Control Board arrives he can see that Sal has benefited from precisely no legal advice. Fool. She's claiming the rent for the whole year of Vince's lease—and that brings the total claim to more than the $10,000 limit. Well, well, well. Never overestimate the forces of justice. If it isn't the knaves who are tipping the balance, it surely will be the fools.

As the summer draws to an end, the only human contact he has with anyone is through Sal's journal, and he sees more of human life on the television set than he ever does outside his bedroom. This evening Peter Mansbridge is promising a feature on Canadian peacekeepers in Somalia and in Bosnia after the commercial break.

Canadians are so sure they are better than everyone else. They weren't surprised when the United Nations declared Canada the most desirable country in the world to live in. Of course it isn't enough, it can never be enough, not for a Canadian. Being best is just not good enough, but God knows they wouldn't want to be anyone else.

But what is this? Atrocities committed by Canadian boys in Somalia? Vince laughs such a loud, barking laugh that he surprises himself.

By the third week in September, the geese are flying south. Vince is in the driveway, watching steam rise off the Remillards' cedar deck in the morning sunshine, when he hears, then sees, a gaggle of about forty geese honking, changing formation, heading over the lake and beyond. Underfoot are torn, sodden election posters and maple leaves the size of grasping giants' hands. The big brave Tories' way of dealing with the massive disaffection of Canadians has been to hide behind Kim Campbell's skirts. Not much of a disguise.

Vince's despondency is punctuated with moments of blind anger. The vines creeping over the trellis are thin and brittle. They have stopped growing, are recoiling from the threat of frost, and all he has to do to break them just above ground level is give a good, sharp tug. The vines at the front of the house are tougher, and on these, one afternoon, he uses the garden shears.

And then instinctively ducks. The house on the far side of Sal's is overrun with cops. Three uniformed officers—two men and a woman—are conferring with three other men, one of whom is carrying a camera bag.

They haven't seen him. They're not looking his way at all. There is no reason, Vince tells himself, why this should have anything to do with him. He begins breathing more easily. But he keeps a low profile anyway, as he tries edging towards the front door without attracting their attention. Even if they're not here for him, he doesn't particularly want to be seen.

Focusing intently on the scene ahead of him, Vince nearly yelps to hear MacLoon's voice practically in his ear. "What's up?"

"Oh, Jesus, you frightened me," Vince gasps, angrily pulling MacLoon by the arm towards the fence where they are both sheltered from view. "What do you think you're doing sneaking up on me like that?"

MacLoon ignores that and just rubs his bruised arm in a bit of a daze. Another man might well have punched Vince for reacting as fiercely as he did. It must take a lot to rile MacLoon. He may be an artist, but he's no fighter. Integrity is all very well, but survival is what matters. When it comes to the crunch, Vince knows what he would choose. MacLoon looks shorter than Vince remembers him. Older too. Spooked.

Vince gestures abruptly towards the far side of the house. "What's going on over there?"

"Suicide," MacLoon whispers. "The tenant committed suicide."

"Tenant?"

MacLoon nods, keeps on nodding. "I never met the man. The owner went looking for him, but the tenant must have died a while back. The body was rotting into the floor."

Vince breathes again. "Is that all?" he asks, turning away.

"What do you mean, is that all?" Vince has finally succeeding in riling MacLoon. "What more do you want?"

But the anger is preferable to the despair.

It must be midnight when Vince hears Janet. How long has she been singing? Her voice is quiet tonight, only just audible above the sighing of cars off in the distance. It's a song Vince knows.

> I wished I had you in Carrickfergus
> only for nights in Ballygrand
> I would swim over the deepest ocean
> the deepest ocean to be by your side.
>
> But the sea is wide, and I can't swim over
> and neither have I wings to fly.
> I wish I could find me a handy boatman
> to ferry me over to my love and die.

She stops there. Maybe she doesn't know the rest of the words. Or maybe she can't keep her voice steady when she sings the rest.

That night, Vince watches a daddy longlegs on the bedroom ceiling before finally turning back to Sal's journal. Where was he, anyway? She was writing about her husband. Yes, a photograph. There was some photograph of them together, taken not that long before Wolf left her...

> I look better in the wedding picture than I do today—or than I do in that photograph with Wolf. This isn't just a question of being thinner and younger then than I am now, although I suppose I'm convinced, like everyone else, that it's preferable to be thin and young. Or—what was it?—a woman can't be too thin or too rich. At some point, when I heard it, I felt wounded by that. Maybe especially because I really had been thin—I spent most of my life as thin as a rail, and I never heard that saying then, when it would have been a compliment. Not that I felt so very wonderful—1.8 metres tall, wearing a size five. It didn't seem a desirable state. But it was natural to me.

1.8 metres. That's nearly six feet. Sal is almost as tall as Vince himself. And a beanpole.

For most of my life, I ate one meal a day—usually lunch—although it was dinner on those days when I knew I would be eating with Wolf. Apart from that, I would have an occasional cup of plain yoghurt, an occasional orange. Often I ate chocolates, and when I was interested in chocolate, I ate nothing else. Then I went off chocolate, and ate nothing at all. I enjoyed the feeling of hunger. I remember I felt virtuous when I was hungry, somehow superior, morally unassailable.

Even when I was pregnant, I was thin. I had no appetite at all, much of the time, especially during the first three months. I had to force myself to eat cottage cheese. I was a ridiculously tall starveling with stick legs and arms and a big, round belly. I wanted nothing but herbal teas and fruit juice, and sometimes even the fruit juice seemed far too much for me, too substantial, too meaty.

So it took me by surprise at first when I started putting on weight. I could hardly credit it. I would avoid any clothes that would make it obvious how much my waist had thickened, how broad my back had become. Then, eventually, I made an effort to lose it—it took me a long time to get around to it, I think, because it had been unimaginable that I should ever need to.

I succeeded for a while, lost several pounds. But only for a while. And then I stopped trying. And look at me now. Yes. Well, I wasn't rich then, and I'm not rich now. I have never wanted to be rich, and I never will be rich. But I will never again be thin. I know that. On the days when I eat chocolates, I eat bread and butter too, and avocados, and Camembert, and who knows what all else. And I love it all. Hunger has lost the appeal it used to have for me. Perhaps virtue has too, I haven't really thought about that. I feel superior to no one. The last time I tried having only a cup of plain yoghurt for dinner, it was less than an hour before I was back in the fridge, ravenous.

I feel that this really is the end. As if some part of me has finally come to terms with the fact that this whole part of my life, the Wolf part, the married part, is over.

What next?

Will there ever be another man? Unlikely. I'm so choosy, for a start, so demanding. Really it's practically impossible for any real man to measure up. He must be absolutely trustworthy, for a start. It's not worth taking another step without that one. Bright. Talented in some way. Funny. Deliberate.

Is that a lot to expect? It seems to be. I know one or two men like that.

But then, of course, the man has to want me, too. There are days when I can imagine that's possible. And there are days when I look in the mirror and am certain it's not.

I have to be prepared to accept that there may never again be a man in my bed. I have to get used to the idea of being alone for the rest of my life. I have to figure out how to cope with the loneliness. There's been loneliness before now. But this will be different. No one to talk to, to celebrate with, to give off to, to commiserate with.

There have been moments when I looked at the changes I've been going through over the past few years with something like hope. This change was necessary, so there must, I have told myself, be something good about it. Yes, that's what I told myself. I have to stop and think about these things. Everything has been so coloured by Wolf's leaving. I find it very difficult to keep in mind now the things I thought before. Probably that is why I have been so harsh recently in judging Carrie. We should not judge one another. I should not judge Carrie.

Carrie's very good at dredging up painful memories. I suppose I think she should be letting them go. Some kinds of history just aren't very helpful. The secret of a good marriage is being able to remake your life, to start over, and to see your partner anew, the way you would if you met him for the very first time. Oh, I say that with such confidence, as if I'd managed to keep my own marriage together. But I still think I very nearly did, and—oh, what do I know?—I still think that's how you have to set about it. Carrie hasn't managed to do any of that. But she may. Probably she's right to have backed away from divorce. I'm not sure she's doing it in the right spirit, exactly. But that too may change. At the moment it seems a kind of lunacy ever to have thought there was any single thing to say for ending a marriage. At the moment, divorce just seems to me irredeemably sad.

In the pages of a photograph album that Vince has strewn over the floor is one shot of Sal, in her twenties. Her hair is wet, unkempt, as if she's just got out of a swimming pool and has shaken her head a few times in the sun. She's like a gazelle, impossibly thin, defenceless. Her profile is perfect; perfectly fragile.

Vince puts this beside the most recent picture he has of Sal, the one loose inside the front cover. This one is dated 1991. Her hair, now grey, is pulled back into a chignon. She's big, not fat, but big, with a heavy chin, solid shoulders and feet planted firmly on the ground. No makeup, no jewellery, no nonsense about this woman. Her eyes are alert, and she's gesturing with her hands, as if she is in the middle of talking about something she cares passionately about.

Vince studies this for a long time.

It's Thanksgiving weekend, the weekend of the Beaconsfield High School reunion. Vince has been seeing announcements in *The Chronicle*, one in *The Gazette*, and some part of him is tempted to attend. But no. He can't face it. Not alone. He hides indoors all weekend, venturing into the village on Sunday afternoon only to buy bread. And on his way back to the house, he sees a middle-aged man running along the Lakeshore Road, chasing an exotic lime-green bird that is flying further and further away from him, higher and higher.

It's a bad week. The following Wednesday he finds himself peering at the *Chronicle* photograph of the reunion in the BHS gym, looking for a familiar face. But most of the faces are young, the faces of graduates half Vince's age. Is that Mr. Lummis, though? What was the name of the geography teacher?

By Friday Vince feels he will lie down and die unless he goes outdoors. So, that evening he goes downtown to see a movie that's being billed as an erotic masterpiece. It's called *L'Amant*, and it's based on a novel by Marguerite Duras. The main characters are a French girl and her lover in Saigon, but neither of them appeals much to Vince. This isn't *érotisme*, not as he understands it.

Everything here is skin deep, only skin deep. And the girl undoubtedly has nice, smooth skin and a lissome young body. More lissome, certainly, than Colleen's, say, more fashionably beautiful. But Colleen has possibilities, and this girl only has nice skin. Vince has a great respect for skin, but in itself it is of limited interest. Especially when you see every inch of it.

Janet knows that. The director of the movie seems to have sensed it, too, for he's done his best to make her a bit more sultry and mysterious by lavishing a lot of attention on her breasts jiggling around under her thin dress in the car. And by giving her a very fine grey felt hat that she wears low over her eyes. But the problem is one of casting, and there's no hat ever made that could make up for the girl's lack of character.

What Vince admires in that movie is not the girl at all, but the voice of Jeanne Moreau, the older, huskier, altogether darker and more interesting woman that vapid girl is supposed to turn into. And that's what finally strains credulity, that that insipid girl could ever turn into a woman with a voice like that. He falls in love with that voice. And at the end of the film, when the camera shoots the older, sadder, life-toughened figure of the writer in middle age, the writer who bares her soul and exposes her every vulnerability along with her skills, her talent, her strength, Vince finds her bowed back infinitely more attractive, infinitely sexier than the writhing naked perfect young thing.

Here, among all these women in this village, here you'd think there'd be just one Jeanne Moreau. A woman who has been that young animal, who has shed that skin and grown others, and yet others. Who has felt it all, love, rage, fear, worry, regret, devotion. Who has been betrayed. Who has been loved, but how can it ever be enough? Who has blamed her parents, her lovers, her husbands, herself, but hasn't stopped there, where so many stop. A woman who has come through all that sorrow and blame to the other side where—what? what is there on the other side? That is what Vince would like to know. There is a voice like Jeanne Moreau's there on the other side, and a thickened body, and a woman who feels right in her skin. Not a saint. Oh no, not a saint. A force to be reckoned with. A woman.

Alerted by a *Chronicle* article headlined "Pointe Claire's Most Famous Gardener is Moving Out," Vince gets up early next morning and walks along the Lakeshore towards Wilton to check out MacLoon's garage sale. It is a dull day, the sun straining through a milky sky. The tall crane pulling the boats out of the water is leaning over the Yacht Club, forming a right-angled triangle with the silver spire of the church of St. Joachim.

The grey streetlamps on this stretch of the road are shaped like the elongated neck of some Jurassic monster staring out across the lake, and a grey gull perched on the tiny head of one of these monsters like some mutant offspring calls out querulously as Vince walks past. Vince's head is bowed as he turns from the Lakeshore up Bowling Green. Underfoot, the face of the Tory election candidate still smiles hopefully, insanely, at Vince. He looks up just outside a house that's under construction, and sees a moosehead on top of a small red car, bloody neck, penis stuck in its mouth. This in a city that hounds MacLoon, this in a world that forces women to pick their dogs' shit off the ground and carry it home in a little bag.

There's a hubbub outside the house on Wilton, cars and laughter, photographers, journalists, video cameras, tape-recorders. Walking between his mother and father, a little fair-haired boy of about eight gives a gleeful bound like a fish jumping out of water. There's no sign of Iris, the neighbourhood shrew. Not much money changing hands, either. But one man—a friend or maybe a colleague—is telling a reporter, "How can a town that lets people use dangerous pesticides meddle with a man who has created a Japanese garden?" And Vince overhears an elegantly dressed older gentleman say, "As far as I'm concerned, it's his property and he should be able to do with it what he wants." The woman he's speaking to—Vince recognizes her as one of the neighbourhood women, with two kids in tow and her hair in a ponytail—agrees. "The schools should be using it. The kids would get a kick out of it, and they'd see something different."

Vince studies the garden. There is something admirable about it. Foolish, but admirable. MacLoon, he decides, is a kind of everyman up against City Hall. If this were a movie, say, or a novel, you might call him Smith—if you had the nerve. Of course, some people would complain. He's an individual, they'd say, not everyman. And of course, he is an individual, with his excessive patience, his cowboy walk, and his hair sticking out at the sides, but he's more than that. He's everyman in a world strangled by idiotic rules and regulations. The artist in a bourgeois society.

And for what? Certainly not for personal gain. That's where Vince and he part company. Not only is this man not making any money out of all his industry and all his perseverance, but he's actually, in front of everyone's eyes, being financially ruined. This, Vince realizes, is what makes an artist truly an artist. Oh, they may make money, some of the lucky ones, but that's somehow by the way. It's just beside the point. And a con artist—who is working first and foremost for personal gain and only secondarily, if at all, for the aesthetic delights of the sting—what about him?

Vince knows the answer to this question all too well. He's finally ready to admit that the con artist is not—cannot be—a real artist. It was a mistake to think he could be a real artist at the same time as—in the very process of—conning the neighbourhood women. It sounded so perfect. Two birds, one stone. Too perfect. He should have known. The motives are different. He can't pretend.

MacLoon is heading Vince's way, looking dazed, and Vince reaches out to shake his hand. But it is not to be. A photographer gets in the way, and then a newspaper reporter, and then Janet arrives and distracts Vince's attention, and though he promptly loses sight of Janet in the throng, the moment has passed.

When Vince gets back indoors at Sal's, he sits down, looks through his drawings, and sets them aside one by one.

This was a mistake. He isn't really an artist, like his father. He just isn't that kind of artist, and he never will be.

It happens.

At a turning point in his life a man can decide to be an artist, or a writer, or a musician—something in which he once thought he showed promise. And then—it does happen, more often than not—he will sometimes discover, will be forced to face the fact, that he really has no talent for whatever it is.

And what then? Well, he gets on with the rest of his life, dammit. He just carries on.

It's nearly a week later when Vince stops off at the shopping centre for groceries, and sees that *The Mirror* has a cover photo of MacLoon with

"Bylawed to death" in red ink and a full-page article inside headlined "What one man called ART Pointe Claire called a DUMP".

By the time this article appears, the journalist wrote, MacLoon will have left Pointe Claire and the bulldozing of his garden will probably have begun. And MacLoon himself is quoted as saying, "It doesn't matter whether it's a bulldozer or a volcano or a fire. It doesn't matter. It's the process that gets a man to heaven."

MacLoon will cope. You don't fly in the face of convention unless you know you can cope with the fallout. But it can still be hard.

Vince himself is finding it hard, these days. And why? There'll be no heaven for Vince, but then it's the here and now that always interested Vince. Still does. His purposes remain, in many ways, what they always were. To have a good time and to survive—and who cares at whose expense?

Not that you can expect it all to be a good time. You have to take the rough with the smooth.

May the devil take the hindmost, that's what Vince says. Nice guys finish last. The only morality Vince knows is, What is good for Vince? What does he love? Only himself and his Harley. Freedom. And power, the most insolent and arrogant, the most male of pleasures. For Vince is a man pitting himself against the elements, a man who lives to ride, who rides to live.

It sounds hollow.

14

The hearing at the Rental Control Board is the next day in an office building up on Côte des Neiges. Vince sits two chairs away from Carrie—who is representing Sal—for nearly an hour before they are both summoned into a little echo chamber where they face the judge from opposite sides of a plastic table. Vince keeps a mild, apologetic expression on his face throughout, but cannot resist a little smile at Carrie's outrage when the judge duly throws the case out, declaring it beyond his jurisdiction. Vince is safe! The Rental Board won't move to evict him, and they won't recognize Sal's right to the unpaid rent. She didn't have a leg to stand on. If ever there was a woman who needed some good legal advice, that woman is Sal. And if she didn't know it before, she will certainly know it now. That will be her next step. A lawyer. And that'll cost her as much again as Vince owes her already. And it'll be spring—and Vince will have spent a comfortable winter in her house—before she even knows it. She's at his mercy.

That night in bed Vince feels the need to go back to the journal again, to read it with Sal's voice in his mind. And it isn't only that he needs to know her better. No. He has well and truly vanquished her already. He no longer really needs to have a sense of what will she do next. He just wants to see what she has to say.

We do so much juggling, wanting it all—we want satisfaction in romance, marriage, work, we want our children to be healthy and happy, we even want to be beautiful. So we race from the beauty salon to the gym and from the gym to the store and then out to lunch with our friends and eventually home, and then we drive our children to music classes and soccer practice and swim meets and pottery and the library, and in between we find the time and the energy, maybe not every single day, but it has to be often or the whole world starts to shake, we find the time and energy and most especially the inclination to be as passionate a lover as ever we were in the days before jobs and children and advancing age and a wider world.

And when, in spite of everything, in spite of all our heroic efforts, the world does start to shake—when it shakes so badly that something, someone, whatever is least securely attached—flies off, then, for a while at least (think of the hope wrapped up in that "at least"), we get badly out of stride. We have more time than ever before—some important task simply no longer presents itself—and yet all of a sudden we find it impossible to manage all the rest. We stop putting all that energy into cajoling our little girl to practise the piano. We don't protest when another child loses interest in hockey. We're paring down our lives to their essentials. We stop going to the beauty salon, we let our membership in the fitness club lapse, we put on weight, we buy ourselves clothes without zippers and buttons. We let ourselves go—what a phrase that is, what volumes it speaks about the evils of simply being oneself. Suddenly it is important to do some things right, only the most important: the older child perhaps, or the little one needs attention; work assumes all the more importance, for work has to fill our empty hearts. And we know now there will be no one else to support us for ever after. Now, when it's too late, we finally give up on the idea of being superwoman, and focus on just those two or three or is it four things that we cannot live without.

Vince still doesn't feel he knows Sal very well at all. What matters to her most of all? What can she not live without? What are those three or four things? There's so much that she isn't saying—or that she's only implying. She doesn't mean to, probably, but she's teasing him, letting him see this much of her, only this much and no more. He can feel his interest in her mount, and it's the interest of discovery. Of discovering who she is, what she's really like. Of uncovering her.

This journal may seem innocent enough, but it isn't. In a sense, no story is. What is it, after all, that persuades anyone to turn a page, to keep on reading a story? The desire to know more. The desire to see. And, as a narrative unfolds, a character is slowly laid bare. And when it's a woman's story, like this journal of Sal's? Then it's the woman—Sal—who is laid bare. And the story is a kind of tease, a kind of striptease—a narrative of female nudity. Slowly the woman is revealed in more and more intimate detail, and the reader turns the pages more and more breathlessly as another veil falls, and another—take it off!—and yet another.

Sal will reveal more. Vince will know more. He's getting closer to her every time he reads her story, imagining her, creating her in his mind. Reading her journal has established an intimate relationship between them, as intimate, in its own way, as the relationship between an artist and his model. As an artist, he could capture his model on canvas just as now he is fashioning an image of Sal in his mind. The mind is more flexible than the canvas, though, and it allows so much more generously for the lapse of time, for change, and even for the reflection not only of the model but of the artist himself.

And indeed, somehow, at the moment, this train of thought is leading Vince not closer to an understanding of Sal, but to a reconsideration of himself. It prompts him to ask, What matters to Vince? He has always had a ready answer to that and now here it is emerging as a real question. That's Sal's doing.

Vince goes back to his reading.

In the pauses between sentences I've been watching Nicholas & Josie on the steps outside. Here I am, in an emotional quagmire, torn in all kinds of different directions. I worry about them. Will they be careful? Do they know what they're doing? And will they be hurt? I fear for them. Their faces are wide open, defenceless. Then there's the delight I feel in their obvious love for each other, in their trust of each other—oh, please let that last for them. And there's something else, too—let's call it ruefulness—they are so young, so lovely.

That isn't ruefulness. That's jealousy. I'm jealous of their youth, jealous of their intimacy. They're at the beginning, at the start, and my marriage has come to a brutal end. They have each other, the future, love. I don't have that, any of it. And there's more to it, too, than the kind of jealousy you might have of any other couple. There he is, my son, in love with a girl, telling her things, confiding in her. Not that he ever would have told me the same things. But he would have talked to me, and he does so less and less. He would have smiled at me, and understood sometimes when I was exasperated. And he does so less and less. His thoughts are with her. It feels like a betrayal. This too is motherhood. This is what it really means to have a child grow up. The child doesn't only grow up, and older; he grows away from you, away from the family—and into some world populated only by his friends. And when that happens, then he can't help it—he starts looking at the rest of us as though we're creatures from outer space, not even human, hardly worth a second's thought. All my life I've seen articles in the women's pages of newspapers about the empty nest syndrome, and it always struck me as rather pathetic. In some unforgivable way, I think I once found it faintly comical. And I was sure it would never happen to me. It could only happen to women who had lived their lives through their children, who had stayed at home and nursed and nurtured and baked so many cookies that they crumbled into dust before they could all be eaten. I was different. I was making a career for myself. That would never happen to me.

The little world that was the family is changed forever when the child grows up and forges a powerful link with someone else, someone from outside. It hurts so much. I feel so very sad. Vulnerable, too, buffeted by the winds of change. And resentful, though I'm ashamed to admit it. Who knows what Nicholas is saying about me? It feels like disloyalty.

Is it a stage? There have been so many stages. He had to grow away from me. I know that. But I suppose I hope that one day he'll be able to see me as a human being. Maybe that's a lot to hope for. Or maybe it isn't. There are other things I could hope for, if I dared. I could hope that he will be proud of me.

I would like that. I am vain enough that I would like that. I am proud of him. Why should he not, one day, be proud of me? That's another thing I found fascinating about Speranza. That her son was proud of her. He used to introduce her with an extravagant gesture as "My mother!" And, in the end, when he was in jail, one of the hardest things of all for him was that he was not able to see her before she died. It was a tragedy, really. A great man, with one fatal weakness. It was almost as though he had some vital piece missing. Caution, perhaps. Prudence. Whatever his flaw, it prompted him to dare the authorities. The authorities, no less, of a mighty empire bursting with confidence that the sun would never set, the tide never turn. And what was his defence? His wit. It was a close run thing, as Wellington said of the Battle of Waterloo, but, like Waterloo, it ended in a rout.

What was that question? "What are you going through now?" I dreamt last night that I was hemorraging and the reason was that I was having a spontaneous hysterectomy. And all day I've had vague, dull pains, the kind of physical memory of pain that you get after you've suffered something agonizing. That's over too, the mother part.

Somewhere else I remember reading that all the terrible things that happen to other people eventually happen to you too. And I remember reading—or did someone actually tell me this?—that one of the most surprising things about growing older is discovering that your thoughts are more and more crowded with ghosts, with the people you knew and loved who have died, but who live on in your thoughts and memories. What I have been discovering, though, is that the world itself is peopled with living ghosts. What is Wolf to me now but the ghost of the man who once lived here and who now exists only in my memory and my imagination? My children too have turned into ghosts, so that I'm invariably taken aback now when I see them face to face. We have fewer friends, we make friends less easily as time goes on, but our thoughts are bustling with people of flesh and blood who have no real existence outside our heads. We all have such ghosts. A parent far away, a friend we've lost touch with, a lover we haven't seen in twenty years.

That's what life is, the process of discovering these awful things. Such a humbling process. So, it's happening to me. This is what I'm going through now. I am desolate.

Vince can no longer deny it. He's reading the journal less because he's looking for information about Sal that could be useful to him, and more because... Because what? Really, he's not entirely sure. There's something irresistible about reading what Sal has to say. And yet she still irritates him. All that garbage about the winds of change. Just what you'd expect from a woman who collects paperweights.

Sal is—or was: Vince has to keep reminding himself these journals were written years ago—dissatisfied with herself, naggingly aware of the failures trailing behind her, of friends lost and discarded. Is anyone without such a trail? Only those blessed with no memory and no imagination. It isn't that the emperor has no clothes; rather that he has dirty underwear.

But there's more to it than that. In some ways the things Sal has to say—about loneliness, yes, there's an example, but about regret, too, about loss—are striking a chord, and Vince wants to know more about how she manages, how she copes all alone.

Vince doesn't really like admitting it, even to himself, but just recently—is it because he's reminded at every turn of his youth? is it the effect of all these houses full of married couples?—he finds himself feeling his age, feeling older than his years, in fact. He's sometimes felt lonely before, but that was the kind of loneliness he could cure by picking up the nearest woman who combined the virtues of willingness and solvency. When he tired of her, after a day, after a year, he would just move on without a second's thought. Why not? There would always be another, one out of every five, that was his rule of thumb.

He can hardly believe it, but these days he's caught himself wanting a different kind of relationship, a real companion, someone to share the rest of his life with, someone, even, to come home to at 5:16. And he regrets that it's unlikely he will ever have such a relationship.

It's unlikely, first of all, he'd ever dare. Who could he ever trust with his life? Who could he be sure of? They might start off lovey-dovey enough, but she would know, she would learn, too much about him, and at the first sign of strife—who knows?—she might turn him in to the authorities. How could he ever take such a chance?

And it's even more unlikely any woman would ever want to share her life with him. He knows what appeals to women about him, and he knows exactly the limits of that appeal. A fling, a moment of danger, a hot, noisy ride. Henry Miller time. No more than that. No good at all through the long snowy winter.

Although—he reminds himself—he does have one major advantage he never had before, and that is his nest egg.

But money isn't everything. He's not so sure he'd want a woman who found the money appealing. And what Vince doesn't know about women and money isn't worth knowing.

Anyway, there are so many other obstacles. Who knows if he'll ever find the right woman. She wouldn't be one in five. She'd be one in a million.

Slowly, imperceptibly, a new thought begins to surface. Vince thinks, he'd like to meet this woman Sal. In his loneliness Vince thinks, they are kindred spirits, he and Sal. And, insanely, a new thought occurs to him. He could win her over. He could charm her. He could, surely he could.

What matters to Vince? Sal was paring her life down to its essentials. What is Vince doing? What are the three or four things he cannot live without?

It was Carrie, wasn't it, who talked about coffee, about Wolf—it was Wolf—making Sal coffee just the way she liked it. Carrie seemed to think that was all you needed to make a good marriage. She certainly didn't have much patience for Sal, who wanted more.

There is something rather appealing about being able to sum up one's desires as tidily as that. But Vince has other things on his mind. Financial survival, for example. No way around that one, coffee or no coffee.

Then there's creativity—that sums it up as well as any other term. Room to develop.

And sexual excitement. Desire.

And what about a wife?—even the word rings oddly in Vince's ears.

Yeah, seriously, a wife, a female companion, a partner: he likes this idea more and more.

This wife—he'll never get used to the word if he doesn't practise—this wife will be exciting, right? That's the whole idea. So a wife isn't an additional need at all, it's just a different way of talking about desire.

Or is it? A wife is legal, and a legal marriage is stamped, sealed, and approved by everything Vince has dodged all his adult life.

Isn't that likely to pose a problem? Surely not. Even Vince has had to bow before the law from time to time. How different is a marriage certificate from a driver's licence? Not much. But the thought irks him. And there's something more about desire, too. Something about being desired. And about making sure the one you desire is the same one you married.

This is getting unnecessarily complicated. Keep things simple. There are still three considerations he has to juggle. Money. Creativity. Desire. Is there any way all three can be stirred around in one single cup of coffee? Wouldn't *that* just be the trick?

The danger of loneliness is that it leaves a man without a buffer against the world. Is there anything more horrifying than sitting alone in a room, defenceless against the ghostly images flickering on the small screen?

Yes. It's more horrifying still to sit alone in the dark and in silence. Today was election day. Needing distraction, Vince musters the curiosity needed to turn on the television to see if there's a new Prime Minister.

And there is. Diehard federalist Jean Chrétien. That much is clear. So much for the Tories. So much for Kim Campbell's skirts. So much for women who try too hard. With a recount still in progress somewhere in Ontario, it's less clear who will function as the official opposition: Lucien Bouchard's Bloc Québécois or the western Reform Party.

Either way it sounds like two Canadas, but then, when was it not? The problem, all along, has been the troubled marriage of French and English. And the discussions of possible solutions—from a new marital agreement to divorce, from separation to a marriage of convenience—has never yet been anything more than a dialogue of the deaf.

Bouchard at least has style. Already, Bouchard *is* Quebec, so far as the rest of Canada is concerned. And that will be more and more the case now that he has such strength in Ottawa. Parizeau must wonder what this new star will turn to next. Won't he perhaps give Parizeau a run for his money? Surely he too fancies being the first President of Quebec? And doesn't it embarass Canada very much to see that both of these champions of Quebec, both Bouchard and Parizeau, speak a more eloquent English than almost any federalist you could name?

A happy Parizeau describes this election win for the Bloc as the first period of a hockey game. The second will be the Quebec election, the victory of the Parti Québécois itself. And the third, the clincher, will be the referendum on an independent Quebec.

That will be the real battle. The dismemberment of Canada. And— if the Native people and the Anglo extremists have their way—the dismemberment of Quebec. Quebecers are no duffers. In fact, they're a pretty hard-headed lot, most of them. For all its romantic appeal, the nationalist cause is vulnerable when it comes to the bread-and-butter issues. No matter who wins the hockey game, though, you can forget about a strong united Canada.

Some long-dead prime minister described the twentieth century as belonging to Canada. It's finally dawning on Vince what it really means. It means that the twentieth century is as good as it's going to get for Canada. It means that there won't be much of a Canada after the century is through. More a negative meaning, in other words, than anything positive. Typical of a oversized non-country that defines itself as Not-American, No-Longer-British, and certainly Not-French.

There is a crash at the door. An egg is splattered all over the glass of the front door. What's going on? Some kid is smearing soap over the picture window before Vince finally figures it out. October 30. That's it. Mat Night. Is that really what it's called? Vince hasn't thought of that term for thirty years, and he's never seen it written. He always thought it must be Mat Night because that's the night the local rowdies steal your doormat.

The next day is Hallowe'en. Vince has always had a soft spot for Hallowe'en. This, after all, is the night for evil spirits to play before the saints come marching in. Of course the irony is that the little kids who are supposed to be so menacing in their ghoulish costumes are really the innocents. And the danger comes not from them so much as from the occasional poisoned treat. In the city, Hallowe'en has been reduced in many parts to Hallowe'en parties, so fearful are parents of their neighbours. Out here, perhaps the custom of traipsing door to door still survives.

Anyway, he takes out the Mercedes, buys some apples and a large pumpkin, and then, grimacing with the effort of carving through the thick wall to the sweet, stinking flesh, he cuts a hideous grin into its face, finds a candle to stick inside, and, when darkness falls, lights his very first Jack O'Lantern.

But no one comes. Whether because the house is tucked away at the end of a long driveway, or because Vince's notoriety has spread further even than he guessed, he sees dozens of insufferably vital little ghosts and robots and witches on the street, most of them chaperoned by anxious parents but, though his Jack O'Lantern is resplendent in its promise of wickedness, not one single imp comes up to threaten Vince with a trick unless he hands over a treat.

It's November when the lawyer who's now on the case starts applying pressure to get Vince out of the house. The front door is opened without ceremony, and a small army of men comes in and removes not only Sal's furniture—which is an inconvenience, but not a whole lot more, especially as her nice big bed is built in—but the photocopier and the laser printer, too, and boxes full of leather coats and the Arrow shirts that arrived just last week. Easy come, easy go. But Vince does mind about the computer, not because of its resale value, which is small, but because he's been keeping a record of his various transactions on it, and he doesn't want it falling into hostile hands.

In another bid to oust Vince, the lawyer sets about making a big song and dance about a pair of longhorns that were on the wall downstairs in what must have been Wolf's study. God knows there's a lot else missing, but for some reason that Vince can't be bothered to fathom, it's the longhorns that will form the basis for the legal case against him which is heard on a brilliant morning in mid-December when the lake is studded with rocks of ice that glitter like rough diamonds. Vince leaves the Mercedes in a no-parking zone immediately outside the Palais de Justice.

Vince has to dash between courtrooms all day, for the fraud cases are being heard at the same time as Sal's. Men and women Vince once worked with look away when they see him in the halls. The businessmen he has defrauded stare stonily across the courtroom. Laila's there, too, as he expected. She looks a bit older than he remembers her, and a lot tougher. He looks her straight in the eye. Win. She called him Win. He liked that.

Those men. Those men called him that, too, Vince realizes suddenly. Win. The men who appeared at his door that morning. Laila must have been the one who sent them. Why? Vince shrugs. She's hoping to witness a conviction, hoping see Vince brought low. Well, she'll be disappointed. He's planning to get off scot-free. And he does. No surprise there. Judy the Judge is presiding.

Laila, he sees, has followed him back into the other courtroom to hear the longhorns case. What for? She's lost her case. This one has nothing to do with her.

Carrie is called to testify on Sal's behalf, and all the damning evidence is duly presented. The case against Vince is tight. It's looking bad. Laila, who watched the proceedings angrily in Judy's court, is starting to look appeased. But little does she know. Little does anyone know. Vince has an ace up his sleeve. At the climactic moment, he exits briefly, and when he reappears he has the horns held aloft.

And why not? He knew the dealer still had them.

The case is thrown out of court. The last Vince sees of Laila, she's in the telephone booth near the doors. He waves breezily to her. She turns as he passes, puts her hand over the receiver, and spits at him.

On his way home that afternoon, he slows his pace to contemplate the colours of the sunny suburban landscape—all those soft, harmonious blues, greens, beiges and browns—when the lights turns jarringly red at the end of St. John's. Ignoring them—there's nothing coming—he steers the Mercedes around the corner onto the Lakeshore Road, and can then hardly believe the evidence of his senses when there's the sound of an explosion. No. Oh my God. A bomb.

And yes—he's in a state of shock by the time he's close enough to see, yes, it's in his own, in Sal's, driveway. The garage door has been blown off. But from this angle it looks as though that's all that's happened. The Harley? Vince hesitates, bows his head to pass under the brown splinters of wood, and finds the Harley miraculously intact at the back of the garage. He turns, hesitates. He could just run away, turn and run away. Oh, no he can't. Mme. Remillard is already at her door, her eyes wide and frightened. Carrie isn't home yet—probably she and Sal's lawyer are licking their wounds somewhere still—but Colleen is running over from her place, all yelps and foolish exclamations. So he can't just run. And he can't stay where he is or he'll have to deal with these women. So he just ignores them all and goes indoors.

There's a bit of damage to the house itself, but not much. Some homemade bomb probably. Stupid fucking amateurs. Just as well, though, Vince thinks to himself. Just as well they didn't do a real professional job of it. Did they know he wasn't at home? Who was it anyway? Vince can imagine a few possible perpetrators—almost any one of his many frustrated victims, in fact. They're all fed up; the law has got them precisely nowhere, Vince has made very sure of that. And one of them must have decided to take the law into his own hands.

Or her own hands.

Laila?

Who was Laila calling from the Palais de Justice?

Someone simultaneously leans on the doorbell and bangs heavily on the glass panel. Clearly this is not one of the neighbourhood belles.

"Police," says the burlier of the two men. "We'd like to ask you a few questions, Carlson." They know Vince well.

The phone starts ringing almost at once, and after hanging up on journalists from *Le Journal de Montréal*, *La Presse*, *Allô Police*, and *The Gazette*, Vince unplugs the phone. None of which stops any of them from printing their stories. Luckily the one in *The Gazette* is tucked away inside in an inconspicuous spot. But anyone reading it would have no problem identifying Vince, and—even worse—the location of the house he's living in now is quite explicit. Worst of all, though, is *Le Journal de Montréal*, which not only prints the address but has a photograph of him, the same old shot they've been trotting out every time he appears in court. *Une bombe explose chez Vince Carlson*, runs the story: *Avertissement ou tentative de meurtre?*

He reads it quickly. There is rather too much of Vince's story in it for comfort. Not that it really matters. *Le Journal de Montréal* does not enjoy a healthy circulation among the English-speaking matrons of Pointe Claire. And besides, it's too late for that to make much of a difference. He's succeeded in alienating them all anyway, and the main surprise, for Carrie, say, and for Madeleine, will be that the story stops there. But still, he doesn't like seeing it in black and white like this.

It's evening when he realizes that it wasn't really a bomb. The correct word is petard. He checks in the *Funk & Wagnalls*. Yes. He's right. A petard is a case containing an explosive to break down a door or a gate. From the French word *peter*, to break wind. It was a classic little fart of a bomb.

The metallic gaudiness of Christmas is everywhere on television, on the radio, and everywhere it excludes Vince. He sits alone in silence until he can bear the silence no longer. But the news on the radio is worse—God help us all—news about the changes to the sign law, Bill 86, the Minister's Christmas present to Quebec. So English is no longer forbidden. So yippee.

As if that's going to make the slightest difference to anyone. The old law might have had some teeth once upon a time, but long before it was repealed it had become just one more of Quebec's eccentricities, like ARRET signs and poutine.

And not even the most vocal opponents of the language law are about to spend money on new signs. They know well enough to wait till the Parti Québécois gets back into power after the next election. The second period. So the occasion goes all but unmarked—except by someone who's gone and put up posters with lines of poetry in English. Vince liked English better when the only place you'd find it was scribbled on walls in the dead of night.

And now the Christmas music is beginning. No. No Christmas music. Vince can't take that. He switches the radio off. He can't take Christmas.

How to survive this day? Vince stares out the window. From the distance, from the village church where the faithful have gathered together, he can hear the *carillon* ending. All around him, behind closed doors, families have gathered to give one another presents and celebrate. He listens. All is still. Aaagh.

But who's that? It's Janet, bundled up in furs, picking her way down her driveway. It's Christmas. She won't cut him. Oh, surely she won't cut him. Vince grabs his sheepskin coat and cuts across the snowy gardens after her. By the time she's lifted her eyes as she emerges onto Cedar Avenue, he is almost strolling.

"Merry Christmas," he says cheerily.

She's surprised to see him. "Oh, hello." Wary. This won't be easy. He'll have to play on the idea of Christmas. Comfort and joy. Yes, oh yes. He wouldn't mind a bit of that. Goodwill to all men. Remind her ever so subtly that that includes Vince. *All* men. But he mustn't let her see how desperate he really is.

They walk up Cedar Avenue to Lakeview in a silence that Vince chooses to consider companionable. But then—what *is* that?—it's the sound of bagpipes, surprisingly loud and clear, cutting through the cold air. Such a grating, ugly noise. A recording? Somehow Vince doubts that. It doesn't sound professional enough for a recording. And if there's one thing more unappealing than the wailing of a professional piper, it's the wailing of an amateur piper.

Vince and Janet exchange puzzled glances, pick up their pace in the direction of the playing. It must be coming from indoors, surely—how could it not?—but it's so loud that the window must be open. But no, there is the piper himself, standing outside the back door of his house on the corner, blowing "Hark the Herald Angels Sing" as though his lungs would burst.

Janet is smiling. And Vince, whose skin is crawling—he can't bear the sound of the pipes—can hardly believe his good fortune. All of a sudden, he's sure the fates are smiling on him. What a gift! A gift in disguise.

But what to say? How to capitalize on this most unexpected Christmas present?

"What an amazing instrument," he says.

"Isn't it!"

"I can't say I really like it." Shit. Oh shit shit shit. As soon as he's said it, he knows he's said the wrong thing. Janet herself is evidently in seventh heaven. But it's not exactly controversial to express reservations about the bagpipes, is it?

Janet's smile fades. She looks at Vince, seeming only now to have remembered who her companion is. "Like isn't a word I'd use for the pipes." And Vince breathes again until she adds, quite emphatically now, "Like has nothing whatever to do with the pipes."

"Oh." Time to shut up and listen. What happened to the fates?

"They were originally used in battle, you know, to scare off the enemy. The pipers would be in the vangard, terrifying the unsuspecting foe. The music wasn't meant as light entertainment."

"I see," Vince murmurs, hoping she can't hear his teeth grating. She's right about one thing. Like has nothing whatever to do with the pipes.

There is silence between them. Vince waits. All he can think of is Ted Cunningham saying "He who pays the piper calls the tune." And he wishes he could pay this piper to shut the fuck up.

"And yet, how moving it is," Janet goes on at last. "Perhaps you have to have been brought up with them to find the sound of the pipes moving. But they're always to be heard playing national anthems and hymns, battle hymns as likely as not, carols occasionally, all the tried and true. Only the tried and true. Nothing new-fangled or trendy about the pipes, oh no."

The piper pauses at the end of the carol. "Merry Christmas," Janet calls over to him.

"Merry Christmas," comes the hearty answer from the back door. A flat-faced, unremarkable-looking man. And he launches into "O Come All Ye Faithful."

Janet laughs, and surely her happiness includes Vince. He smiles at her. This is the moment.

"I've been wanting to ask you something," he begins, turning towards St. John's Road. She's hesitant, looking back in the other direction, where a man is heading for them. It's MacLoon, hardly recognizable inside his parka. Janet waves.

"Oh?" She's distracted. But he can make it quick.

"Yes. I know people are saying a lot of things about me, but..."

She stares at Vince.

"I wonder if you would like to come over for a drink this afternoon." She must know he's pretty strung out to be making such a request.

"You've got to be kidding."

"No. Really. I mean it."

"That's completely out of the question." She has no pity. She's going to leave him standing there.

"I always figured you were different from the others. That maybe you wouldn't listen to vicious gossip..." But he knows it's hopeless.

She pauses only briefly in the middle of the road. "It's Christmas, and I didn't want to be cruel, but now I'm going to continue my walk with my friend."

He sits alone in silence in the empty living room, and slowly the hours pass until he gets up and goes to bed. It's hardly nine o'clock, but he needs oblivion. Tomorrow will be a better day.

But the next day is no better. Vince lies in bed till he can stand it no longer. He can't stand being indoors any longer, he can't stand anything, any of it. So he gets up, puts on everything he can find, and goes outdoors. He walks until the sky turns yellow. His face is frozen. He wants to walk further, but the winds are too cutting. The temperature is minus 31 degrees, but with the wind-chill factor it's minus 54 degrees Celsius. He goes back to the house for the Mercedes, and takes the highway into town. It's so dry that the roads aren't even slippery, but so windy that in open areas the powdery snow whites out the road entirely.

Vince veers south onto the Champlain Bridge, where he stops the car and climbs out. The freezing air evaporating off the river curls up over the parapet like the sulphurous fumes of hell. Vince leans over. Further. It would be so easy. So quick, so easy.

What do you do when you're hanging in between times? Those are the dangerous times. In between. You've let go—you've let go of what used to secure you. Your old life, whatever that was. And you're hanging in mid-air, reaching, straining for a grip on whatever's coming next. How do you survive that moment? How?

How did Sal get from there to wherever she is now?

Hers is a different story. But it must have been hard for her. The life she used to have has disappeared altogether. Her husband gone, her children grown, her youth flown, her own new career—well, that must please her, but it can't have been easy, and quite likely it isn't easy even now. But she survived. Vince doesn't know how, but she survived.

And that's the thought that pulls Vince back from the railing. Only that.

So it's back to the journal, as Vince flounders around for a way to save himself. But how?

It's at times like these that men find themselves a cause, preferably messianic. It's at times like these that they turn to religion. No. The state of Vince's immortal soul is a subject he has no intention of investigating too closely.

And if not the soul, then what about the body? He could probably distract himself quite effectively with a nice little affair, just another affair. Or could he? What if he were bored? And what would be the point, anyway?

Maybe it's just time to move on.

But where would he go? Right now, one place looks to him like any other.

He comes back to the idea of a woman. That's what he's been wanting. He thought it would be easy, and it hasn't turned out that way. He doesn't want any common- or garden-variety woman, and he doesn't want any common- or garden-variety affair. No. That's over. Vince sighs. What he wants now is a real love affair. A big shining love. The one and only.

His mind skims over towards Jessye. A loaf of bread, a glass of wine, and thou. Oh, Jessye.

But that's a vortex, and Jessye's a witch. That way lies death. Probably that will be his death, he decides philosophically. That's the ultimate, really, in carnal knowledge. Boundless desire, yes, but desire endlessly denied. He'd rather that, any day, to the bridge where hell freezes over. But not today. Not yet. He's turned back from all that. He's looking for some other way.

Listlessly, Vince is perusing Sal's journal when all of a sudden he puts two and two together. Sal. He stops reading, looks up. Sal's the very one. That's it! He's known it for months, without really facing up to what it could mean. Sal!

And inspiration immediately has to contend with an ambush of objections. This isn't a one-way street, after all. And Sal is doubtless convinced that Vince is the devil incarnate.

So? He'll show her otherwise. He has his charms. He still has his charms.

What about the state of her house? The explosion, surely, will have been the last straw. What a Christmas present that must have been for her, the news about the bomb blast.

But Sal's not such a materialist. The house is not the most important thing. Not if he can sweep her off her feet. Besides, there was nothing personal in that. And she's bound to understand, surely, the artistic side of his nature, to know that artists are not like other people.

He's sold whatever she owned that was worth selling. He owes her five months' rent. He's forced her to find herself a lawyer. And he's indirectly responsible for damage to her property. The men who replaced the garage door last week told him they'd be billing Sal for a couple of thousand bucks.

And he will not only pay, but give her more than he owes. Yes. He will shower her with goods if that's what she wants. He's promised himself not to dip into his nest egg, but he's been known to break a promise before now. Besides, he's saving that for something special, and what—who—could be more special than Sal? He'll pay for her new garage door, if that's what she wants. He'll pay for a brand new house, for that matter.

She probably hates him. Just think what he's put her through. The anxiety, the anguish, the financial catastrophe.

But she just thinks she hates him. She's never even met him. She's a lonely woman. A good man is hard to find. What were her criteria? They're in her journal, somewhere. He scrambles through the journal to find the right page. Yes. Absolutely trustworthy, for a start. Then: Bright. Talented. Funny. Deliberate.

Deliberate? Where does that one come from? Well, Vince is deliberate. In fact, he qualifies on all but one count. Trustworthy Vince is not. But he can do something about that. It's not as though there's a lot of competition. And in his imagination he's already lying beside her, teasing her about her need for a deliberate lover. There's no problem. What problem could there be? Sal's got a penchant for danger, too, you bet she does. He'll put on his shades and roar up beside her on the Harley. She'll hop on, and they'll live happily ever after.

In fact, probably she's half in love with him already. Sal would just love Vince. Yes. Sal is the one he's been looking for. And Vince, oh most definitely—the journal proves it beyond a shadow of doubt—is the very man she's been looking for. He laughs out loud. It's perfect. Vince and Sal. Sal and Vince. They were made for each other! She's going to put in an appearance one of these days. And when she does, she's going to be not only Vince's woman, but Vince's wife.

Oh, he wishes she were here now. Sal, short for Salvation.

PART IV

15

The doorbell rings one afternoon in February when Vince is sleeping. He ignores it, but then he hears a key in the lock and leaps out of bed. He has barely tied a towel around his waist when there Sal is, at the bedroom door, like a vision out of a dream.
    Sal.
    He stares at her, she at him.
    Neither speaks.
    She's monumental. Extremely tall, stately, wide-hipped. Far more sizable than any of the photographs reveal, probably more sizable than she was when the photographs were taken. Her hair is like spun silver, streaked with tarnished silver. There's nothing wispy about it. Rich and long, it's swept back from her face in a thick chignon. Her mouth is wide, her lips generous, her face marked with laugh lines. But she isn't laughing now.
    Her back is straight, and her feet are planted steadily on the floor. There is no nervousness about her, no affectation, no self-consciousness. But is hers really a lack of self-consciousness? There's no fidgeting here, certainly, no awkward fumbling with hands or pockets or purse. She feels no need to cross her arms to protect herself from Vince's gaze, or from his nakedness. She looks at him with an expression Vince cannot fathom. One brown eye is larger than the other. She hardly blinks. She is fully conscious of herself and *bien dans sa peau*. Confident of her right to stand where she chooses to stand, to look as she chooses to look.
    She is dressed in a long, loose, deep green velvet tunic over some long-sleeved wine-coloured pullover. On her feet are well-worn wide red ankle-boots in leather so supple that it has moulded around her toes. She wears no makeup, and her only jewellery is the wide, thick band of hand-shaped silver around her wrist.

Vince takes a step backwards, puts his right hand out to the wall to steady himself, and then quickly offers it to her. She ignores it. Seeing her journal on the floor beside the bed, she goes over, picks it up, and walks out into the hall with it. She moves with unhurried grace.

"You, er, must be Sal..." he ventures feebly, following her into the living room.

Then, on an impulse, he adds, "Excuse me just for a moment"—oh, Vince can still be the very soul of gentlemanly politeness, he hasn't really lost his touch. First he brings her a chair from the kitchen, and then he dodges back to the bedroom to pull on his clothes.

There's nothing he can say or do that will sweeten the moment. Music is what's needed here.

Will it be Pablo or Jessye? Pablo might give the game away. Too obvious. So Jessye it is. Jessye is his. She will be his offering to Sal. It is an offering she will be unable to refuse. He slips the *Vier Letzten Lieder* into the CD slot, turns the blaster on, and raises the volume.

He returns to Sal just in time to see surprise cross her eyes. She regains her composure almost at once, though, and he has a moment of doubt as he sits down across from her in the living room. They listen. Really it's impossible to do anything else.

There are moments when Sal looks over at Vince, trying to stir herself to do whatever it is she has come to do, say whatever it is that she has come to say. The music is too much for her, though, and by the time "Morgen" is swelling through the house, the set of her shoulders has changed ever so slightly, and her lips, though still closed, are fuller than they were. Leaning back, fanning herself langorously with her journal, she looks into the middle distance. She is aware, no doubt, of Vince's eyes on her, but she knows there's time enough for him, for business.

He, for his part, is feasting on her with his eyes. Nothing has prepared him for this. Not her photographs, not her journal, nothing. Everything he knows about her, he knows from that journal. How long he seems to have known her! Yet it was only last July when he first opened the journal. And in such disgust, too! Well, she surprised him.

What a transformation! Somehow he should have known, someone, something should have tipped him off. The cello was a clue, the best clue. He imagines her, sitting alone on a stage, her head bowed, leaning into the cello.

Has he made a sound? There is silence, suddenly, in the room. Sal is looking over at him, and he doesn't know where they stand anymore. One Saskatchewan, two Saskatchewan. Is she helpless, or is he? He had the advantage there, for a while. And now look at him. Hoist with his own petard. He shudders. When is he ever going to find the words to say something both true and important?

In due course, quite calmly and methodically, Sal gets up and, with Vince following meekly in her footsteps, begins checking out the house and the garage. Occasionally she asks him a question.

"So you sold it all?"

He nods.

"The paintings too?"

"Yes."

"How much?"

"Eighteen hundred."

"They fetched more than I thought. You're pretty good." He listens for irony, detects none. "Who did you sell them to?"

"Rimmer is the dealer's name. In Little Burgundy."

She stares at the pages of the photograph albums strewn over the floor of the bedroom for a long time, fans herself a little, says nothing.

She's inscrutable. He wishes he were still painting. He needs all the help he can get. But that's finished now, and it's no use trying to revive it. He tries out his special little artist's voice on her anyway, but gets no response at all. She is unnaturally calm. She leaves after a couple of hours, on foot.

And leaves him in terror. Terror that she will never return, terror that she will.

A week later she is back. In the garage she pauses over the Harley longer than she does over the broken bicycles in the pit or even over the new garage door. This is not lost on Vince.

When she comes back for the third time he offers her a beer, and is not surprised when she accepts it.

After an hour he says he has to go into the village. He has been using the car all winter, but this is an occasion for the Harley. That far he can go, even in March.

"I'm finished anyway," she says.

"Can I give you a ride?"

"A ride?"

"On the Harley."

She looks at him coolly, nods.

She leans against the backrest. She has yet to touch him in any way. But she will. Surely she will.

"Teach me to ride it myself," she asks him the next time.

He figures it's the least he can do. So he teaches her. She smells so sweet.

"You've been alone here, the whole time?" she asks after a while.

"I live alone, yes."

What is she plotting? She must be plotting. God knows, he'd be plotting if he were in her shoes. And where is she staying? He doesn't know. He's dying to find out, but doesn't dare ask. And it isn't so important, really. Just so long as she comes back. That's all that matters to him now.

His sleep is ravaged by nightmares.

In one, a decapitated sheep appears on the front lawn. Vince doesn't know what to do with it. Then another one appears. And another. The city is getting irritated, and Vince is forcing himself to stay awake to see who is responsible. Finally he catches them in the act. An unmarked truck, no licence plate, stops, four guys dump the sheep on the lawn and are gone within a minute. By the time he has called the police the truck is long gone. The next night, he persuades the police to stake out the house. Nothing. The minute they've left for their breakfast early in the morning, though, the unmarked truck pulls up, and another headless sheep is on the lawn.

Another nightmare.

In this one, Sal gets on the Harley, rides it out to the *pointe*, and keeps going. Over the water, she dives sideways, landing in the water seconds after the bike has sunk. She swims safely to shore where she wrings out her skirt before going on her way, singing.

March is ending when Vince is puzzled by a roar, morning after morning, out on the lake, until he catches a glimpse of the enormous hovercraft breaking up the ice out towards Dorval Island. And then Vince wonders why they bother, for the ice will surely break up anyway, without any noisy help. He likes to think he understands the real reason when, one afternoon, for the space of an hour, ice floes covered in fresh white snow float miraculously on the deep purple water until swallowed up by the lake.

The birds have returned, and the trees, though pregnant, are in the early stages and still not showing. Neighbours invisible all winter are shedding their clothes and their shelters to step gingerly over their newly naked gardens. In January Colleen ran away from home with some punk band that's now touring out west. Madeleine has been hospitalized with bone cancer, and Vince has overheard Pierre talking to Carrie about house prices over the garden fence.

One morning, Vince catches the end of a dream, just as it's escaping. The scene is of a cluttered room. He is being presented with a choice. He can choose himself. Or he can choose the nugget in his hand—what is it? gold?

The decision is made. He has made his choice. Pouf! He's gone in a puff of smoke, and filling the room is a huge golden coach.

That afternoon, Sal arrives with her cello case. Did someone drive her over? Or has she walked from the bus stop with her cello? Such a big instrument—but then, she's a big woman. She seems to carry it effortlessly.

"Wincenty," she announces, laying the case down on the living room floor and opening it. She has taken to calling him Wincenty. "There's only one thing for it."

He waits, wary.

She lets him wait, smiling—how? mischievously? surely she's not being mischievous...

"Wincenty, I want to marry you."

She has three conditions.

The first is that she will not take his name. This isn't something he has given a moment's thought to. Once she makes a thing of it, though, it suddenly starts to matter to him. He discovers he rather likes the idea of there being a Mrs. Vince Carlson in the world, a rose in Vince's lapel, so to speak. And what a rose! But not even Vince can think of a good way of persuading her to use his name. And it doesn't matter that much. What's in a name, after all?

"Fine," he says in the end. "But at least we should have a joint bank account."

She thinks about this for a moment. The sunshine is flooding into the living room. "Yes, we should."

"The second condition?" he asks.

"We pool our assets," she says matter-of-factly.

So. She knows about his nest egg.

"*All* our assets," she adds.

That's OK, Vince thinks. He'll come out on top. Sal's own assets include the house. He'll be co-owner of the house!

Changing the subject before she can change her mind, he asks, "By the way, I've been meaning to ask you about your name. Katarina. Sal. What's the missing link?"

"Oh, I have so many names," she says wearily, standing up and going to the window. "It is customary in some European families. Elisabet is one of my middle names."

"Ah." Vince is thinking of the string of names he himself has accumulated over a lifetime.

"I have something to ask you too," she says.

"Yes?"

She is quicksilver. It will be hours before he realizes that she never explained the missing link.

"Your best memory. What is your favourite memory, the thing you remember most fondly of all?"

He says nothing.

"You don't want to tell me?" she teases. "That's all right. I think I can guess. But I have no idea what would be your worst memory."

What is she up to?

"I just want to get to know you better." She smiles.

"The worst memories you have are precisely those you don't want to dredge up," he says finally.

"I know. But we can put it to rest again. You'll see."

Still he hesitates.

"I'll tell you mine," she promises.

"Mine," he begins slowly, "is from the day I left home. Not the causes, not the things that happened to persuade me to go. Just one vivid, painful memory... " He pauses again, and she waits patiently. "Making my way on foot up to the highway here, and then hitching," he finishes lamely. "I hitched a ride into town and never came back."

"And you see? Here you are, back again."

"Yeah..." he agrees uncertainly.

"Mine will not surprise you."

"Your worst memory?"

"I'll get to that. My best memory is from Paris. It is either a memory or a dream, I can't be quite sure now. But it is good. Frightening, but good. I am on the very top of the Tour Eiffel with a man, and the structure is swaying in the wind. It is very alarming, very scary, but I am happier than I have ever been."

"And who is the man?"

"This is what I don't know. It doesn't matter, anyway," she shrugs. "What matters is that wonderful mixture of happiness and danger. It doesn't last. That excitement cannot last, or we would die. But that is the best. That is what every love must be measured against." Sal stops and looks at Vince, her face still and pale. "My worst memory," she switches moods suddenly, before he can wonder too much about how long the excitement will last; she puts her hand to her brow to shelter herself from the sun, and stares at Vince darkly across the room, "is not what people might think. It is not what you, especially, might think."

He figures it best to say nothing. It was inevitable she'd say something, sometime, about the ruin of her house. In fact, he realizes suddenly, it will be a great relief to have the subject out in the open at last. That way he'll at least have some idea of how she's taking it—and of why she's reacted as she has. Why *does* she want to marry him, anyway? How can she even stand the sight of him? It is true, the chemistry between them has been right from the very start. And chemistry can explain a lot, but not everything.

"You see, my worst memory is not the sight of this house, of what you did to it while I was away. That was not entirely pleasant, I will admit, but it is far from the worst thing."

She is in profile, staring out of the window. A good, strong profile. Something old-fashioned about it, too—the nose, the hair pulled back. It's like the profile of a queen on some old postage stamp. Vince watches her carefully. He has never seen her more serious than this.

She sighs deeply. She might be alone in the room for all the attention she's paying Vince. Then, finally, she continues. "The worst was the confusion. The not knowing *how* to react. Everyone was expecting me to be angry at you. Furious, in fact. And I tried to feel that, mostly because that's what everyone wanted me to feel. 'Did you cry?' they would ask me. 'Did you feel like murdering him?' And I would equivocate. I would say something like 'I suppose so.' Or sometimes I think I would even say, 'yes.' But I was lying. I didn't feel any of those things at all. And so then I thought I must be a monster of some kind, some unnatural creature. Because in fact, Wincenty, I felt happy. I have hated this house, and everything in it. It holds so many painful memories for me, reminders of my life with my husband, of all the bad times. So I felt relief at getting rid of all those reminders. And I was—I am—grateful to you. Oh, I know you didn't mean to do me a favour, Wincenty," she concludes, turning to face him. "But that's what you have done."

"And you call that confusion? It sounds to me as if you were perfectly clear about what you felt."

"There was confusion. I did feel confusion. It took me a long time to realize what I really felt about it all." She thinks about this.

"You said that it wasn't entirely pleasant, the sight of the house when you returned," he prompts her.

"No. It wasn't entirely pleasant. I was happy to be rid of it all. Perfectly happy. What wasn't pleasant was knowing that someone had wished me ill." She fixes him with a stare unlike any he has seen. The mercury has dropped. "That you had wished me ill."

Now Vince is confused. "I didn't wish you ill," he lies. "There was nothing personal in what I did. I didn't know you."

"You are partly right. But,"—it's as though she's simply lost interest in the topic—"that's enough of this, don't you think? It doesn't matter now, anyway. What matters is love." Her voice is melancholy. Vince cannot doubt her sincerity. "Anything else is just another word for loneliness."

Sal stoops and reaches into the cello case for the bow. Without looking at Vince, she tightens it, and stoops again to flick open a small compartment and take out a chunk of rosin, which she rubs up and down the hairs of the bow. She lifts her cello out of its case, and sits down to tune it, her head bent, her feet flat on the floor, her knees wide. Then she leans down for her music and opens it on the floor in front of her. Fauré is the only word Vince manages to catch as she flicks to the page she wants, takes a deep breath, and begins to play.

Vince closes his eyes, shutting out everything but the music, but then opens them wide as the tempo changes. He has never heard such resonance. Sal's cello has the warmth and the sadness of a human voice. A woman's voice. Not a young woman's. No. It's too mellow for that, too wise, too tragic.

"I am tired of loneliness," she says when she's finished.

Vince is suddenly overcome with weariness.

"And you are too," she says quietly.

"Yes."

She plays again.

When she sets her bow and cello back in the case and stands up to go, she looks directly at Vince, and they stand there, facing each other in silence, making promises with their eyes. Then—it's as though she's made a decision of some kind—Sal closes her cello case and leaves it on the living room floor.

Vince smiles. She trusts him. He reaches out to touch her hand, leans forward to kiss her. She steps back.

"No," she says. "Not yet. We're going to do this the old-fashioned way."

And that's the third condition.

It is the morning of the wedding.

Sal is in deep red, and she is carrying a single full-blown red rose.

"Do you, Wincenty Tadeusz Jimenez Carlson, take this woman to be your lawful wedded wife?"

"I do."

"Do you, Katarina Maria Elisabet Salome von Friesen, take this man to be your lawful wedded husband."

Salome! It is hardly more than a whisper. But what a whisper! So voluptuously sibilant that it fills the hall.

Vince turns to her in alarm. She meet his eyes and smiles, ever so slightly, not at all sweetly, and he nearly faints from the heady smell of the rose. He hardly recognizes her. What has he done? He is marrying a complete stranger.

"Salome," he says slowly, at last, wrapping his mouth around the syllables carefully, grateful that their rich, dangerous sensuousness keeps his voice from shaking. And suddenly Vince finds himself laughing a loud, cavernous, rumbling laugh. And, laughing, he slowly feels his face being taken over by a wide, wide smile. And as his laughter winds down from a roar into a sputtering hiss, his smile tightens into a grin.

"I do," she says finally, deliberately, her voice deep.

Salome.
So.
He wants to believe the very name can explain a lot. But he knows it explains nothing.

Sal by any other name... But who doesn't have different names? Vince himself certainly does. He's been Vince most of his life, but his mother, when she was irritated, called him Wincenty Tadeusz, pulling up short before Jimenez would remind her of another life. His grandmother called him Vinskie and addressed birthday cards to him as Master Wincenty Cunningham. He expunged the Cunningham as soon as he left home. He's been Carlson most of the time since then, though there was a whole string of other names, too, a different name, practically, for every different game. He was known to his professors, though, as M. Carlson, to his clients as Mr. Carlson, and the prison guards knew him only by a number. The women have known him either as Vince or—like Madeleine—in French, as Vincent. He really can't think of another occasion when he has heard his whole name spoken aloud. Wincenty Tadeusz Jimenez Carlson.

By mid-afternoon Sal has arranged to have the telephone and the electricity cut off, emptied the joint bank account, and his wallet. The Mercedes has gone. The Harley has gone. All his papers are missing—his social insurance card, his passport, his driver's licence, everything. And Sal herself has disappeared. Gone. She's gone and left him.

And Vince knows, all at once, why he was right, all those years, to love a woman he would never meet.

Life gets difficult for Vince very quickly after this. Walking has never been Vince's style, but now he has no alternative. On a sudden inspiration, he goes looking for the mountain bikes he threw into the pit in the garage in the summer. They are looking very much the worse for the damp, and he picks up first one, then another, then the third, finding them rusted beyond hope and letting each in turn drop back into the puddle of rainwater in which they've been lying.

For four days no one speaks to Vince, and he speaks to no one. There's practically nothing left in the house that he can sell. The built-in dishwasher? The radio? Well, if he has to, he will. He has to eat. There's a limit to the meals you can concoct out of the storage cupboard. He's down to his last box of pasta. Much as he detests sardines, he has reason now to be glad he stocked up on them. He doesn't even waste thought on the pretty surprise he might have left for Sal. What she's done to him is so far in excess of anything that rotten fish could accomplish that it would be effort wasted just to punch the holes in all those cans. And, ditto for the sugar in the iron. Whatever she may have been like when she was younger, and married, and at least relatively biddable, she doesn't strike Vince as a woman who now has a lot of interest in ironing.

Help. There must be someone he can turn to for help. Isn't there? Vince racks his brains. What about his brother Gary? Could he find him? His mother's lawyer must know where Gary lives. And so what? Why should Gary lift a finger to help Vince? A better bet might be one of the dealers. Donald Rimmer is the one he knew best. But Vince hasn't been in touch with him since... How long is it, anyway? Still.., Vince has brought him good business over the years. Surely he'll lend Vince a hand.

Vince picks up the phone. "*Il n'y a pas de service au numéro que vous avez composé.*" *Pas de service*? Maybe he dialled the wrong number. Vince tries again. Same thing. He stares at the phone, as though he might read there the answer to his questions. What's happened to Donald? Was he busted? Is he dead?

There's nothing for it. Vince is going to have to sell the house. That, he realizes, might be a bit tricky. He did sign conditional ownership papers in Reed's office about a week before the wedding. The paperwork was to have been finalized afterwards. But...Vince is thinking through some of the legal ramifications. As co-owner, he can't sell the house without Sal's consent. But if Sal is nowhere to be found, Vince may be able to forge her signature and pocket all the proceeds of the sale himself. He certainly won't want Reed to act as his notary. And it's going to take time. How is he going to keep the wolf from the door in the meantime?

The next morning he is awakened by Carrie hammering an *A vendre* sign into the grass at the end of the driveway.

Vince throws open the bedroom window. "You can't do that," he calls out. "This is my house."

"Oh, no it isn't. It belongs to Nicholas. Sal saw Reed about it the day before the wedding and transferred ownership to Nicholas. I just spoke to him. He wants to sell it."

Vince chokes. "Where is she?" he growls. "Do you know?"

But Carrie says nothing.

"You know, don't you! Tell me where she is! For God's sake, tell me. She cleaned me out. I have no money for food, even. Nothing. I have to find her, talk to her."

He rushes to the door. He'll shake the information out of her if he has to.

But Carrie is pulling away in her beige slug by the time he gets outside.

Vince slumps against the door frame. He stays like that a long time. He has seen and done many things in his life, but never before has he simply not known what to do. And never before has he felt like this. Like what? Words fail him. He's like some kind of zombie.

It's the fault of the house, he decides wildly, when he finally goes back indoors. The house is haunted. Evil.

That's crazy. Get a grip, Vince.

But where?

On what?

Where can Vince turn?

And from across the way he hears Janet's voice, singing. Carrickfergus.

> I wished I had you in Carrickfergus
> only for nights in Ballygrand
> I would swim over the deepest ocean
> the deepest ocean to be by your side.
>
> But the sea is wide, and I can't swim over
> and neither have I wings to fly.
> I wish I could find me a handy boatman
> to ferry me over to my love and die.
>
> My childhood days bring back sad reflections
> of happy days so long ago
> My boyhood friends and my own relations
> have all passed on like the melting snow.
>
> So I'll spend my days in endless roving
> soft is the grass and my bed is free.
> Oh to be home now in Carrickfergus,
> on the long road down to the salty sea.
>
> And in Kilkenny it is reported
> on marble stone there as black as ink
> with gold and silver did I support her
> But I'll sing no more till I get a drink.
>
> I'm drunk today and I'm rarely sober
> a handsome rover from town to town
> Oh but I am sick now and my days are numbered
> come all ye young men and lay me down.

Vince listens to the very end. Then he goes up to the door of Carrie's house and rings the bell.

For a long time no one answers. Maybe the bell isn't working? He bangs on the door.

Finally the door opens. It's MacLoon. He is barefoot, barelegged too, wearing a yellow silk housecoat of Janet's that doesn't even cover his knobby knees. The sight enrages Vince. "What do you think you're doing here!" he asks roughly. "You were run out of town!"

"I beg your pardon?" There is astonishment on MacLoon's face. Astonishment and anger.

"I have to see her."

"Do you mind!" MacLoon retorts, closing the door in Vince's face.

Vince won't allow that. Oh no. "Get out of my way!" he shouts. He's stronger than this fool any day. And Vince pushes against the door, while MacLoon falls back into the hall.

Janet. No. He won't be able to charm her. That's hopeless. Even in his present state, Vince can see that's hopeless. But at least —

Yes.

At least he can get himself some money.

So he tears through the house and down to Janet's room. She looks alarmed—oh, well might she! he wonders how he must look—but says nothing.

"I'm not going to hurt you. I'm just hungry. I want fifty dollars. If you give me fifty dollars, just that, I'll never bother you again, ever. I swear."

He almost runs up Cedar and through the tunnel, slowing only when the shopping centre is in sight, and he does his shopping in a frenzy. Will he have time? Will he even have time? For all he knows, Janet and MacLoon will have called the police, and they'll be waiting for him when he gets back.

But no, there's no car in the driveway when he arrives back with a bag full of provisions.

First things first. Jessye. Singing Richard Strauss. And what else but *Salome*?

And he opens the first bottle. It's not the best wine, but it'll do. Vince starts to feel better. The bread is wonderfully fresh and crusty. He peels the wrapper off the *chèvre* and allows it to breathe while he prepares the pine nuts. No endives. Only lettuce. And there's no time to mess around with bacon. Rather a makeshift meal, really, but it too will do. Vince is in a hurry.

Jessye. Oh, yes. Nothing makeshift about Jessye. Oh, sweet heaven. She's all he's got now. He's all hers.

Afterwards, he stretches out on the living room floor and stares at the ceiling, listening. There's a long silence after the music ends. He isn't sleepy, not at all.

Vince is staggering as he leaves the front door open and makes his way, slowly at first, but then with greater urgency up towards the highway.

There it occurs to him briefly that he could hitch a ride into town. He could start again. He could make himself a new life out of nothing again.

No.

It's too late for that.

Is there a more desperate age than forty-five?

Vince continues on his way. Just a few more steps now to the railway tracks.

His head is beginning to ache. He lies down and cools the back of his neck on the rails.

And that's where he's found.

THE END

ABOUT THE AUTHOR

Linda Leith, who lives in Pointe Claire, Quebec, with her husband and three sons, was born in Belfast, Northern Ireland. Educated in London, Basel, Paris, and Montreal, Leith has a Ph.D. in English Literature from the University of London, England, and is a member of the English Department of John Abbott College in Ste. Anne de Bellevue, Quebec.

Leith's first novel, *Birds of Passage* (published by NuAge Editions), was serialized on the CBC Radio program "Between the Covers" in 1994. She is the author of *Introducing Hugh MacLennan's Two Solitudes* (ECW Press) and of articles that have appeared in a variety of Canadian and international periodicals. Publisher and co-editor of *Matrix* magazine from 1988 to 1994, she also edited the anthology *Telling Differences: New English Fiction from Quebec* (Véhicule Press).

The Tragedy Queen is her second novel.